Into the Breach With You

The Ladies Alpine Society
Book 3

Edie Cay

ARE YOU SIGNED UP FOR DRAGONBLADE'S BLOG?

You'll get the latest news and information on exclusive giveaways, exclusive excerpts, coming releases, sales, free books, cover reveals and more.

Check out our complete list of authors, too!

No spam, no junk. That's a promise!

Sign Up Here

www.dragonbladepublishing.com

Dearest Reader;

Thank you for your support of a small press. At Dragonblade Publishing, we strive to bring you the highest quality Historical Romance from some of the best authors in the business. Without your support, there is no 'us', so we sincerely hope you adore these stories and find some new favorite authors along the way.

Happy Reading!

CEO, Dragonblade Publishing

Additional Dragonblade books by Author Edie Cay

The Ladies Alpine Society
In Knots Over You (Book 1)
In the Money With You (Book 2)
Into the Breach With You (Book 3)

Chapter One

1869, Zermatt, Switzerland

J USTINE BREWER DIDN'T mind a lot of things. She didn't mind the cold; she didn't mind her friends being so in love that they draped themselves endlessly around their sweethearts. Or overhearing their whispered saccharine sentiments so often that it made her teeth hurt.

But what she did absolutely mind was being forced to sit still for three days straight: from the ferry across the Channel to the train from Calais to Paris, the train from Paris to Strasbourg, the train from Strasbourg to Zurich, and the donkey ride from Zurich to Zermatt. She was going to crawl out of her bloody skin.

As it was, she already wished she were climbing the mountain herself instead of being strapped onto the back of a donkey like a piece of luggage, feeling the cold and observing how the snow gathered on rocks and trees, until finally—finally!—the valley unfurled, and beyond was the stately, snowy, scooped-out peak of the Matterhorn. It loomed above all other peaks, and on the cold, clear day, it glowed with its hard bright-white angles.

The donkeys ambled down into Zermatt, the church steeple at the far end lording over the shadowed valley, a pale echo of the mountain beyond. The town itself was not large, but well established. The snow crusted on the rooftops of the wood-and-slate Alpine houses, which were utterly unlike English cottages.

They all possessed a tightness and squareness, each window and shutter at right angles. Not a single board leaned even a centimeter out of place. There were few people out in the streets, all wrapped tightly in woolen scarves and hats, barely anything but eyes showing against the chill air.

When they finally arrived at their inn, Justine was too impatient to wait for someone to help her down off the donkey. She slid off herself and threw the reins haphazardly. But oh, that air! Nothing had ever tasted as good as this air—crisp and fresh and cool, she felt like she could drink it. She was even more anxious to run, to feel that air deep in her lungs, to replace all the fetid air of the three days' worth of enclosed trains.

In front of her, Ophelia and her father, Lord Rascomb, dismounted. Another train of donkeys pulled up behind them, hauling all the luggage and climbing equipment they'd brought from London or picked up along the way. One step closer to the top of the Matterhorn. If she weren't positive Ophelia would get annoyed with her for wandering away, she would have gone on a walk around right then. She stamped on the snow, hearing the cold crunch of it under her boots.

"Fräulein," a man said to her, indicating the way into the hotel.

The building was freshly built, the light-colored boards still smelling of trees. The rugs were new, and Justine thought about how much melted snow these would absorb over the years. Her carpetbag was already waiting at the front desk, along with Ophelia's.

"Güete n'Abu," the man at the desk said. He was older, perhaps in his sixties, with frothy snow-white hair and a round face. His cheeks were pink, which contrasted with the bright blue ice-chip color of his eyes. "Ich bin der Herr Brunner."

"Good afternoon," Justine said, not understanding a word that was spoken. Instead, she looked around, waiting for Lord Rascomb to speak with the older man. There was a staircase that obviously went up to guest rooms, and another doorway that gaped open. Through it, she saw tables and chairs. She pointed, then mimed bringing a fork to her mouth. "For eating?"

The man's eyes brightened and he nodded. "Ja, fürs Essen."

It looked pleasant enough. Simple accommodations, but that's all they needed. She was looking forward to her simple dresses, the solitary runs, and this delicious crisp air. No dances, no balls, no dinners. Just mountains.

Lord Rascomb approached, pulling letters out of his coat pocket. The men spoke in German, which Justine ignored and instead looked about at the potted plants and the red and yellow painted designs on the exposed beams above her head.

Ophelia joined her. Justine pointed upwards. "The English never decorate a ceiling."

"Untrue," Ophelia said, sniffing.

"All is well?" Justine asked.

"I should like a bath, that's all," Ophelia said.

Justine didn't respond because she didn't need to. They'd endured the hell of puberty together, their first menses—for Justine's first blood came as she shared a bed with Ophelia and would have been the most mortifying event in the world had Ophelia not been so drattedly kind about it. And while Justine had received the taunting of Ophelia's older brother, Tristan, now thankfully wed and thoroughly besotted with Eleanor, it wasn't as if Justine hadn't given as good as she'd gotten. Until Tristan had told Justine's nickname to his influential friends and it became the work of the scandal sheets.

But it didn't matter to Justine, and Ophelia stuck by her through it all, even though other girls told Ophelia to cut ties with Justine because of her reputation. Ophelia always told them that Justine was an innocent. In the matters of men? Yes, absolutely. In the matters of other mischief? Perhaps not. And her older brother Francis, Tristan's schoolmate, was of no help whatsoever. He didn't defend his little sister at all.

It didn't help that no matter what kind of gown Justine wore, her slim waist, short stature, and buxom endowments made her look as if she were hoping for a tumble in the hay. The only true resistance to this presumption was to laugh at them. And she did. She had gotten used to needing to be unkind, needing to be loud and forceful. And, in one particularly horrifying instance when she was at her debut, being very *well seen*, so no man could carry her off.

"I like the red bird motif," Justine said, still staring at the Alpine ceiling. "It's cheerful."

"It's bloody," Ophelia said.

Justine looked to her friend. Anxious indeed to be so judgmental. It wasn't like her. Justine was about to say something, when there was a thunder on the stairs and the rest of the Ladies' Alpine Society came tearing into view.

Eleanor flung herself on Justine, while Prudence embraced Ophelia.

"We've missed you!" Eleanor squealed. Their quiet and withdrawn knot-tying genius Eleanor was capable of squealing? Marriage had loosened her.

"Who are you, and what have you done with Eleanor?" Justine admonished. But Eleanor moved aside, and Tristan moved in for a hearty embrace, something he had never done before. Puzzled, Justine suffered his affection.

"Bad News," Tristan uttered the nickname he'd bestowed.

"Arsehole," she said, the only name he'd ever earned.

Tristan laughed and let her go, leaving her to greet Prudence and then have a very awkward handshake with Mr. Moon, their expedition accountant who was not supposed to be here but had followed Prudence.

Not that Justine would blame him. Prudence was a kind of American goddess, embodying all the things Englishwomen wouldn't dare do: smiling at strangers, for one. Prudence was tall and moved easily in her skin with a confidence that even Justine envied.

Justine took Prudence's hand and squeezed it. "Darlings, it's lovely to see your gorgeous faces. Well, except yours, Tristan. It's abominable as usual."

Tristan was considered one of the best-looking men in London. He shared his golden hair and doll-like blue eyes with Ophelia and their mother, as well as an easygoing disposition that was often construed as sweet. But Justine knew what an arsehole he was and had no inclination to stop telling him so.

"However," Justine continued, "a bath is crucial. Where might the bathing facilities be located?"

"Won't you need to unpack first?" Eleanor asked.

"No need," Justine chirped, gesturing to the carpetbags she'd set aside. "We have our changes of clothes at the ready."

"I can show you the way," Prudence said, picking up one of the carpetbags. "Follow me."

A bath, then a dinner of sausages and potatoes and sauerkraut, and they were in their beds, a small portable iron brazier glowing to keep them warm. Justine shared a room with Ophelia, each in their small beds, and while her friend fell asleep immediately, Justine felt like it was the middle of the afternoon. She was ready for tea and gossip, or even a training run. It had been *ages* since she'd been allowed to move properly.

She lit the small oil lamp next to her bed and tried to read. But even her mind was restless. Eleanor had given her a book about Mary, Queen of Scots, which normally would have been interesting, but Justine could not concentrate. Not when her body screamed for permission to move.

A young lady shouldn't go wandering about a hotel in the middle of the night—it wasn't done because it wasn't safe. But she would *die* if she had to lay still any longer. With a jealous glance at Ophelia's sleeping form, her angelic face arranged like the porcelain dolls her mother gifted her every year, Justine got out of bed. She put on her heavy woolen stockings, her dowdiest dress—meant for climbing mountains in—and an extra shawl that she tied about her shoulders and waist. She pulled on the warm, wool-lined slippers and crept out of the room.

. . . Where she discovered it was very cold. Very cold indeed!

The iron braziers heated the rooms individually, but the passageways were freezing. Justine would need to find a fireplace quickly. And perhaps a dose of local flavors that could help her fall asleep.

Was she a nightmare for chaperones? Yes. Was she Bad News, as Tristan Bridewell had said so many years ago? Possibly. Would she lose her mind if she didn't wander the Alpine inn right this minute? Absolutely.

Carrying her oil lamp with her down the passage and then down the stairs, she followed the heat. It was easy to feel the draughts as they circulated through the building. As she got to the bottom floor where the innkeeper had greeted them, she could feel the warmth emanating from the dining room, where the door was now closed. She followed it, opening the door without thinking what would be behind it.

It had been where they ate dinner that night, where breakfast would be served in the morning; it was just a dining room.

But when she opened the door, all she could see was a man's shoulders, powerfully built, achingly obvious, outlined by firelight. The man whipped his head around, holding a shirt to his chest.

"Oh my," Justine breathed, her heart thundering at her discovery. She was unable to move or to quit staring.

Recovering from his shock, the man relaxed and pulled the shirt on, vaguely tucking it in before pulling up the leather braces that had been hanging at his sides. "Guten Abend, Fräulein."

"I . . ." Justine trailed off. "I don't speak German."

The man nodded, looked aside for a moment and then began again, this time in English. "Good evening, miss. Do you need something?" His accent was clipped, and in the firelight, his lined forehead became even more pronounced as he frowned. "Not right. I mean to say, may I help you?"

"Your English is very good," she said, hoping a compliment would somehow make amends for her bursting in on him.

"Thank you," he said. "May I help you?"

Justine frowned for a second, then realized why he was insisting on helping her. It was the middle of the night and she was prowling around like a burglar. "Do you work here?"

"Ja," he said with a chuckle. "And you do not."

"No," she said. Then she realized he wasn't wearing socks or shoes, and she was suddenly embarrassed. Justine Brewer, of Bad News Brewer fame, was *embarrassed.*

"Then what are you doing out of your bed?" He leaned forward, and the light hit him so she could see his features more plainly. And it was awful. He was even better looking than Tristan had ever been. This man had unkempt and unruly blond curls—far longer than what any Englishman would wear. He had light eyes and a jaw that could cut glass. Of all the damnable things. Now she would end up hating him. Handsome men were often atrocious, in her experience.

But he hadn't seemed to imbue his words with innuendo. He wasn't mentioning her bed with the idea that he might be getting in it. He was merely asking. How . . . unexpected.

"I couldn't sleep," Justine said, uncertain as to how to feel suddenly.

He blinked and nodded, as if that were a substitution for words. "Do you not read?"

What? Was he asking if she was literate? "Of course I read," she snapped. But then she realized where she was—a remote town in the mountains. There were likely many people here who did not read. And it was an activity one did to help a person fall asleep. Oh, she was being an arse. *Don't be an arse, don't be an arse,* she chanted to herself.

"Then why not read to sleep?"

"Are you shivering?" she asked, noticing a tremor as the light caught a billow of his white shirt.

"Ja. I am very cold."

"Then stand closer to the fire! Are you daft?" Without thinking, she pushed him back towards the impressively large decorative iron stove, with its open glowing grate. He let himself be guided, her hands on his shoulders. Justine was very aware of how much taller he was than her, and he stared down at her, amused.

"I am to help you," he said. "I am trying to be of service."

"You won't be of service to anyone if you catch your death," Justine snapped. "Do you not have thicker blankets?"

He chuckled again, a soft rumble from his chest that was more akin to a cat purring than a man laughing. "Why, when I am next to a big fire?"

The heat was powerful. Already, Justine's forehead prickled with sweat. She dropped her hands from where they had inadvertently started to droop to his chest. Oh dear. It was a firm and solid chest. Not at all like the soft, padded London men she was accustomed to chasing her. But then she realized that his clothes were damp. "Why are your clothes wet?"

"You ask many questions. I ask one. Will you please answer my one question, and then I promise I will answer whatever question you have. Promise?"

Justine looked up and blinked at him. She felt strange. Like the world had tilted in some way. Was it vertigo from the altitude change? Was she becoming ill? She was likely ill from all her travels. But there was nothing on God's green Earth that would persuade her to go to bed now. She felt like she needed to run for a full day to be rid of whatever energy possessed her right now. "Fine. What's your question?"

"May I help you?" he asked again, his words slow and emphasized.

"Oh. Erm, no? I can't sleep, that's all." She trailed off, not knowing how to describe the sensation in her limbs, so she shook them to demonstrate.

"Ah." He nodded as if he not only understood her flailing, but could sympathize. He held up his hand. "Moment."

He padded off into the darkness, and there was something about being able to see the bare bottoms of his feet that made Justine feel as if she were doing the most inappropriate thing possible. Her. Bad News Brewer, who had repeatedly stolen whole bottles of sherry from her parents' wine cellars to consume with Ophelia, getting drunk and playing stupid games as the room spun.

Bad News Brewer, who wore two dance cards so that the men who filled the same dance slot could argue or possibly fistfight over who got to have the waltz with her. Bad News Brewer, who once climbed the ancient oak at the Bridewells' London townhouse to dance on the slate-tiled roof because stupid Tristan had said she would be too scared. And that same Bad News Brewer was worried that the bottom of a man's foot was too much? What was the world coming to?

"Get ahold of yourself," she whispered to the giant iron stove.

He appeared out of nowhere, holding a bottle and two of the tiniest wine glasses in the world. "Hold what?"

Justine shook her head. "Nothing."

He gave her a confused smile, and Justine was reminded of Prudence, who smiled at every bloody turn of the day because she couldn't stop the facial tic. Bloody Americans and bloody Swiss.

But he didn't question her, only raised the bottle and the glasses and said, "Brandy."

"Of course," Justine said, relieved that there would be an activity, even if the activity was drinking some kind of alcohol, which had been drilled into her since practically birth that a young lady did not do in the company of men.

And for good reason. Because the middle of the night was a strange time, bound by its own rules, populated by its own sounds and scents. The dictums of day had no business interfering with whatever nighttime prowling discovered. Which was precisely why Justine preferred it.

The man poured the two glasses and handed her one. She accepted it and sniffed at the goldish-looking liquor. It smelled like apples and honey and the low burn of alcohol. Frankly, it smelled delicious. He held his glass out as a toast. "Proscht."

"Bless you," Justine said, knowing it was rude, but he smiled at her. "Cheers." She didn't move to touch his glass with hers, though he did with her. She didn't realize it was something she should have done, but she knew for next time that touching glasses was preferred here.

She sipped, tasting what seemed like a very nice French apple brandy. "Is this from here?" she asked. "Locally made?"

He shook his shaggy blond head. "Imported from Calvados. For the English. For you."

Justine laughed. "Of course the Swiss import French liquor for the English."

"You like it?"

She giggled. Oh God, she *giggled*. "Of course. Calvados is excellent."

He gestured to the seat near the fire, clearly where he had draped his clothing to dry. "Sit, please?"

She moved towards the chair but then stopped, her heavy woolen dress swinging against her ankles. "Where will you be?"

He gestured to another chair, farther back in the dining room. When he saw her concern, he reassured her. "I will bring the chair to the fire."

She nodded, taking his glass from him as she sat, giving him the opportunity to use both of his hands to move the chair over.

He placed the stiff-backed wooden chair closer to the fire and took his glass from her, taking a hefty swig, nearly emptying it. He looked at her expectantly.

"You're not saying I should—" she mimed tossing the glass back, as he had done.

"Ja," he said, his rumpled golden hair somehow adorable and not at all making her want to hate him for being pretty.

"Young ladies shouldn't," she protested before feeling very stupid about explaining what proper British ladies did as she sat in a Swiss inn at the foot of the Matterhorn. She was doing the extraordinary. She was full of daring. So with a smile, she tossed back the brandy with a swift motion. The apple liquor burned delightfully down her throat.

He laughed and clapped for her. "Brava!" He finished his glass and then poured another for both of them. "Warms you up for the temperature and for the conversation."

"I have to warm up for the conversation?" She watched the liquor spill into her glass.

"Maybe my English is not so good after all," he said.

"I suppose not. I don't even know your name. We should at least be introduced." Was she flirting on purpose? There were so many times she'd been accused of flirting that she didn't even know the meaning of the word anymore. Scandal sheets reported that she flirted if she shook someone's hand or laughed at a joke. She flirted when she did what every other young lady did, but if Bad News Brewer did it, the action was somehow imbued with extra meaning.

"Do we need names right now?" he asked.

"So I know what to call you? Better than 'O! You there!'"

"Is it?" he asked, stretching his legs out in front of him and crossing them at the ankles.

Justine noticed his thighs. She was not a person who noticed men's thighs. But his were powerful and as thick as her waist. This was a man who could build you an inn. Her mouth was unexpectedly dry, so she sipped again at her brandy, steadying her breath.

"If I know you, then I must treat you as a guest, and not as a ghost roaming the hotel at night." He chuckled to himself. "I want to be off-duty, just for these hours."

"I hadn't thought of it that way." She had never served any-one, never worked. She was obsequious to exactly no one, and planned on keeping it that way. But to live a life of service, whether a maid in a big home or in a simple Swiss mountain inn, had to take its toll somehow. "Then that's fine. Or as my American friend might say, 'O.K.'"

He pulled his chin back and looked at her askance. "What does this mean? The two letters together?"

Justine shrugged, another gesture she wouldn't have used if they had been properly introduced and not been drinking brandy in front of an open grate of an enormous iron stove where she could discreetly admire his very pretty thighs, the open vee of his shirt, the way his leather braces clung to his shoulders. "No clue. But she says it all the time. I believe she means it as something like 'yes,' but not as formal or certain of a yes."

The man pursed his lips as he looked into the fire, considering the new Americanism. "Interesting. I will try it. Maybe it is a useful thing. Yes, but with a circumstance."

"Exactly. 'Yes, but I have opinions'."

"O.K." He tried it out.

She grinned. "O.K."

He clinked his tiny glass to hers, and the crystal rang out in the dining room, a clear sound that seemed loud enough to raise the dead. "O.K."

"Cheers," Justine said, and dashed back the second mouthful.

"Good," he said approving of her intake. "More?"

Justine eyed her glass. There wasn't much in a single pour, but she was already sensing the delightfully warm tingle in her toes, and it probably wasn't the fire making her feel that way. "I really shouldn't."

"Bah," he said, bringing the bottle over to pour her another. "My ghost, please, another."

"I'm the ghost?" Justine said, holding her glass out. "You're the one who should be the ghost. You speak the language and all that. I only came down from my room, innocent as can be."

"Innocent? We are drinking the good apple brandy. Mein Onkel will be upset if he thinks a ghost drank the whole bottle."

"We are not drinking the whole bottle," she protested.

"Not if you go upstairs. You must help. Simple." He poured her a glass and tipped his own back, then refilled it.

"This must be the last one," she said, feeling the brandy swish to one side of her lips as she sipped. She licked at it with her tongue, and she noticed him watching her very carefully. As an experiment, she did it again, and he watched, going utterly still. Justine wondered if he would try to kiss her. She certainly wouldn't mind, nor would she stop him. Maybe being a ghost wasn't a bad thing.

He cleared his throat. "Why must this be the last glass?"

"Because alcohol affects me very strongly. I'm not as big as you are, after all."

"No," he agreed, his voice suddenly quiet and serious. The joking edge that he'd had earlier was gone, and he stared into the open grate of fire, not at her.

The atmosphere of the small dining room shifted, and she wondered if she'd done something wrong. The feeling had never happened to her before. Men—and honestly, some women—kept pursuing until they finally realized that Justine was serious when she said their suits were pointless. Justine was incapable of feeling that way towards someone.

Until now, anyway. When she wanted this Swiss tree trunk of a man to turn to her and beg to kiss her, beseech her for her name, give her trinkets and favors until he ran out of money or time. Instead, he stared into the fire. Somehow that camaraderie was lost, leaving her a bit put out.

But there was nothing she could do about it, she decided, ghost as she was. In order to escape all the sooner, she tossed back the last of the brandy and stood, holding her glass outstretched for him to take. "Thank you," she said as he accepted it. "That was most—"

Then the world swayed, and she felt as if the room was being turned on its side, the way a child might turn a picture book. Even in that smallest increment of time, she dreaded her head hitting the floor, knowing she was unable to stop it.

Instead, there was warmth. Too much heat. She was sweating so much, so hard, so fast. And her stomach did not feel right at all. And this lovely, warm tree cupped her face in his giant hands and said something she didn't understand at all.

"Scheiss," Karl said, swearing. She was but a little thing, small enough to bind up like an infant and haul on his back. He'd caught her as she fell, trying very hard to forget about her softness as he accidentally—accidentally!—brushed his hand along her bodice. But she had gone pale very quickly, and if there was one thing Karl knew very well, it was the signs of a novice drinker being sick.

He had just mopped this floor, one of his many tasks at the inn. He mopped, chopped wood, penned animals, milked the cows and the goats. And now, he needed to find a pail for his ghost.

He started to explain his plan, but he couldn't think of the English words, so he just ran behind the long bar that attached to the dining room and found the snow bucket. Easy enough to clean out, anyway. If he'd had his socks on, he could have slid across the waxed floor, but as it was, his bare feet squeaked and quaked across the new wood. He arrived in time, her mass of dark hair coming out of the pins she'd no doubt used in haste, not thinking she'd come upon anyone in the middle of the night.

She lifted her head. "I do apologize," she said and then began retching. He held her hair back, marveling at the silky tresses, knowing this would be the only time he'd get a chance to feel them in his hands. Was it an ideal moment? No. Was this as close as he'd been to a woman in almost a year? Yes. His world was not built for women to inhabit it. So the pleasure of running his hand through such silky and well-maintained curls was a rare one.

Given Karl's profession, he was more than capable of understanding pain and suffering while simultaneously wondering at the grandeur of the view and accomplishment. There was a dichotomy in life, one of profound beauty, and one of profound pain, and they often occurred at the same time.

Like this girl, beautiful and delightful, and also vomiting and not always keeping it confined to the bucket. He would need to mop again before breakfast.

"I'm too hot," she panted.

Karl took a closer look and saw she was wearing wool, head to toe. He tore off the woolen shawl tucked around her shoulders, revealing a tiny waist and an exquisitely ample bosom.

She retched. "Still too hot."

He scooped her up, hooking the pail with a spare finger, and took her to the back door of the dining room.

The massive wooden door didn't so much as creak as he yanked it open by its heavy iron ring. There was plenty of snow to cool down this English miss. He put her down, and she sank to all fours, her palms firmly planted in the ice. He pulled her hair off her neck, taking the initiative to try to re-pin some of her tresses. Her nape was sticky with sweat, so he scooped some snow in his hands and placed it there. She sighed in pleasure.

It was a sound he could not have accurately imagined. And now that he'd heard it, it would never go away. He knew that sigh would echo in his mind for years to come. Every lonely night, he would hear that sigh and remember his hands in those dark tresses, and his self-ministrations would move swiftly.

She scooped some of the crusted snow into her mouth, her body relaxing. Karl did his best to not look. For she was ill, and he still harbored very unprofessional images that flipped through his mind at the speed with which one might shuffle a deck of cards.

"I'm better," she said, still panting.

No doubt her heart pounded too quickly, and her stomach was still convulsing.

"Will you put more snow on my neck?" she asked, as if it were too much trouble.

It was no trouble at all. He very much liked holding his hand across the nape of her neck. She shifted, sitting back on her haunches, her hair a mass of unruly strands, tumbling loose about her shoulders. He had not done a good job pinning up her hair, but he did not care.

"This is perhaps the most embarrassing thing I have ever done." She slapped her hands on her knees, then winced. "And that is saying something."

He grinned. "We all make mistakes. Mine was giving you the expensive brandy. If I'd known it was all going to come up, I would have picked a different bottle."

That at least got a wounded chuckle from her. She was still in fine spirits, then. She might be hungover the next day, but that would ease as well. Perhaps he could give her some of the local remedies, which he had to admit helped.

"I normally can handle my liquor," she said, her eyes closed. She scooped the snow in her hands and smeared it across her face.

Karl was helpless. He could only watch her hands drift over her features, wishing it were him. No, not helping. Tomorrow, he would have to step into his professional role. There was no time to be dallying with foreign women. "Altitude. We are very high in the mountains already. Far higher than London. You cannot drink as much up here without feeling the effects."

"Why did you not tell me earlier?" She sounded genuinely upset.

"Who would not know this? Who would come to the Alps and not know?" This was silly—of course everyone knew that drinking at altitude saved money. This was a great joke for all mountaineers. But, he supposed, softening, as a maid in England, where there were no great heights, she might not have understood this.

"I didn't know!" She attempted to stand, but wobbled.

Karl was there, using his body to block her from falling inward on the hardwood floors. He put a hand out in front of her to catch her if she fell forward onto the snow. "I have you." At least he could remember that in English.

It wasn't second nature yet, to speak in English. His native Bavarian was not that far from the Swiss dialect spoken in Zermatt, which was an easy switch to make. And the Italian had been so similar to French that it hadn't bothered him much either. But he'd guided multiple trips in those languages. It was not having anyone to practice his English with that made it so difficult to remember.

But this girl guaranteed he would try. He was already formulating plans to ask for English lessons from her in the evenings after her duties were concluded. He didn't need them, as his father had drilled him in the importance of English for expanding their trade routes, but perhaps he could ask for colloquialisms and the like. It wasn't a lie, merely an exaggeration.

She gripped his hand, her smaller palms disappearing into his. But she didn't move again for quite some time. She balanced well, standing and breathing a steady rhythm, much as he did while ascending difficult terrain.

"I'm perfectly well now, thank you." She turned to face him, and if she had not just emptied her stomach all over the dining room, he would have tried to kiss her. Perfect bow lips. She was like a caricature of the perfect woman—cute but still possessing the curving traits that made his mind flip over to far more seductive thoughts.

She walked past him, veering into the wall. He scooped her up before she fell. She weighed nearly nothing. Despite her whispered protests, he tucked her close against his chest.

"You really don't need to—"

He shrugged, jostling her a little. She was still pale, her face turned up to his. Would she appreciate this heroic gesture? As he delivered her up the stairs, she told him her room number. Ah. The room with the viscount's daughter. So she worked for the honorable Miss Ophelia Bridewell. He tucked that information away.

He set her down on her feet, being as gentle as he was able. "Goodnight."

"Thank you," she said, clearing her throat. "That was quite the delivery."

"I do what is required of me," he said, with a smirk.

She returned the smile. "Most gallant." Instead of a kiss—

again, he'd given her too much brandy—he bowed to her.

Chapter Two

THE NEXT MORNING was not nearly as bad as she'd anticipated. Yes, her mouth was parched and her head throbbed until she downed a cup of water, but all of that was attributable to the long travels of the prior week. She didn't dare tell anyone of her midnight assignation with the undressed man in the dining room. Or her subsequent humiliation of casting up her accounts while on all fours in the snow.

Hopefully this man mostly worked out of doors and she wouldn't see him much. They, after all, had plans in place for altitude training and climbs in the mountain range before attempting to summit the Matterhorn in July—months away, but training was of the utmost importance.

Justine and Ophelia helped each other pin up their hair and button dresses, and went down to breakfast, wondering what to expect from the Swiss chalet that opened expressly for their expedition. None of the other inns in Zermatt were open for another month at least. Lord Rascomb had explained, as they'd bumped on donkeys through the empty town, that the Alpine inns didn't have a way to heat individual rooms adequately.

They met Prudence and Mr. Moon on the landing. While the couple greeted them, Justine could practically smell the unquenchable desire radiating from them. Mr. Moon was tall and thin, and very restrained, but even his reserve crackled with heat as he kept his eyes fixed on Prudence. And Prudence, her honey-gold hair normally pinned in a conservative chignon, was clearly hastily put up, letting portions of her coiffure sag and letting tendrils escape down her back—which Mr. Moon twirled around his finger when he thought no one saw.

But Justine saw. And she sighed. It wasn't that she envied Prudence; she envied Mr. Moon. She wanted to be besotted like that. And it had just never happened. She'd tried to be, but polite friendship was all she could muster. Or flirtatious bluster, as she'd done last night. Which ended in driving away another suitor, given that she'd spent a good portion of their conversation casting up her accounts.

The light in the window was very faint, not at all the bright, cheerful morning she'd expected. But when peering out the small windows, she found it was because the sun had not yet made it over the mountaintops, or at least, not from where this hotel sat. A bit odd, but that was the way her flat-landed self had been raised, she supposed.

The dining room smelled of sausage and coffee, thankfully, not of cast-up apple brandy. That was a relief. Lord and Lady Rascomb were already at the dining table, holding court for the entire room. Another wish for herself, to have a life where she even vaguely resembled this handsome older couple who exuded calm happiness.

It was one of the reasons Justine preferred to spend time at Ophelia's house rather than her own. Her parents were unfortunately mismatched. Her father was like her, which was why he had so much money, in Justine's opinion. He couldn't keep still, always working, always finding new ways to invest. Her mother, on the other hand, had spent a lifetime trying to understand him, or at least get along with him, and then bore a final girl child who couldn't hide her similarities to her frenetic father.

As Justine came around the table, Ophelia sitting next to her father, Justine took the place next to her best friend. But her eyes widened as she saw her Swiss guard from last night sitting across from Lord Rascomb.

In the daylight, he was chiseled like the mountains that sur-rounded the valley they occupied. Even his nose seemed rough-hewn, as if he'd been marked out of rock, and never polished into full man-form. He wore what Justine considered undress for a man—an open shirt, uncollared, with no cravat to cover that expanse of skin where a notch cratered between his throat and his chest.

He had blue eyes that were deep blue, not the light sky-blue that Ophelia had, or the gray-blue that Prudence sported. They were blue like a flower, or a lake after a storm. Why was he sitting at their table? If he worked for the innkeeper, he should be shuttling plates or brushing down horses or unloading something very, very heavy.

He gestured with one arm, and Justine did not understand how the seams of his clothing did not shear away from the strain against the width of his shoulders. He glanced over at her, an eyebrow cocked as if asking what she was doing, sitting at the table.

"Mr. Vogel, let me introduce the rest of the team. My daugh-ter, and leader of this expedition, Miss Ophelia Bridewell." He gestured to his daughter, his obvious pride swelling in his voice. It was one of Justine's favorite things about him. He was generous with his daughters as well as his sons. He let all four of his children explore the world in their own ways, supporting them for their choices, not shoving them into pre-ordained pigeonholes whether it suited them or not.

Her own father would not have allowed Justine to lead an expedition to climb the Matterhorn. Then again, Justine was not really suited for leadership. She was there for cheering everyone along, and for dragging all of them outside for a second run whether they wanted it or not. She knew they had to be prepared for altitude, and that meant working their hearts as best they could at sea-level London. But organization was not her strong suit.

Then Lord Rascomb gestured to Justine. "And this is Miss

Justine Brewer, also on the expedition. Miss Brewer, this is Mr. Karl Vogel, our lead guide on the expedition. He's successfully ascended the Matterhorn once before."

"Twice," Mr. Vogel corrected in a voice that should have sounded arrogant, but didn't. It sounded factual, not the hint of braggadocio she would have expected.

Lord Rascomb nodded and murmured his apologies for his inaccuracy, and proceeded to introduce Prudence and Mr. Moon, and when Eleanor and Tristan showed up, them as well. But the introduction rang in her head: lead guide. Lead guide. Mr. Karl Vogel, lead guide.

"Since we are all here," Ophelia said sometime later as empty plates were being cleared by a woman, and not the innkeeper's nephew, "let's begin our expedition meeting early."

Justine looked up from her plate where she'd pushed a sausage around in circles, not thinking, only remembering and cringing. Their lead guide now knew that she didn't sleep, she prowled around in the dark, alone, and couldn't handle her liquor. Wonderful. Though it made sense now why he spoke such good English. The British were the ones who went after these mountains more than anyone else. At least, she thought so? Maybe the French, too. Or the Americans. It didn't matter why Mr. Vogel spoke English. He did. And very well, too.

Ophelia began with the timeline. Lady Rascomb opened a valise that must have been set near her chair and began producing paper—the timeline written down. Maps of terrains. Climbs they would do before the Matterhorn. Weather patterns and requirements for them all to look for as spring melted into summer.

"At this stage," Ophelia said, looking at all of them, "there are two things we must do. The first is that we need to acclimate to this altitude. That's why we are here so early in the season. Even if we do nothing but walk around Zermatt, we are acclimating. The second thing is to keep ourselves in good health. We still require our training regimes, our knot-tying skills. So, we will be venturing up nearby peaks to understand the tools we will need for our attempt. It will help with our rope skills, as well as build Mr. Vogel's confidence in our abilities."

Ophelia's face was hard, and Justine knew the next part was something that made her angry. Ophelia's anger was rare, but when it existed, it was white-hot rage. So, whatever it was, Justine flinched. Justine's temper was easier to flare, but also easier to cool.

Lord Rascomb cleared his throat. "You all know that I have utmost faith in you. Our summit of Ben Nevis was proof of that. However, many people don't believe women have the stamina for climbing mountains."

Justine laughed out loud. She couldn't help it. The absolute nerve. She looked at Karl Vogel and crossed her arms. Had he never heard of giving birth? Marriage? Ask her mother what those were all about, and she would say *stamina.*

Lord Rascomb looked at Justine not with annoyance, but with pleading. "Therefore, Ophelia has agreed, and I have given my word and a monetary stipend to reinforce this, we will allow Mr. Vogel to be the final say on who climbs on the morning of our Matterhorn attempt."

"I beg your pardon?" Justine exploded. Now she leaned forward, elbows on the table, as rude as could be. Thank goodness her mother wasn't here. She pointed at the blond ox, who sat calm as the Devil himself. "He has no idea of our capabilities."

"But he will," Ophelia said. "Mr. Vogel will be helping us with our training and leading us on our associated climbs. I expect him to be fair and impartial, judging us not on our womanliness, but on our abilities."

Justine's head pounded again, almost as if outrage cued a hangover. "There is no man who can look past our womanliness."

Lord Rascomb cleared his throat. "I'd like to think I don't hold your abilities in account of your sex, Miss Brewer."

She crossed her arms. "Fine. You don't, but you're Ophelia's father. But this man?" She glared down the man who had put cold snow on the nape of her neck when she'd needed it. But also the bloke who hadn't warned her about drinking spirits at high altitude.

"We cannot ask him to be impartial if we cannot be impartial, Justine," Prudence said from across the table, living up to her name. Why was Prudence as level-headed as Ophelia? "Let's give him the benefit of the doubt."

"If Lord Rascomb believes he is honorable, then I will trust him," Eleanor said. Of course she would side with her new father-in-law.

Justine narrowed her eyes at Tristan, waiting for him to ally himself with his father and now his wife as well. But Tristan wisely kept his mouth shut for once. He even lifted his hands in a give-up gesture as she stared him down. Finally, she looked back to Ophelia, who chewed the inside of her lip. She didn't like it any, either.

"Fine," Justine blustered and stared down this Karl Vogel. This mountain of a man who held her fate in his hands.

Ophelia clasped her hands and put them on the table. "Then our final order of business is to discuss our upcoming week. You will have the rest of today off to walk and explore the village, which will acclimate you to the elevation. Tomorrow, we will start with our first run. Mr. Vogel, I cede the table to you."

He nodded and gave a side glance to Justine. She frowned. What did he mean by that?

"The training run for the expedition team will begin promptly at one in the afternoon. For those of you who wish to work more, I also begin my day at six in the morning. You may come with me before breakfast, if you wish."

Justine narrowed her eyes. He didn't look at her, but she felt the challenge in his voice. He got up and worked at six in the morning? Then she would be downstairs, dressed, and ready to go fifteen minutes before that.

KARL HAD MADE a mistake. He understood that, and there were few ways to fix what he had done by presuming the girl was a servant. How could he have made such an error? It was purely, he believed, because he had hoped she was a maid, for if she were, she would be within his reach. But since she was the daughter of a British man of consequence, Karl Vogel had no ability to touch her. She was a client.

She was also the most vocal against the idea of his judging who would climb, which he understood. Pride was a powerful beast, and the girl seemed to have much of it. Did she know that the mountains would eat her alive if she kept up her pride? That the snow did not care how carefully one's argument was constructed or how straight one's spine was?

Pride in the mountains was akin to death. And if they were to succeed, then he had to find a way to teach her humility. Not the kind of humility Jakob had advocated when they'd first discussed the possibility of guiding a mostly-woman-filled expedition. Jakob had recommended taking them over his knee, spanking them, and sending them home.

Though the thought of taking this girl over his knee made him light-headed. She was even more spectacular in daylight. Dressed now in a simple gown, the pink and blue confection hugged her curves, accenting a small waist and an ample bosom. The cut of the dress hinted at a high, tight, and round hintern that would fill even his generous palms.

So he offered an early run. That would make her humble enough, knowing that he was out there, working, while she slept late. By demonstrating that she was too small to keep up with the other women, and could not put in the athletic work that was required for even an attempt at the Matterhorn, the problem would solve itself. He would not have to declare who could climb and who couldn't, as the specter of death and hardship would cause her and possibly the rest of the women, to stay away from the mountain.

But after he'd announced his morning run, he saw her face. The set of her jaw, the thinning of those apple-red lips. Her eyes bored into him, her gaze as weighty as a plow harness. He ignored it, feeling hopeful, as that kind of defiant stance was what pushed a person up a mountain. For every climb was difficult or painful. If it wasn't, then it wasn't truly a climb. It was a lark. An old woman's amble.

The meeting adjourned, and Karl forced himself to look at the young Fräulein Bridewell for permission to leave. It was difficult to not look to Lord Rascomb, the Englishman whose robustness and bearing reminded Karl of so many other roving adventuring Englishmen he'd met.

Indeed, he had been successful twice in attempts on the Matterhorn. He dared not tell Lord Rascomb how many had been unsuccessful. That many, many slogs up the mountain had been aborted only a few hours up due to weather or snow. That both were unpredictable, and the mountain chose its own favorites.

What he found surprising was that these women had a focused exercise they conducted to ready themselves for the attempt. Some of the men who arrived were shocked to find they did not function as normal at this altitude. More sickened as they attempted even some basic mountain ascents. The altitude, like the mountains, was unforgiving. He commended Fräulein Bridewell on giving her team a long lead time, giving them an opportunity to learn the terrain, accustom their bodies, and watch the weather. It showed patience and dedication. Karl appreciated that about her, wondering if that was her wisdom or her father's.

He caught himself watching Miss Brewer sway out of the room. She walked with angry purpose, and he was drawn to it like a bee to a flower. But he shook his head. This was not the time to be consumed by lust. There was much to do.

His Onkel Peter caught his eye, and Karl went to the wooden

bar to speak with him.

"What did they talk about?" His Onkel asked in Bavarian. His hands never stopped moving, polishing the glasses that he then rehung above the bar.

"Planning climbs, that's all," Karl answered. "Shall I clear the plates?"

Onkel Peter nodded. "Then tend the goats. And don't forget to mend the fences today, as well. I don't want the goats escaping again. Frau Lieder wants my head for the nibbles of her laundry."

Karl laughed as he cleared the tables. His aunt Greta was in the kitchen cleaning up with their one hired-on maid, Elke, who was washing the giant pots and pans Greta had used to cook breakfast for their guests.

"There," Greta said, pointing to the only bit of space available on the countertops. "Thank you for clearing the plates, Karl. You're a very good boy."

He smiled and returned to the dining room to clear more. As he finished, he took a rag to wipe down the tables.

"Ach, my Karl, thank you. And will you be able to help with the guests at tea time?" Greta asked, her hands, like Peter's, always in motion.

"Of course, Aunt," Karl said, though between the goats and fences, he wasn't sure when he would have time. But he would make time.

⤜⤛✦⤚⤛

JUSTINE DIDN'T KNOW what to do with herself. She and Ophelia walked into the village, which was very small and very sleepy. But it was ringed by the fantastical-looking mountains, and a crisp blue sky. Snow carpeted the ground and crunched hard beneath their feet. It took them all of twenty minutes to explore, and the villagers looked at them with curiosity.

They passed the famed Monte Rosa hotel, where Whymper

and his team had stayed. Where famed lady climber Lucy Walker lived in the summers with her father. As far as Justine knew, Lucy Walker had yet to attempt the Matterhorn, but she had climbed the other mountains in the range. If they were to bet, it was between them and Walker to be the first woman up the Matterhorn. There were a few other women climbers who might make a run on it as well. A few Americans. But Justine had never met any of them. It was strange how women kept themselves apart in such a venture. All of them smarting from the lack of inclusion and the outright hostility from men climbers.

"What a warm welcome," Justine said, as one older woman opened her door to examine them and then shut it again without a word or greeting.

"We must be quite the event," Ophelia said.

"There isn't anything else happening here," Justine said. "I'm going to crawl out of my skin if I can't *do* something."

The nice thing about having been friends for such a long time was that Ophelia didn't judge her. Ophelia smiled and looked at her fondly, as this was a typical complaint of Justine's. And she knew it, too. Justine bounced on her toes as she walked, itching to move.

"You can always help me with the maps. We have several climbs to plan in the next few months."

"I hate maps," Justine groaned. There was something about them that made her brain blank like an empty page. No matter how much she concentrated, a map was as good as a landscape of an ocean to her.

"You could help our guide, Herr Vogel, with preparations." Ophelia's light blue eyes blinked in absolute innocence.

Justine narrowed her eyes.

Ophelia shrugged. "He's probably very busy and could use your help."

"What are you talking about?"

"Did you notice what a fine-featured man he is? That chin. That nose. Those eyes."

"He does have all of those facial features, yes, I noticed he wasn't missing any." Justine crossed her arms.

"I thought they were very nicely put together. And well-formed."

"Good," Justine shot back, knowing very well that Ophelia was trying to distract her boredom. "Then you can arrange a courtship."

"For you? Justine, I'm so surprised," Ophelia said with no hint of malice.

Justine's boot crunched over a puddle that had melted and then re-frozen. The ice was delicate and the shattering noise was exquisite. Justine loved that sound. But still, Ophelia was being unreasonable. "What?"

"He tried very hard not to stare at you at breakfast," Ophelia said. "So much so that he barely looked at you, even when you threw your big fit."

"I did not throw a fit." Justine knew that her emotions lived more near the surface than others'. She knew there were times when she seemed out of sorts while everyone else was calm. But it wasn't that she was emotional for no reason. There was absolutely a reason: having some man evaluate who could and could not climb was practically guaranteeing they would never step foot on the Matterhorn. "But it's a stupid rule, and you know it."

"It is, and I agree. But it was the only way any guide would take the risk."

Justine fumed. She knew the guides had been under particular scrutiny since Edward Whymper's successful summit of the Matterhorn, and Lord Douglas's subsequent death, falling while on the descent. The two men who had guided, a father and son, were sued by the families of the three British men who died, and were salaciously accused of negligence. Or, which some considered to be worse, that the younger guide cut the rope on purpose, severing himself from the men who had fallen. Whether it was to save himself or purposeful murder didn't matter. The blight on their reputation was the same.

That faithful ascent, only four years prior, had shaken the mountaineering world. Justine had attended the London Alpine club meetings, despite the fact that she was unwanted and hissed at. She'd hissed right back at them, the cowards. That was before they started to outright bar her entrance.

"Shall we head back to the inn?" Ophelia asked.

Justine looked up, realizing that they'd made an entire loop of the village. There wasn't much but the houses of the few families who lived there, two inns, and snowy piles of lumber that awaited the spring. "I suppose. Not much else to do."

"I need to plan the next climb—but I need some information from Mr. Vogel first. His insight would be most welcome. Would you like to come with me?"

Justine set her jaw. "No matchmaking. And I'll come because I'm bored, not because I want to see what Mr. Vogel is doing."

"Quite," Ophelia said, her mouth twitching.

Justine tried to be annoyed. She wanted to be annoyed. But she really did want to see what Mr. Vogel was up to. Even if he'd seen her at her worst. Even if he held her fate in those large, calloused hands.

Chapter Three

GOATS WERE FIRST on his chore list, only because the longer they were ignored, the louder they became. Tante Greta was sensitive to goats' incessant bleating, so he did his best to keep them happy. He'd mucked out their enclosure, put down fresh hay, and checked each animal for overall health, which mostly meant leaning against the fence and letting the curious animals work their hungry lips around his clothing.

He'd taken off his outer coat and laid it across the fence rail. Still, the cool sweat made his shirt stick to his back. The goats nibbled at his fingers and then investigated the cotton shirt that Karl pulled at. While he was in the pen, he checked the fence beams, pulling and pushing at them to test how well placed they were, and if they would stand up to a determined goat.

He tidied away the implements and patted the goats on their heads before leaving the pen. Next up were the fences at the edge of the grazing pasture. He swung by the shed behind the inn, and that was where they found him.

"Mr. Vogel," Fräulein Bridewell greeted. She wore a plain bonnet, but still far more lace adorned it than graced any of the women in the valley here.

Karl winced and shut the shed door. "Guten Morgen, Fräulein Bridewell." Then he noticed the girl behind her. "Fräulein Brewer."

The cool air had pinked her cheeks. She looked in perfect

health, even if she was staring at him with murder in her eyes. It made him grin before he remembered that he should not show too much interest. He tempered his expression and hefted the long-handled hatchet over his shoulder. "I must repair a fence before the light leaves. If you have need of something, perhaps you will walk with me?"

"Thank you, we'd be glad to accompany you." Fräulein Bridewell glanced over her shoulder to Fräulein Brewer, who rolled her eyes with such drama, he'd think he was transported to the theater in Munich.

Karl turned, smothering another smile as he led them up the trail. The snow was thin and crusty from the wind and sun. There would likely be one more snowfall before summer, but the valley did not receive as much snow as the surrounding mountains. The town was protected by its geographical arrangement, not that Karl needed to persuade anyone of the natural idyll Zermatt possessed. Indeed, its virtue in his mind was that it was difficult to get to, making any traveler more predisposed to fall in love. It was the reward at the end of a harrowing trail, not unlike reaching the peak of an Alpine ascent.

They trudged behind him, and he was pleased that their breathing sounded even as they continued up the side of the valley.

"I didn't realize you were taking us on a hike," Fräulein Brewer grumbled behind him. The snow made for a perfect sound carrier. He could hear her as if she were speaking directly into his ear. A flash of remembrance from the night before hit him, when he'd been so tempted to kiss her, so close to her, smelling her, her unbound hair brushing his arm.

"In other languages, we say this is a walk, as any walk. We don't make distinctions. It is the English who have to prepare themselves. The rest of us, we expect hills."

"Hills?" Fräulein Brewer protested. "This is an actual mountain."

Fräulein Bridewell huffed a laugh. "Where are you taking us,

Mr. Vogel?"

"The edge of the grazing pasture. It is not too far now." Karl glanced back at them. Neither of them was bent at the waist or fatigued. Good sign. They continued without speaking, him listening to their rhythmic breathing and clear steps. Perhaps taking them up a mountain wouldn't be so bad after all. But surely, even with three months of preparation, they could not be serious about the Matterhorn.

The downed fence was easy to find. The split-rail fence abutted the forest. It was obvious from the arrangement that snowmelt had pushed a boulder down the hill, crashing it into the fence, and irreparably cracking the wooden rails. It would only take a dry day to make the wood split and crack even further, allowing the boulder to continue its path downward.

After assessing the damage, Karl leaned the hatchet against the trunk of a tree. "So," he said, and then set to rolling the boulder to a copse of trees that would easily hold its weight. He returned to the damaged fence, getting his breath under control. "What questions do you have for me?"

JUSTINE HAD NOTHING in her head, which was unusual. Typically, she had a ticker tape of constant reminders, worries, thoughts, and tasks scrolling through her head. But here, watching Karl Vogel push a boulder, Justine could not remember a single one.

Thighs. That's what she thought. Those massive thighs flexing as he pushed away the boulder. Then, when he returned, broad chest heaving, she had to push herself to think. Thankfully, Ophelia took the opportunity to speak, because Justine was lost.

"Mr. Vogel, we would like to arrange to climb several of the surrounding mountains over the coming weeks, as preparation for the Matterhorn come summer." Ophelia stepped forward. "We would very much like to have your expertise in knowing which mountains and terrain would be best for acclimation to the Alpine environment."

Justine finally came to herself long enough to realize Ophelia was using her obsequious voice. Was that really necessary? He was their guide. She paid him. He had to do what he was told. Why was she flattering him?

A breeze came up and chilled her. She pulled at her woolen cape and marveled at Mr. Vogel's work without a coat. Was he impervious to the cold, as he'd been impervious to the altitude? It was hard for her to concentrate on the words they were exchanging, and Justine looked away to clear the space Karl took up in her mind. The vista was beyond words she could string together. Scotland had been beautiful, but so was this, in an entirely different way. The white crimping of the surrounding mountains fairly glowed a bone-bleached white in the morning light.

"Wait for the alpenglow this evening," he called to her. "That is even more beautiful."

She glanced back at him, surprised he noticed her lack of attention. Surprised anyone noticed her when Ophelia was around. Honestly, it shocked Justine how many suitors she had, being short, reckless, talkative, and, according to her mother, foolhardy. Mostly because she always stood next to Ophelia, who was tall, regal, intelligent, ambitious, aristocratic, and logical. And blonde.

And Justine didn't think that just because they'd been friends since leading strings. Ophelia was all of those things, and yet, men didn't flock to her. They cleared their throats, bowed deeply at the waist, and asked her to dance, where they rarely spoke, apparently. Ophelia reported not enjoying dancing because her partners were so quiet. Justine, on the other hand, couldn't make any of them shut their pitiful gobs.

So the fact that Karl Vogel called over to her was surprising. Shouldn't he be scraping and bowing to Ophelia?

"Then it's settled?" Ophelia asked. Karl nodded his head once, and then Ophelia turned around and looked at Justine, beaming.

That told Justine she should have been paying attention. The sound of the hatchet made her jump. She whirled around to find Ophelia stepping lightly down the path to where Justine stood, and Karl cutting down a tree.

It was, in a word, magnificent. But it didn't stop there. With two hard cuts, one from either side, the thin tree fell right to where the broken fence sat. He cut it to size, and with every swing, Justine's mouth grew drier.

"We should get back," Ophelia said.

Justine nodded in agreement, but she could not make her feet move. Not as Karl stood the tree trunk on its end and stripped the bark from it. She had believed, not knowing exactly how a fence was mended, that it was a project that took a long time. She expected twine or wire, or nails or something. But no. None of those things. Only the broad-shouldered blond Karl Vogel with his long-handled hatchet.

"Good thing you aren't the fainting type," Ophelia said.

"Good thing," Justine managed.

Karl looked up, noticing them still standing there. "Did you need something further, Fräulein Bridewell?"

"Not at all, but Fräulein Brewer had a question." Ophelia elbowed Justine in the ribs.

"I hate you," Justine whispered to her friend.

"Ja, Fräulein?" His bright blue eyes landed on hers, and she had never felt as utterly stupid as she did right then.

Her mind fumbled for something, anything. "What time will we be going on our walk tomorrow?"

"One in the afternoon," he said, wiping sweat from his brow. There was amusement in his face. And it made her cheeks burn with embarrassment.

"Then I'll see you at six." Justine turned her back to him with every ounce of willpower she had.

"Thank you, Herr Vogel. *Dankeschön.*"

Justine couldn't help but give Ophelia side-eye as they descended the mountain. "Did you really thank him in German?"

"Of course," Ophelia countered. "It's polite. We are in Switzerland; we should do our best to learn the language of our location."

"It's pointless. We'll be gone in a few months, and he speaks English." Justine balled her fists. Why did she feel so irritated suddenly?

"We may be gone from this trip, but the German climbers are some of the most successful. If I want to continue to climb and have a decent reputation, I need to learn as many languages as I can."

"I thought you already knew French," Justine said.

It was Ophelia's turn to give side-eye. "Which is helpful, but French and German are not at all alike."

Justine shrugged. They'd gone to the same ladies' boarding school, but Justine had always skipped French. The class was held at four o'clock in the afternoon, an hour that Justine could not stay awake for. The comfort of a drowse in the meager sunshine that landed on her bed during that time was unarguable.

Dinner came quickly after they got down the trail. The inn supplied a cup of tea and a slice of apple cake at three, and then it was seven, and they were expected to sit down and eat again. The meal felt early to her, but then, she would have to shift her waking and sleeping hours if she was to beat Karl Vogel at his own game. She eyed him at dinner. After serving everyone, he sat at another table, speaking German or Swiss, or whatever language everyone but her spoke, laughing. He drank from a tankard, which she supposed was full of ale or beer. What did she know of the drinking habits of Swiss mountain guides?

Good, she thought. Drink up. Because tomorrow morning, she was prepared to run faster and harder and make him keep up with *her*.

She went to bed early that night, surprising Ophelia with a simple *goodnight* before turning down her oil lamp. Normally, she couldn't fall sleep quickly, but with the Alpine walks combined with the lack of sleep the night before, she fell deep and fast.

Periodically through the night, she awoke, each time checking the small timepiece she'd bought to wear on her breast. The green ribbon was bright enough to pick off her nightstand, and the portable brazier glowed enough for her to see the timepiece. When it was finally five in the morning, Justine got dressed.

She crept down the stairs, her hair braided, her boots double tied, knit cap in hand. There was a creak on the third stair, and again on the fifth—she would have to learn these. After all, didn't Karl sleep in the dining room? At least, he did last night. She wouldn't want to wake him and alert him to her presence before it was time. At a quarter till six, she thought she was safe, until she rounded the corner to find Karl bouncing on his toes.

"Are you ready?" he asked.

A stab of disappointment hit her. Bloody hell. She'd meant to surprise him, and there he was, bright-eyed, ready to run. "I am."

"Any others?" he asked, glancing up the stairs.

"No, just us." Justine grimaced. Fine, he got her today, but tomorrow, she would be down there at half past, just to prove a point.

HE TOOK HER up the goat trail first. The sky was dark, but she didn't complain. What starlight there was reflected on the snow, and the trail they left in the crusty snow was easy to spot. Karl knew she wouldn't get lost on the only trail, and sound travelled well on snow, and he'd hear her if she fell too far behind.

When they reached the repaired fence, he walked them along it until they got to the gate. He pushed down the latch, which moved the rock that served as the weight to keep the latch down and the gate closed.

"That's a clever thing," she murmured as she passed through the gate.

Karl inwardly fumed at the audacity of the English. Of course it was clever. People had been living here forever. It wasn't just the English who invented. There were plenty of scientists and inventors and philosophers from the German provinces and Switzerland as well as other places. Without the Germans, England would have no composers, since they liked to pick their favorites from other countries and then call them their own. But as he led her higher up the goat path, and the sun crested the mountain ridge, he realized that she had only complimented a gate. He had no reason to hold centuries of history over her head, as if she alone were responsible for the actions of an empire.

He listened to her breathing growing more and more labored. She was unaccustomed to hills such as these. There was no replacement for this simple act of walking up a mountain.

With her comfort in mind, he stopped at an overlook to let her catch her breath. She pulled up short next to him, gulping in air. The wind had loosened her braids, and a dark brown strand crossed her neck like a velvet ribbon. She was very pretty with her dark brown eyes, large and searching as she took in the sight of the valley below and mountains.

She made a lilting high-pitched noise in her throat, still too winded to speak. But Karl took that as an affirmation that she found the view as beautiful as he did.

"Are you well?" he asked her, concerned at how long it took her to catch her breath. The cold air could push into a person's lungs and make them feel icy cold from the inside out.

She swallowed hard, gulping more air before clearing her throat. "I'm well, thank you."

"Good," he said. "Eat some snow."

Her breath stopped laboring as she looked at him as if he'd lost his mind.

"You cannot be coughing your way up a mountain. It takes too long. Have some snow to wet your throat." Did she not have basic sense? Her cheeks were bright red from exertion, and she needed to clear herself of the excess heat that a woolen dress kept close. And while he didn't think she had wet lung—they were not that high in elevation, and the way he might check was to put his ear to her breast, and he didn't think that would be permitted— eating snow would be helpful.

She stared at him more. "From the ground."

"From wherever," he said, gesturing to the trees that dripped ice from their needles. "Are you so blue-blooded that you cannot drink your own water?"

Her eyebrows raised up so far that they disappeared underneath her knit cap. "I beg your pardon."

"You have a need. Take the snow that is available to you." Karl gestured at the tree again. Maybe he could blame her for all of the ignorance the English brought with them. Treating the Swiss as if they were backward yokels, stupid and barely deserving respect. Throw money at them, and they jump at the chance to carry supplies, show them trails, help them achieve the impossible.

She didn't move to scoop any snow or shake ice from the tree. No, she stared at him as if he were a naughty schoolboy. He did not like it.

"Who do you think I am?" she asked, placing her fists on her hips, accenting how tiny her waist was in a way that made him wonder what it would feel like to have his own hand there, in the dip of her waist. Wonder what it would feel like to pull her closer to him while his hand was there.

He shrugged as if he did not care, and not that he did not know. Because he didn't. "A spoiled aristocrat from England."

She laughed so loud and so suddenly he worried about an avalanche. He didn't know why she was laughing other than a possibility of frost-induced lunacy, if there was such a thing.

"I'm no aristocrat. If only my father could have heard that!" Her voice was still laced with humor. She shook her head. "Me, on the same plane as Ophelia?" She cooed out a last chuckle.

He was dumbstruck. Apparently, he was incorrect about her social standing, but why was that a cause of such humor? It put him into even more of a dark mood. He turned to head up the next path, where there were three choices, three branches to choose, all of different difficulty.

Over his shoulder, he watched as she drew her woolen mitten under her nose. So not a blue blood. He gritted his teeth and started up the steepest path. Let her prove how hardy she was.

AT HALF PAST noon, Ophelia touched her shoulder to wake her.

That man wanted to kill her. Murder by mountain. Justine peeled open one eye. "Do you have any food?"

Worry creased Ophelia's face. "I could go ask the kitchen . . . ?"

Justine held up her hand to stop her friend. At least she was still dressed. Even her boots. She'd returned from their hike as breakfast was being served and gone up to the room to wash her face and hands, but instead had fallen asleep on the bed. Her feet were swollen and hot in her boots, but she didn't care.

In her fatigue, she rolled off the bed, landing on the floor on all fours.

"Goodness," Ophelia commented, jumping back.

Justine used her hands to climb up to standing. "I'm fine. Some bread and cheese, and water, I'll be ready for the next round."

Lots of water.

Ophelia was ready to go downstairs, so they left the room together. Justine's thighs felt shaky on the stairs, but she'd manage. She needed some food, and after that, all would be correct.

Sure enough, the innkeeper handed her a circular roll with cheese and dried meat stuffed inside of it. The episode took some pantomiming, but they got through it. And as they waited for Eleanor and Tristan to join them, Herr Brunner came to her holding a tankard so full it splashed onto the floor.

Justine accepted it gratefully. The bread was delicious, but she was parched. "Apple?" she asked, as the aroma made it unmistakable.

"Apfel, ja," Herr Brunner said, nodding.

"Does it have alcohol?" Ophelia asked, peering into the tankard.

"No idea. Drinking it anyway," Justine said, keeping a smile plastered on her face to appease Herr Brunner. She gulped it down, the sugar hitting her bloodstream almost instantly.

Karl Vogel appeared in the doorway, looking nearly a foot wider than his uncle. She turned away from him and scarfed her roll down as quickly as she could. She didn't want to show any weakness, and that included hunger.

The two men talked, and Justine kept her face averted as she chewed. Tristan and Eleanor descended, followed by Prudence, who looked flushed and hurried. Justine risked a glance back at Karl, who was counting the group with a nod of his head. She swallowed the knot of bread, and it got stuck in her throat.

She downed the rest of the apple cider, the wide mouth of the tankard allowing the liquid to splash down the side of her chin. Great look. Just bloody adorable. Couldn't even eat without covering herself in it.

Wiping her mouth and dabbing at her neckline where the apple cider landed, she turned forward, only to find him watching her. Embarrassment burned through her again. Just a bloody goddess over here, ready to scale to the highest of heights, even though she couldn't manage to put food and drink in her mouth correctly.

"Have I missed anything?" Prudence asked, hurriedly finishing a plait in her hair.

Justine shook her head, still feeling the lump in her throat from the bread. Why couldn't she be a normal person, the kind of normal person that didn't care if Karl Vogel saw her eating?

"Are all people here?" Karl called to the group.

Ophelia turned around, assessed their cadre, and nodded in

the affirmative.

"Then we go," he announced, and turned on his heel, leaving the rest of them to fall in line.

He trucked them up the same goat path they'd taken earlier that morning. The back of Justine's thighs burned, and she dragged, waiting for that second wind to lift her into the bliss of a working body. They passed the mended fence and went through the gate, to which the other women and Tristan murmured their appreciation of its ingenuity.

Stopped, Justine had time to look at Karl. His face was mostly impassive. Mostly. Something about the group's comments on the gate seemed to rile him. His expression changed subtly, and if she hadn't watched him so closely, she would have missed it. Something about that gate made him mad. What an odd man. Who cared about a gate?

Well, if goats were a person's only company, that could put things in a very different perspective. He settled his features, and his eyes met hers. She thought she should look away, but she wasn't a bashful girl. Lady. Woman. What was she now? A Fräulein? Whatever anyone called her was what she would be. As her mind flipped through this progression, Karl's blue eyes stared her down. She smiled at him, which might have been flirtatious, or simply polite. She honestly couldn't tell, so she did it anyway.

Karl didn't return the smile, instead turning and continuing up the goat path. Justine anticipated revisiting the steep climb he'd taken her on earlier that morning, and even looked forward to it. The view had been wonderful, but now at the divergent paths, he chose the one to the right instead of the far left.

Justine frowned, but went along. Was this to be even more challenging? But no, it wasn't. In fact, it was a far easier amble up a gentle slope. This time, Justine was distracted by the wonderful crispness of the air, countered by the warmth of the sun as it crested out above the trees.

Ahead of them was a wooden building. What would she call it? It certainly could not be considered a house, though, from the children spilling out of it, that was its purpose. The children clambered their welcome to Karl as he approached. He scooped up the littlest girl in one arm and the littlest boy in the other. The rest danced around him as if he were a hero in a folk story.

Karl was treated like a prince among men by these children. In the doorway, the shortest man Justine had ever seen appeared. No, he wasn't short. His back hunched over so severely he appeared as if he were permanently bowing. But the man didn't seem to be in pain or otherwise troubled. Karl ushered their group inside, crowding an already-crowded hut.

It was dark, for the windows were closed, and the air was stale and musty, smelling of overripe cheese and bodies and hay. Soon they found out why. This man was a cheesemaker. There was a pen of goats in the back, separated by a wooden wall and a closed door, but their incessant curious *maa maa* made for funny pauses in conversation. The cheesemaker only spoke in Swiss, as did the children. Karl translated.

They were ushered to the long table, where they sat obediently, unsure of what to do or say, since none of them spoke Swiss German. Ophelia focused on the cheesemaker and Karl, ignoring the rest of them, clearly trying to lead by example. Or lead in some kind of way. Justine exchanged looks with Prudence, who smiled, because Prudence not smiling was a strange event. Even Justine, who smiled an obscene amount, could not out-smile Prudence. Eleanor and Tristan held hands beneath the table's edge, and that made Justine feel happy for them. Even if Tristan was objectively the worst person in the entire world. She'd forgiven him enough that she'd blessed his and Eleanor's marriage. Not that they'd asked her.

Light spilled around the room in edges—some from a window frosted along the bottom frame, which had been scratched through by a child's nail at some point. The canvas curtains were thinned and old, but hemmed nicely. There was a loft that overlooked the table where they sat, and Justine could make out two sets of eyes from beneath a blanket. The shyest of them all, no doubt.

The rest of the children either returned to their tasks or played with the strangers. The littlest girl and boy still sat on Karl's lap, content to be held. It was such a strange sight, she thought. Her father had never held them on his lap. And she'd never seen any other father do that either. But it looked so natural for him. As if he actually liked them. Did he? Did someone actually *like* children? What an appalling thought.

The two men talked, then Karl translated for the rest of them. She'd better pay attention to this, but she couldn't. There were too many things to look at, and all these children to watch. What were they doing? At least she figured out one of the girls was mending a piece of clothing. Another was hauling a pail of water through the door to the goat pen. For a moment, the bleating of the goats was louder when the door opened, then muted as the girl closed the door behind her.

But Justine's observations were cut short by a plate offered to them all: dark bread smeared with cheese and a dab of honey. There was enough for a slice for each of them. She held her piece aloft while she waited for all of them to get a slice. The same as her friends, because manners taught them to wait until everyone had their share, and then they could eat.

But the cheesemaker gestured to all of them, emphatically. She knew that gesture: "Eat, eat!" Apparently, the table manners drilled into her did not apply in Swiss cheese huts. So she bit into the hunk of black bread, and fell in love. The sweet honey balanced the tangy cheese, and the lightness of that contrasted with the dry, dense bread.

"He says that he planned to give you dried apricots also, but the children got into them and ate them all." Karl looked around at them as he translated, ruffling the bright hair of the children on his lap.

Justine looked closer and saw that the children watched them eat. They were thin children, not emaciated, but certainly not plump like she or her siblings had been. This was a great extravagance to share with them. Suddenly, she no longer wanted to eat anymore, but didn't want to offend anyone by not eating. Still, she chewed. And her stomach growled loud enough for everyone to hear.

Rather than be embarrassed, she played it up, grabbing her middle with her non-bread-filled hand and making wide eyes at the children on Karl's lap. They no doubt knew the sound of a hungry belly. Those children giggled, and her stomach growled again, as if on cue. She looked up at the two sets of eyes in the loft, her eyes wide with alarm. And she hunched over and scarfed down the rest of her bread as if she were a starving mouse, and all of the children laughed then, even the girl mending the clothes in the corner.

With the children giggling, her friends looked on with amusement. The little girl on Karl's lap slid off and came over to stand next to Justine. When Justine turned to face her, the little girl put one small, hot hand on her belly. When it didn't growl, the girl nodded with approval, and then climbed onto the bench, pushing Prudence farther down the way.

It wasn't a bad way to spend an afternoon.

<hr>

Chapter Four

K ARL SHOULD HAVE been exhausted but he found he couldn't sleep. His pallet by the fire in the dining room was warmer than the goat pen, and smelled better, but at least in the goat pen he could hear the rhythmic breathing of another creature. Here, he stewed in his own thoughts, like limp cabbage in a pot of lukewarm water.

Thoughts, as if he were a profound philosopher. No, he was a lusty young man who couldn't banish the petite brunette with the big eyes, pert nose and pouty lips. He had believed—wrongly— that she would not show for the afternoon walk with her comrades. Instead, she was there, even though she'd missed breakfast and was dead last in their line up the trails. But still, even as they'd visited Luc Meynet and his seemingly unending passel of nieces and nephews, she had entertained him.

Entertained was not the right idea. No, she had delighted him. Her playful hunger act had engaged the children, and that was enough. The shy twins, Liesl and Luc, had even climbed down from the loft and stared at the strangers from the corner near the door of the winter goat enclosure. They wouldn't even come down from the loft when it was only Karl, let alone Karl and his guests.

That had made his heart like her. His loins liked her already. Liked her so much it would not let him forget about her, even in his sleep.

He'd tried so hard not to look at her while they waited for all the members of their hike to show. But then she had dripped the apple cider onto her chest, the sight of which had made him light-headed. His first thought was that she'd known exactly what she was doing, letting the liquid stream from her mouth, down her lovely neck, and lace right between her breasts. That she'd done it to torment him. As if he were not already haunted by lewd—and creative!—images flashing through his brain at inappropriate times. But Miss Brewer's face betrayed mortification as she wiped at the rivulets of apple cider that he so wanted to lick away with his tongue. To have his mouth on her. Any part of her. Mixing with the sweet tartness of the apple cider—he had to stop. He could not think like this.

He'd never minded sleeping on the ground, but here, knowing she was essentially sleeping in a room two floors directly above him was torment. He had to wear himself out so that he wouldn't be so craven as to relieve the pressure in his body in the dining room at night.

Not to mention that she was a client and a guest, *and* rich *and* British, with a father no doubt powerful enough to make his life a misery should Karl put his hands where they didn't belong.

He gritted his teeth, trying to make thoughts of her go away. She was a nice girl—in her own way—and didn't deserve the lewd machinations Karl put her through in his mind.

His cock was heavy and ached to be relieved, but he was not doing that in the dining room of his uncle's establishment. The more he resolved not to relieve himself, and instead work himself to exhaustion the next day, the more his lower half screamed for attention. He tried to think of anything else. Goats. Fences. Turds. Then his stupid cock gave him the idea of Fräulein Brewer sneaking downstairs again in the middle of the night, hair unbound, dark eyes wide and uncertain. He groaned and turned on his stomach, doing his best to smother the painful erection. He thought of Luc Meynet. His uncle. The ice-cold temperatures of the river water beneath the layers of thick ice. It worked long enough for him to fall asleep, eventually. But it was work to stay there, as his dreams featured dark hair and expanses of pale skin against green summer grass.

JUSTINE HAD ALMOST fallen asleep at dinner. Yet she was wide awake at five in the morning, according to her timepiece. She slipped into her woolen stockings and skirts, grabbed her hat and mittens on the hooks by the door, and went downstairs, ready to wait for Karl and mock him for his tardiness.

But bloody hell, he was already there, arms crossed in the dim light of a lamp, leaning against the newel. It couldn't be five thirty yet.

"Ready?" he asked, not acknowledging the early hour or her early arrival.

He was positively infuriating. She gritted her teeth, unwilling to give him credit for besting her. "Ready."

They hiked up steep switchbacks, her toes numb in her boots as they splashed through loose scree on the shoulders of the mountains that surrounded the valley. They returned, and Justine went to her room and fell asleep. Again, Herr Brunner offered her a round bread she learned was called a Brötli, sliced and stuffed full of cheese and dried meat. She again ate it so quickly there was a lump in her throat, and the group hiked again. Justine made it through most of the dinner course before Ophelia had to nudge her.

The next morning, she awoke at a quarter to five in the morning. She crept down, and he was there, arms crossed, waiting for her. This time it made her angry. But she said nothing, and neither did he as they once again went out for a steep walk. Her thighs burned and her calves ached, but she made it and kept up. Again, she missed breakfast but was there, ready for the afternoon hike, as was Herr Brunner with his Brötli.

She skipped dinner to sleep.

The next morning, she rose at half past four, certain that this time—this time!—she'd catch him snoozing. But no. Again, he was there, powerful arms folded across his wide chest, ready. Damn him. It was the same as it had been. No talking, just hiking. They didn't speak a word. But Justine kept pace. Her thighs wobbled on the way down the mountain, and she was scared that her body might give out on her, but it didn't. She carried on as if she hadn't a care in the world.

And went to bed instead of breakfast. She showed downstairs for the afternoon hike, and Herr Brunner had her Brötli ready for her. She was shaky with fatigue. Prudence was down early and had to touch her shoulder to get her attention.

"You look exhausted, Justine."

Justine smiled, her mouth full of cheese and meat and bread. Food was both amazing and a pain to keep chewing. If only there were a quicker way to get this into her body. She didn't have the energy to reply to her friend.

"Have you been going on morning hikes all week?"

Justine nodded, taking another bite. She couldn't waste time talking. Food needed to be consumed before it was time to walk again. She could do this. The afternoon hikes were easier anyway.

"Maybe you should go back upstairs and rest this afternoon."

Justine shook her head. There was nothing anyone could say that would make her stop. If this was what this arrogant guide needed her to prove in order to get her up the Matterhorn, she would do it. He wasn't going to run her down. It wasn't possible. She was stronger, she knew it. She'd have to act more energetic than she felt, but that took energy she didn't have either.

To prove to everyone that she was doing absolutely perfectly well, she made sure to be in the middle of their pack while hiking. With Prudence's new concern, Justine was afraid she'd tell Ophelia, and they would make her stop. But she wasn't stopping until Karl Vogel stopped. When he was run down, she was run down. She could go just as long, just as hard.

Today, however, she could see him leading them up the trail, and it gratified her to see how his boots scuffed certain rocks, how slowly he was taking them up this gently graded hill. He was as tired as she was. Or at least close to it.

Over the past week, she'd become very familiar with his hiking style, how high he lifted his boots, his sure-footedness, even when and if he needed to stretch out his arms for balance. He was not quite so sure of himself now.

At dinner, she was able to make it to the pudding course, her spirits buoyed by the knowledge that Karl Vogel was flagging, too. She would win this unspoken contest. There was no way she could ever be as strong as him, but she could prove that she had just as much mettle and commitment as he did.

⟫⟫⟫✕⟪⟪⟪

HIS ONKEL CAUGHT him by the arm as he returned the rag to the kitchen. He'd wiped down the tables and put what few chairs they had upside down on the tables so he could sweep and mop before laying out his pallet in front of the fire.

"How are you doing with the ladies?" Onkel Peter asked in German.

"Fine." Karl could barely think straight. His strategy of exhausting his lust was working in some respects. He didn't have the time to get an erection before he fell asleep now, but his dreams were somehow all the more vivid for it. And every dream featured her. Every dream she smiled at him, every dream she had her shoulders and feet bared, and frequently, much more. It was a struggle to be awake early enough to be at the reception desk waiting for her, but he was. There was no way he was going to lose her unspoken challenge.

She thought she was strong? There was no one who would or could out-climb Karl. At least, not anywhere nearby. He was only now making his name as a guide, but he was well respected, and there was no way some ridiculous brown-eyed English sprite was going to outmatch him.

Behind Onkel Peter, Tante Greta tsked. Her large forearms were thrust into the washing bin, and she didn't bother to look up. "You are losing weight, Karl. That's not good. Eat more, walk less."

"Tante, I cannot walk less."

"Stop taking that girl out first, then you will walk less. Then maybe both of you will eat breakfast."

"Sometimes the girl only eats the Brötli I fix her before the midday walk!" Onkel Peter added.

Karl sighed. He didn't like that Fräulein Brewer was losing weight rapidly either. Some weight loss would be expected—they were here to climb mountains, and living in higher altitudes often kept a person slim. But the rate both of them were shedding pounds was not sustainable.

"A break, perhaps?" Onkel Peter suggested, the wrinkles around his eyes crinkling in hope. "One day off?"

"Yes, everyone knows you must rest," Tante Greta said. "Like bread. It can only rise after a rest."

"I will think about it," Karl promised. "Can you pass me the broom, Onkel?"

The older man waved him away. "I will sweep. You eat this plate your Tante made you."

Karl glanced over to the corner where a small table sat with two chairs—where they ate in the kitchen, while the rest of the guests ate in the dining room. On the table was a small plate, laden with cheese and dried fruit.

"Tante, I ate dinner. Every morsel. I promise."

She shook her head, and Karl thought he might see the young woman in there that had bewitched a young Peter Brunner away from stately Augsburg and into the snow-capped mountains. "You must eat. Keep up your strength, because I have seen this girl. She will not stop. I know, because I see her. I was like her, too. I would not stop for anything or anyone. I'd rather die. And you keep her moving at this rate, she will drop dead in front of you rather than disappoint you."

"Yes, Tante." Karl went over and obediently ate the cheese and fruit, chewing quickly for fear of falling asleep sitting up.

SHE WOKE AT four. But now she didn't expect to surprise him. Indeed, he was there, arms folded, bright-eyed, waiting, the bloody wanker. Fine. Again, without a word, he led them out of the inn and into the blue-purple pre-dawn twilight. He took her a different way this time, not up the goat path, but the opposite direction. They walked up the valley, from where they had arrived on the donkeys a week earlier. Had it only been a week? It seemed like it had been a month at least.

They walked along the frozen stream at a quick clip, Justine practically running to keep up with Karl's fast pace. He said nothing, but she trailed alongside him, a half-step behind. As soon as she caught up, she could swear he started walking faster.

But the chill invigorated her. It was as if yesterday her body had turned a corner. Instead of screaming at her to stop and lay down, to sleep for an entire week if possible, now it was happy to accommodate her demands. Her legs ached not to rest, but rather to keep moving. Her head no longer hurt from fatigue. Even the blisters on her smallest toes had hardened into callouses.

He wanted to hike twice a day? Fine. He wanted to run these trails in silence, fine. She could do it, and happily so. Even though his speed was high, something felt different. He seemed not as distant in that half-step ahead of her. As if he were going to actually speak. Wouldn't that be novel?

"Here," he said finally, pointing to a path that diverged from the stream. They walked across the valley, closer to another town—had they already gone the distance of an entire town?— and then started up a steep path that would no doubt end in

Justine's heart wanting to explode out of her body.

Once they were up in the trees, she grew accustomed to the slightly slower rhythmic pace of Karl's steps, still almost a run for her much-shorter legs. Whatever hope she had for a conversation died. After his one-word direction earlier, he didn't speak, so she didn't either.

They moved, fully in their bodies, up the mountain on long sloping switchbacks. They climbed until they reached the tree line. Above there, the icy, rocky scree was slippery, but still they ascended. The breeze felt good, even though it was cold. Her nose ran continuously, and she kept running her woolen glove under it.

They crested a rounded area, a shoulder of the mountain, and Karl slowed to a stop. Her breath came in short pants as she stopped next to him, her hands on her hips. This hadn't been the worst of their paths, but it was the speed that had made it difficult. Her calves burned, and the sides of her thighs ached from the use.

She was shocked he'd stopped at all. At no point in the earlier walks had he let them stop. Only when they were on the afternoon hikes did he give them time to relax and admire views. Or teach them about local flora and fauna. Usually, she was too tired to listen. Besides, he was mostly speaking with Tristan and Ophelia, who both loved to learn those tedious bits about a place.

"I like seeing the houses," Karl said out of nowhere.

Justine could only look, not having enough breath to speak, and shocked by an actual conversational topic. Indeed, down below them, she could see the town they'd almost reached, and then to her left she could barely make out Zermatt, crowded as it was by the trees.

"It's nice," Justine said as soon as she could. Was she supposed to answer him back? Did he want to chat, or did he want to opine at her?

"Do you know this town?" he asked her, pointing to the one they had turned up the path before entering.

She shook her head, feeling the wool scratching at the sweaty nape of her neck as she did so. Were they going to have a chat? Did she need to bring a flask of tea for this? But she didn't want to ruin his candor by bringing attention to their typical silence.

"This town is called Täsch. It was wiped out centuries ago by a rockslide."

Justine raised her eyebrows, but from where she stood, it made sense. Their traverse over had been filled with rock fragments piled so deep that each step was unsure as the rocks ground and slipped against each other. "They were able to dig it out?"

Karl shook his head. "No. They rebuilt instead. New homes. New barns."

Justine stared down at the little brown wooden buildings below them. "They certainly don't look new."

Karl laughed, shocking Justine. The man could laugh? She had thought they'd walked any sort of humor right out of him. "Not anymore, no. This happened many, many years ago. Maybe four hundred years?"

Justine reared back, finally comfortable enough to give her real opinion. "And you still tell this story, even though it was four hundred years ago?"

He shrugged. "Not much else to tell. Nothing happens here. It's the same families, the same goats and cows, the same snow."

Justine took in a large steadying breath and turned in a slow circle, viewing the mountains, the snow, the scale of this valley. "And magnificent mountains."

She could hear his grin in his voice as he said, "The best mountains."

"The rest of the walk is downhill. We can go slower and still make breakfast."

Was he trying to be nice to her? After this entire week of bloody death marches? "After that speed walk from the inn, you'll go slow enough to actually talk to me?"

He had a fat grin on his face, which only made him look more approachable and competent, and *handsome*, damn him. After what he'd done to her, he had the gall to be nice? "I notice you like to talk. I will allow this."

"Allow?" Justine was about to burst into flames from anger until she noticed his eyes sparkling with mischief. Before she thought better of it, she slugged him as hard as she could in the arm. "You are a complete arse." Then she stomped off down what she assumed was the correct trail. After all this. After four in the morning wake-ups, after falling asleep at the dinner table almost every night. If they returned to the inn with time for her to have an actual hot cup of tea, she thought she might cry.

How dare he be nice to her?

He laughed and jogged after her. "Not many can keep up with me. I've been very impressed with you, Fräulein Brewer."

She scoffed at him and tossed her head, but a warm thrill coursed through her insides down to her toes. He was clearly very good at this, and very knowledgeable—exactly what one could hope for in a guide. They walked in companionable silence for a while before she couldn't stand it anymore. If she was "allowed" to talk, then she was talking.

"Were you born here?" she asked.

"No, I was born in Augsberg." When she didn't reply, he continued. "Which is in Bavaria."

Justine had no idea where Bavaria was. But probably near here? She nodded sagely, as if she were a very serious student of geography and had not spent that time of her studies staring out the window, willing herself to keep still so she wouldn't get hit on the knuckles with a ruler *again*.

"You don't know where that is," Karl said, not even asking a question, but stating the obvious.

She was a terrible actress, but she was a terrible actress in some very beautiful mountains, and she didn't care because the smell of the clean, clear air was still thrilling. She shrugged. "According to my father, Bavaria is neither here nor there with all the talk of war again. He was not happy about me gallivanting off to a disputed area."

His back straightened, and his flash of pride was palpable in this serene walk. The tree line was still below them, but they were about to descend into the dark forest, where the ground was almost spongy underneath the crust of old, icy snow among the roots.

"Did I offend you?" she asked, trying very hard to not ask sweetly, so he would not take even more offense, or think her completely empty-headed. Why did she care what he thought? She hated that she did, even though his regard meant very little to her, and was not at all consuming. "I don't follow all the wars. There are too many, and after the American debacle, I have absolutely no interest in learning more."

"Then you are lucky," he said.

She glanced over at him before they entered the dim light of the trees. His mouth was set in a grim line, and he was profoundly unhappy. The path began to descend more steeply, and she tried to figure out what to say next. She didn't mean to make him unhappy; in fact, it actually bothered her that he was. Why on earth would she be bothered about his feelings? She'd never been remotely disturbed when her suitors were mad at her for dancing with another man, or God forbid, fanning herself in a heated ballroom, leading them to believe she was sending secret fan messages mocking them.

Fine, she did mock them with her fan, but it was because they made these assumptions of her feelings and time. As if she couldn't help but be overjoyed when the man with the persistent runny nose wanted to dance with her. Oh, he had money? How exciting, so did her father. If she could run a business or do anything, she would have money too. Look at her brothers. They were perfect idiots, and they were able to make a pound or two.

But Karl's unhappiness felt very much like her fault. And it wasn't based on assumptions of her feelings, but rather her lack of knowledge. Or compassion. Ugh. She hated feelings.

"I apologize for my lack of knowledge," she began, not knowing where she'd end up. "It's just, as a woman, I'm given a very small circle of approved topics to discuss or learn about, and far-away wars aren't one of them."

Karl huffed, as if he were balancing his prickly emotions and his compassion towards her confinements. "No, I must apologize. Those 'far-away wars' take place near my home. Not my town, but I nearly fought for the Austrians, and if I had, I would have been at the Battle of Königgrätz."

Justine nodded again, knowing absolutely nothing. "I see." It was a diplomatic thing to say, and might assuage his feelings, but she had no idea what that battle meant, or where it was, and frankly couldn't have spelled it or repeated it back to him if he'd asked.

"This is not a battle you have heard of? How is this possible?"

She wanted to glare at him but kept that to herself. But her mouth couldn't stop. "What part of *Englishwoman* do you not understand?"

"How does being an Englishwoman have anything to do with knowing of the largest battle since Napoleon?" Karl threw his hands in the air. "It is as if you live with your head in the ground!"

"Yes, now you understand!" Justine cried. "Do you know what I was taught? How to match my shoes to my dress. What fabrics work well together. Which colors are best for my complexion. How to use a buttonholer that dislocates your shoulder to get dressed and undressed because my only value is how well I display my very expensive clothing."

"You are useless!" he cried, his gait elongating until he strode far in front of her.

"Do you think that's my fault?" she cried, running after him. "You try being coddled within an inch of your life. You try having every man you've ever met either stare down your dress or ask your father how much your dowry is. Why do you think I'm in this blasted place? It's the only thing I am allowed to do, and the only reason I can is because Ophelia is doing it!" She caught right up to him, her shorter legs working double the rate his were, but it didn't matter. There was no way he was going to leave her alone in the woods. "Instead of judging me for it, why don't you try telling me about it, you absolute hypocritical twit?"

His face creased. "What is a twit?" he spat out.

"You, you great numpty." They were side by side again.

"I do not know that word either." His boots landed heavy in the snow, tamping deeper than he ever had before.

She *liked* that he was stomping like a child. Good. Now he could be the ignorant one. "English is full of nuance."

Karl scoffed. "As if English is the only language and the rest of us are grunting and banging rocks together."

"That's not what I said." Her temper was cooling, but her heart was racing like a rabbit's. There was something about this verbal sparring that she enjoyed.

"Then tell me these words," he demanded. His stomping had lessened into normal steps.

"And what if I don't?" she challenged, still enjoying the edge she carried over him. True, the superiority was exceedingly slim, as the only thing she was better at was her native language, but she was petty enough to exploit any angle she had.

"I'm not a twat," he grumbled.

She spat out a laugh. "That's not what I said."

"No? What did you say? Tweet? Like a birdsong?"

She started laughing and couldn't stop. "You called yourself a twat." Her breath caught, and she had to slow down, bending over to recover.

"It is really not funny," he said. "What is a twat?"

His question sent her spiraling again. She sighed out her laughter and tried for some composure. "A twat is—" She could barely get the word out of her mouth, and she was about to gesture to her own body, but then decided against it. There were limits, even for her. "A twat is a rather indecent thing to say."

At least the exchange seemed to appease him, and he raised his eyebrows in consideration. He watched her recover a while longer, which neither of them seemed to mind. Finally, she gave a sigh and quieted, which seemed to appease him.

"Ready?"

She nodded, trying desperately not to snicker and they continued down the path.

"You are right," he said, catching her by surprise. "It is not fair to criticize your learning if I do not seek to rectify it."

"That sentence started out very nicely, but sort of fell off at the end."

"Do you not wish to learn?" he asked, looking at her with sincere concern, as if she had told him she had a terrible illness.

"Not that I don't wish to, but I have had very bad luck at learning in the past."

He frowned. "But you know about your colors and the, what was it? Button-holder?"

"Buttonholer," she corrected. "You can try, if you wish, but I make no promises of retaining the information or even being able to fully concentrate on listening to you."

He made a considering sort of noise that she found adorable. She hated that she thought it was adorable. He wasn't at all worthy of adoring. He'd just called her stupid. No, she amended to herself, not stupid. Ignorant, and that was different.

"I will give you the brief version of events. For these are wars very long in the making."

"That I believe," she said. "They say women can hold a grudge, but my goodness, we don't wipe out entire towns to get back at one another. Even Miss Christenson only ever spilled her red ratafia on Miss Barrow's white dress when she believed Miss Barrow had stolen away the affections of Lord Crowdon. Turns out he wasn't interested in either of them."

Karl shook his head. "I don't understand anything you just said."

"See?" Justine smiled. "We're even. Now tell me about some very serious men having very serious wars and ending up very seriously dead."

As they walked, Karl tried to tell her about the different kingdoms that had made up the middle of the European continent. Mostly about Prussia in the north, Bavaria and Austria in the east, France to the west, and the newly unified Italian peninsula in the south, and how they squabbled. Justine couldn't help but think of it as siblings, all fighting over the last pudding.

But then he made it personal, and that Justine could pay attention to, because it was him. Only a few times did she get lost in how pleasing his face looked as he spoke animatedly of his home and Austria. Of how his town was more like Austrian culture than Prussian culture. How, even if they all spoke a similar language, the dialects were different, and the northerners found them slow and stupid because they had farms and weavers' guilds, instead of railroads and factories. And how that made him want to fight.

"Of course it made me want to put on a uniform. The fighting was happening near my mother and brothers and sisters. I wanted to defend them. But before I could go and make a fool of myself, we received a letter from my Onkel Peter, who had long ago married a Swiss woman from Zermatt, my Tante Greta, and how they were opening a hotel for British tourists. How they were going to change Zermatt from its small, out-of-the-way village to one of travel and trade."

"How did that affect you?" Justine asked. "It was your uncle, not you."

"Yes, but he counted on having support of his brother, my father. Family, you know, sometimes they make promises from long ago, and then, they come due at inconvenient times. I had been to Zermatt many times, but I only stayed during the climbing season, not all winter."

Justine smiled. She could understand staying here in Zermatt. The mountains had enchanted her.

"My Onkel needed a man strong enough to tend to every-thing. Most young men from here either left for bigger cities to find work or went to war. I didn't want to come. I wanted to fight. To be brave. To be a hero."

"But you didn't."

Karl shook his head. "I did not. I am not a hero. I am a dirty mountain guide, finding peace with goats and cattle that graze high up on the peaks. Sometimes I despise how peaceful I feel here, how at home I feel."

They left the tree cover, emerging at the bottom of the forest, near the frozen stream, the village of Täsch behind them and Zermatt, unseen around the mountain base, ahead of them.

"I suppose that is the difference between being born to a family versus being born to a dynasty," she said, thinking of all the overheard conversations of Tristan and his elder brother Arthur, who would one day become the Viscount Rascomb, after their father died.

"I don't understand," Karl said, frowning. "I do not know this word in English. Dy-nas-ty."

"Fair enough," Justine said. The sun felt good on her face and her arms. A cup of tea at breakfast would taste so perfect, along with some toast and jam. "Dynasty is akin to a ruling class. Like royalty or some kind of nobleman. A family where the eldest son must do his duty for his country or the title, not necessarily his family."

"Ah," Karl said, his expression opening in understanding. "I understand, and yes. That is it. I have family obligations that are more important than fighting in a war that is too big for us to understand. I do not mean that my family is better than my country, only that there is not only fighting that makes a country."

"Deals made by men of influence," Justine mused, thinking of how her father was not a dynastic man, but he could, at times, be considered a man of influence. Anyone with wealth, should they be so inclined, could become influential. But money didn't mean a person was good or deserving. It was just *there*. And, as many learned in the aftermath of wars, that wealth could be gone in an instant.

Oh, look at her, thinking profound worldly thoughts. What this mountain air was doing to her! She looked over at Karl and grinned. She'd never liked a man before. Been attracted to them? Of course. Justine had liked plenty of men for dancing and flirting, and even a stolen kiss or two. But she'd never *liked* them. Walking with Karl was companionable, friendly. He didn't seem to look down on her or treat her as a child, which was new.

She'd once believed that the reason why she had so many suitors was that she was short. They believed they could treat her as a child, and given her size, it was a tempting thought. But she wasn't a child. She was an opinionated woman, and that made even her outlandish dowry seem unappealing.

But Karl seemed to not be bothered by what her mother called her "plucky spirit." That's when she realized she'd started thinking of him by his first name, which was far too familiar. He still called her Fräulein, so she should respond in kind. How strange that she wanted to become more familiar with him, when he seemed to not care about her one way or another.

They walked on in silence. But before they reached the inn, he said, "Tomorrow is a rest day for everyone. Like bread, one must rest before one can rise."

Justine blinked at him. Was she the bread? Were they all the bread?

"Are you resting?" she asked.

He gave her a wistful smile. "I will be doing chores around the inn. Whatever is needed. Some goats are close to kidding."

"There are baby goats here?" Justine asked, amused at how animated he became about livestock. A baby goat was very cute, and she would not mind holding one at all.

"You can come see, if you like. The pens are just beyond the inn. You will hear them." Karl opened the door for her, and the commotion from the dining room surprised her. They were back in time for the full swing of breakfast.

He held the door for her to the dining room as well, and she couldn't help but feel like that young debutante again. Just for a moment. A handsome man, watching her as she sailed into a room. Except this time she had the gritty, salty sheen of sweat dried on her face. And that was a vast improvement.

Chapter Five

I T WAS CLOUDY, but at least it was warm. There would be a melt that would reconfigure some of the snow, and then next month would come another freeze. It would be dangerous to do any big mountain climbing until the weather conditions stabilized. Karl would keep an eye on the snow to make sure he kept his clients safe.

Tante Greta had the right idea of having a day of rest. He slept in for the first time in a week, waking only as he heard her come down to the kitchen to begin the breakfast service. It was pleasant to have a coffee while staring out at the mountains. He rarely drank coffee, but with the guests here, they were well supplied for the coming months with the luxury beverage.

Instead of sitting with guests this morning, he ate in the kitchen and helped with the food service. There wasn't much room, and he could see the irritation on Greta's face when he'd step in her way. She had a routine in the mornings, and he was clearly making her life more difficult. He apologized and took himself out to check on the goats.

The goat pen was holding up well. Four of their herd were about to give birth. He would tell Tante Greta that someone needed to be out with them on the days he hiked. At least to check in and make sure the kidding progressed well.

He left his empty coffee cup on the post and went on to the barn where the cattle were. The cattle were in the same state as the goats. A few ready to calve, but here they had their neighbor, Herr Fröhlich, to check on them. Herr Frölich helped Onkel Peter and Tante Greta with their herd and took them up in the mountains with his, and they bartered with milk and cheese the rest of the year to keep him happy.

After the tour of the animals and a pat on the head for Gunther, the dog who watched over all of them, he didn't need to go check on the goats again, but he might, in case Fräulein Brewer came to see babies.

Not that it was his duty to check on the livestock, really. When the summer came, that would be handed off to one of the seasonal hires, as most of their hired hands were currently prepping their own flocks, trade, and building projects. Most didn't even live in Zermatt year-round and had promised to return in another month, when the foreign tourists typically arrived in Zermatt.

But Karl's English clients were definitely not like others. Then again, these English were women, which made them unusual on the surface, but it was more than their gender. Most mountaineers were men, or if there were women, they were married or related to one of the other men. He'd seen those women. Hale and hardy, unjudged, for they were already married. Or they were strange women, under the influence of their strange fathers or uncles.

But this group of alpinist women, beautiful and wealthy, some married, some not, was unlike anything he'd ever encountered in his mountaineering career. There were always rumors of women-only Alpine trips, and rarely people asked if he knew any women Alpine guides; he did not.

Footsteps came up behind him, and after a week of hearing her tread, he knew who it was before turning.

"Any baby goats this morning?" she asked, tucking her hands inside the woolen shawl she'd draped over herself. Her hair was half-down, the way he'd first seen her that first night.

"The beginnings, yes," Karl said, brushing crusted snow off a rock with his boot. He was a fool in front of her, and he hated that. Much better when they were moving, and he didn't have to sound smart in another language. He shook his head. "I mean that yes, we have babies. They are in a separate pen. There are other goats that still have not kidded."

Her eyes lit up. "May I see them?"

He nodded, and as he guided them closer to the pens, he noticed that she was distracted by the view. She seemed to love the mountains. And she had yet to complain about any of the walks he'd taken her on. Because of snow and time and not wanting to carry equipment, he hadn't taken her up any big peaks yet. Perhaps he could teach her how to read the snow, make her more capable.

She might not be good at reading snow, but she could at least help guide the others with her steady pace. It was a thought. And then perhaps they might have to spend their time after dinner going over maps and making plans.

Typically, this was the work of the expedition leader, which was Fräulein Bridewell, but the cool-tempered blonde had told him that all the preliminary mountain guiding should be planned with Fräulein Brewer. She'd been very clear about that when they'd followed him up to mend the fence.

"I have spent so much time preparing for the Matterhorn, that I can't even imagine an after," Justine said. "It's like an event that can never happen, because what will I do when it's over?"

Karl shrugged. He remembered that feeling from long ago, but it had since faded, under the weight of so many subsequent experiences. "You'll find another mountain to climb. There are many."

Justine laughed, and he swore it sounded like a bell. A beautiful, clear, unexpected laugh, unlike her many other kinds that were tinged with other emotions. This one was pure. His chest puffed up, happy that *he* was the one who had made her laugh.

"Do you have a favorite?" she asked.

His mind blanked, unsure of what she was asking.

"Mountain, I mean. Do you have a favorite mountain?" She looked down, away from him. Was she suddenly shy?

It made him stammer. He didn't want her to be uncomfortable, but he also didn't know how to answer her question. "Favorite in what way? To look at? To climb? A favorite experience?"

"Are those different?" she asked, meeting his gaze again.

He nodded. "Wildly different! To climb is an accomplishment. Sometimes a hardship. You may freeze a toe or lose a toenail. You maybe might get very hurt or have to stay up all night to finish a descent. You are hungry and tired and sore, but it is exhilarating because you did it! But then, some climbs are fun because you may need ropes and a partner, and it is less about the top than the journey up the side. Those are very fun. And then others, I know them so well, I look at their beauty from afar, and sigh. It brings me pleasure knowing they exist, even if they do not know I am there."

"You make it sound like the mountains are women you are courting." Fräulein Brewer's cheeks flushed pink. She looked like the dolls he saw in shop windows in Munich and Zurich. The pretty ones with porcelain heads and shiny curled hair.

I would court you, he thought, but didn't say it. There was no point. She was here for a few months only. Instead, he shrugged. "It is my life. It is what I do."

She was silent for a moment. "I could help you."

Karl's mind flipped through possibilities, but none of them could be correct. "With what?"

"With the baby goats, you ninny."

"Nin-ny," he repeated. This was another new word to him. "Is this like nan-ny?"

She shook her head with exaggerated exasperation. He liked making her react to him, and it felt very much like pulling a girl's hair when he was younger.

"Your English is excellent in many places, but how are you so bad at insults?"

"I am not often insulted," Karl said. Well, not in English, anyway. Any group of mountain guides who spoke the same language were merciless in their teasing, but none of them spoke English either. French, German, Swiss, Tyrolian, yes. All of those. But English? What for?

She huffed out a laugh, and sunlight crept far enough over the trees and the roofline of the inn to catch the reddish glint of her hair. "I find that hard to believe. I could insult you all day."

"I believe you could," he said, mildly. He did not want to be insulted, but he was beginning to understand that she spoke many words, but rarely did she intend anything mean-spirited. Her insults were a flirtation, which he would gladly accept. "But I don't know how you could help a goat give birth."

"Not the birthing, the babies."

"Fräulein Brewer," Karl started, not wanting to exclude her in any way, but also not wanting her to take on a responsibility that she could not possibly keep up. "I think—"

"I enjoy the way you say *Fräulein* to me, but it seems cumbersome, all those syllables." She pushed her lips into a pout that made his hands twitch and his thighs flex in unwilling response. "Perhaps, when we are alone, you might call me Justine."

Karl swallowed hard. His thoughtful, prepared mind screamed that this was not appropriate. Why was anyone allowing her to be alone with him? Why had they let him be alone with her? He would have looked around for a chaperone if he could have torn his gaze from her playful brown eyes.

But the rest of him nodded dumbly in agreement and tried out her name on his tongue. "Justine, then. And I am Karl."

She smiled and repeated his name, and he could have been happy to go deaf after hearing his name on her lips.

SHE KNEW IT was a terrible idea to give him leave to use her first name. Of course it was a terrible idea—she'd thought it up, hadn't she? If ever she had a reliable trait, it was bad ideas. But he pronounced her name with a soft *j*, like the French, and it made her weak in the knees. In his mouth, her name was beautiful, not at all mannish and workmanlike.

Standing in that morning half-sun, the cold threatening to creep into her hands despite her gloves, she was in paradise. He looked at her with interest, engaged when she teased him, and never lost his temper, no matter what she said.

The situation was almost perverse. They stood in the most gorgeous valley she'd ever seen, the sky gray and cloudy, but still she found it to be more cheerful than any of the innumerable gray days she'd spent in England. And there was this man. After the ballroom legions of men who tried to flirt with her, engage her, dance with her, take liberties with her, none had made her feel like this.

It was enough to turn a girl's head.

"Justine, there you are!" Ophelia called, gathering her woolen shawl around her shoulders.

Justine wanted to sigh. Because if ever there was a person who knew when the worst time to show up was, it was Ophelia. There had been an occasion at finishing school when she'd walked in on Justine and Annabelle Rivers, which had been a short-lived—but educational—romp that year. There was nothing as embarrassing as them both throwing down their skirts as the door opened, and Ophelia walking in, her nose wrinkled.

She loved her best friend, she did. But her timing was shit, if she could be so bold.

"Since we will not be taking our exercise today, I thought it a perfect day to go over routes and sort the gear." Ophelia looked beautiful, her long gold-blonde hair shining in the low light of the gray day. Justine could be jealous of her friend, whose blue eyes and fair complexion were almost comically the picture of the English ideal. Instead, Justine understood Ophelia's aloofness, which was actually dreaminess wrapped in aristocratic manners.

And Ophelia had a point. Maps. Routes. Gear. Ugh. The worst. Justine wanted to put one foot in front of the other. She wanted to be pointed in the correct direction and let loose, like a hunting dog, crashing through streams and underbrush. Perhaps not the most flattering of comparisons for herself, but accurate.

If that was unavailable, cuddling a baby goat would be an excellent consolation prize.

"You're right, Ophelia," Justine said with a groan. "I suppose we will set up in the dining room, if it is available?" It would be so much more fun to stand out here with Karl, watching his expression as he mentally translated her teasing words. Plus, he didn't wear a waistcoat or formal English clothing, and she enjoyed seeing his broad shoulders move and flex in his woolen shirt, kept tight against him by his braces.

In fact, men's fashion here embraced tighter trousers as well, and combined with the boots Karl wore, Justine found herself admiring more than just his shoulders. But Ophelia. Maps. Routes. Gear. Yes. She needed to get Karl Vogel out of her brain and the practicalities of this expedition in.

"If I may, I can outline the routes I myself have climbed," Karl offered.

"I thought you had chores to do," Justine teased, even though she did hope he would spend the day with them.

"I do," he admitted. "But this afternoon, during the coffee time, I could come."

"Tea time," Justine corrected.

Karl rolled his eyes dramatically, but he had the underpinnings of a smile on his face as he did so. "Coffee. Tea. Hot beverage time with a piece of cake."

"Very well put, Mr. Vogel." Ophelia gave him a short, competent nod. Then she looked to Justine, and there was almost a visible realization in her expression as Ophelia finally caught up to the relationship between Justine and Karl. "I will meet you inside, Justine."

It put a smile on Justine's face to watch Ophelia go, her steps as uncertain as Ophelia's ever were, knowing that she had blundered into a flirtation and completely ruined it.

"I should go," Justine said. "I'll see you this afternoon, though, when you can correct everything we've done and I can throw cake at you for it."

Karl's brow furrowed. "Why would you waste good cake?"

Justine smiled. "Throwing a hot beverage at you would be much worse."

Karl nodded thoughtfully. "Perhaps no throwing, then?"

"Don't be an arse, and I won't." Justine turned and flounced away, her heart absolutely light and singing, as if she were meant to be right here, in this place, doing this very thing. She'd never in her life felt so free and at home. If only this expedition could last forever.

THE WEATHER TURNED much sooner than Karl anticipated. They only had a few days of the temperate melt before the hard frost slammed into the mountains, capturing all the moisture in the air and freezing it.

They put the goats and the cows in the same pens to keep them warm, and the birthing goats came into the storage closets on the ground floor, the farthest away from the dining hall as they could get. Karl worked hard every day, making sure the cows and the goats were warm and watered, cleaning up the new interior goat shed so that the smells didn't disturb the guests.

They hadn't gone on any hikes once the cold snap hit only because Karl was too busy. He'd hoped the Englishwomen would go out of their own accord—perhaps they did—but he had other work to hold his attention. He often missed dinner, which was a shame, because he enjoyed seeing Fräulein Brewer in her evening dress. He knew it was nothing compared to the beautiful silk and lace confections she must have at home, but he loved seeing her in the bright colors and gowns dotted with small flowers.

She was unlike anyone he'd ever met before, and he could admit he was infatuated. But it was nothing he couldn't push under the surface so that when she left, he wouldn't be useless. He was still a mountain guide, and if there was anything mountaineers knew, it was discomfort.

Onkel Peter pulled him aside. "Karl. You are working too hard. I go to change the hay for the goats, it is already done. I go to check on the cows, they are toasty and warm from the lit brazier. You must let me earn my keep, or your Tante Greta will turn me out before she lets go of Elke."

Karl shook his head. "Onkel, this is why you asked me here. To be of use. I am of use, what is wrong with that?"

His Onkel gave him a pitying look. "You are young, Karl. And you have clients here. Spend time with them. With the pretty one who watches you when she thinks no one will notice."

Karl shrugged to feign indifference. "They are all pretty."

His Onkel did not seem convinced of his apathy. "Your shadow, Karl. She is a pretty one, and very capable. Like your Tante." He winked, patted Karl on the arm and took the water pail he was carrying to the goats.

He could only blink as he watched his Onkel take over his chores. What should he be doing if he was not buried under the heavy workload of running an inn? His immediate urge was the same as always: *outside.*

The small windows let in the cold, but he could see the gray crispness outside. At least that would be warmer than when the skies were clear and clean. He went through the dining room where the guests were strewn about the tables, lingering over coffee and tea. The married couples were playing some kind of card game that he didn't recognize. The women were teamed up against the men, and the teasing seemed merciless.

It reminded him of Justine, and he wondered if that was something that he had missed out on in his younger years, since he'd started coming up to Zermatt when he was only seventeen to climb and then later, to guide. He'd not gone to churches and dances, learning how young people were meant to flirt and to court one another. But he'd supposed that Justine's gentle teasing was akin to pulling his braids in school. Not that Karl had braids. He frowned.

"Don't tell me that frown is for me," Justine said, looking up from where she and Lord and Lady Rascomb and Fräulein Bridewell had maps spread all over the longest dining table. "You only just got here. How can I have already earned your disapproval?"

He tried not to smile, because he was beginning to understand that she did like him as much as he liked her. While he'd had relations with women before, it had been easily won barmaids, and neither of them believed in a longer-term attachment. This was different. It felt different, anyhow. "No disapproval. But I have been relieved of my afternoon chores. I can take you outside."

Why did the English language not have a collective word for *you*? So inconvenient. He meant to invite everyone in the room, but how did one say that?

Justine's dark brows rose in surprise and delight. "Me, you say?"

Karl nodded, and then looked at each of the rest gathered. "And you, and you, and you."

"And me?" squealed Herr Bridewell in a falsetto. His fellow card players laughed, and his wife tossed a crust of bread at him.

Glancing back at Justine, he noticed her cheeks had reddened. She had thought he'd meant only her. Which he did, but thought was inappropriate. Was it not inappropriate? He didn't know any more. All he could hope was that his language blunder was not ill-received.

"Anyone who would like to go outside today. I will warn you that it is colder than it was when you arrived, and you will need more layers than you typically wear."

"Mr. Vogel," a gentleman said, and Karl swung his gaze over

to the thin man who accompanied their afternoon hikes well enough, but was not listed on the expedition. The husband of the Mrs. Prudence Moon, a woman who was on the expedition list, which confused Karl, but he was learning not to question these English ladies. "Is this cold spell typical for this time of year? In England, we usually have a springtime."

Karl nodded. "This is what happens here. We have a thaw, and then another frost. This will not last long. Then another thaw. Then summer."

Herr Bridewell let out a low chuckle. "Sounds delightful."

Karl nodded. "It is very muddy for a time."

"Even better," Herr Bridewell added. The man glanced at his bride, and then his sister, and announced, "I am having a jolly time where I am. My wife and I decline your generous offer, Mr. Vogel, and I do hope that Mr. and Mrs. Moon do likewise."

Herr Moon nodded. "Of course. Card playing is not a terrible way to spend a day."

"Very well." Karl nodded and turned back to the long dining table.

"My old joints are not too keen on the cold, I admit. I'll sit this one out," said Lord Rascomb, looking pointedly at Lady Rascomb, who raised her eyebrow.

Fräulein Bridewell frowned back at her mother. She whispered something to her mother that Karl could not hear, and Justine shot her a look. The three of them debated in hushed tones, and all Karl could get from it was *inappropriate*, which was what he'd been worried about in the first place.

Justine glanced at him, her big brown eyes full of some kind of emotion he didn't understand. All he could do was stand there like some big cow and wait for a decision. He would go outside no matter what was decided, for the cold didn't bother him. The key was to be in it, accept it, be a part of it. To suffer against weather was the greatest folly. A person would never win against nature.

Finally, the conference broke apart and Justine stood. She was very pretty; Onkel Peter was correct. And he did think she was the prettiest of all the women here, petite and fierce, quick and full of blazing health.

"I'll go," Justine said, her eyes downcast, as if she were embarrassed. That was strange.

"I need to get my warm things, as do you," Karl said.

Fräulein Bridewell sat back down at the table, her brow furrowed. She did not meet his eyes either. That did not seem to be a good sign.

"I can be back down in ten minutes," Justine said, skirting the table to run upstairs.

Karl nodded, watching her go. "I'll meet you at the front desk."

She did not bother to turn around to acknowledge that she'd heard him, not that it was terribly important. They always met at the front desk, why should this time be any different?

Glancing around, he found that none of the other clients looked at him. They were all absorbed in their own business, not wanting to speak to him. How strange. English people were strange. Unease pricked at him as he went to the pegs behind the bar where he kept his few outdoor options. His thick coats with fur lining, his woolen scarves and gloves and mittens. His extra thick socks and the underlayers that protected him from the wind that could slice right through the wool.

He waited at the desk, sweating as minutes ticked by. Finally, she appeared, and he pushed himself off the desk and propelled himself out the door. How relieving to finally be rid of the sweating.

She hurried after him, her steps coming one-two, one-two. Leaving the front of the inn, the wind screamed down through the valley and cooled him at once. He loved this feeling, this change, of keeping warm, knowing it was so cold out.

"Come," he said to her, wanting to get away from the inn and all of the strange whispered words that sat in the air. He led her over towards Täsch, not wanting to take on too much today, but also not wanting to go far in case her clothes did not keep her warm enough or if the weather suddenly changed for the worse.

By the river, however, he found exactly what he was looking for: different types of snow.

"Look," he said pointing at where the new, brittle, dusty snow met with the hard-packed crusty white bank.

She came and stood beside him, looking, but not saying anything. Her silence was odd. He didn't like it. But he also didn't understand it. From what he'd been told by the Frenchman he'd guided, the English would rather sweep problems away, as if they never existed, than discuss the trouble.

Karl understood the trouble with discomfort, but he also felt that it was like when there was something about your boot that troubled you. If you didn't stop to take off your boot and examine and rectify the trouble, then it would cause a blister. If the blister continued to be bothered, it would bleed and become infected. It was best to deal with the problem before a blister occurred in the first place.

Since she hadn't said anything about the snow, he had to take charge of this. They were in Zermatt, not London. He was the guide and she was the client, so he would do this his way, not hers. "What was the trouble?"

"Trouble with what?" she asked, mildly. There was no tease, no double-entendre. It made him uneasy.

"Trouble that made you whisper with Fräulein Bridewell and Lady Rascomb." His jaw clenched, flexing against the woolen scarf that he had wound around his chin.

She fiddled with her own scarf, unwinding it from around her neck and then adjusting it to leave enough length to cover her mouth. "It was merely addressing concerns." She finished her adjustments and with that, her mouth was covered.

His jaw clenched even harder. Perhaps it had been better when they walked, rather than talked. "I would like very much to know these concerns. That way I can help with them. That is my job."

She steadied her chocolate gaze on him. "You cannot help with them. Because I am the problem. Not you."

He pulled back, viscerally shocked by her comment. How could she be the problem? She was the only one who came on these excursions with him, and therefore the most prepared for what faced them on the Matterhorn in a few short months.

She walked further down the stream, making her way towards the trail that meandered next to it, her back to him. What could possibly be wrong with her?

He caught up to her. "Are you ill?"

"No," she said, not bothering to explain anymore.

Karl shook his head. If she didn't want to tell him, then that was her choice, he supposed, and he had tried his best. Fine. He hated that he bristled at her coldness, that it made him feel like he had done something wrong, when he knew very well that he hadn't. "If you do not wish to be here, then you can return to the inn at any time."

"If I have to stay inside one more minute, I'm going to scream." Justine turned away from him.

Karl frowned. This was how his older sister had been—never wanting Karl to see her upset. But then, she would turn away and attempt to cry silently, which she was terrible at. He always knew when she was crying. But it started this way. "Then let me teach you about snow. That was the purpose of today's walk. To read the snow."

"Read the snow?" she asked in a mocking tone. But she turned to face him, and that was something. The tip of her nose was red, but that could just as easily be from the cold weather and not tears. "As in, the frozen water that surrounds us."

"Yes," Karl said, nodding, hoping he would be able to reel her in with this knowledge. "It is vital for anyone doing big mountain climbing to understand the conditions in which they find themselves. So I want to show you the snow, and how to tell the different kinds."

"How can there be different kinds of snow? It's all water, isn't it?"

"Ja, but how that water freezes changes the way it behaves when a foot is placed upon it. When you live in these conditions, you learn by error. You do not, and we will find snow on the mountain even in July. You must learn."

Justine's posture relaxed and she crossed her arms. "Fine. Teach me the snow."

Karl smiled, not that she could tell under his scarf. "It has to do with the amount of moisture in the air, the temperature, and the wind. This snow?" He brought his heel down hard on the packed, crusty snow. "Old and hardpacked. It is more like rock, and will last late into the thaw." He pulled off his mitten, bent and scraped what he could from the surface of it. "Look at it closely." He dropped it in her hand.

She brought the clump of dirty snow up to her face. "Looks like snow to me."

Fine. She wanted to be a difficult pupil, this was her prerogative. "Keep that in your hand." He walked over to the stream and broke off the overhanging crust that had formed in the last day or two. The clump was clear, not white, and had space between each crystal. He dumped it into her hand next to the other clump. "And this one?"

A line formed between her eyebrows. "They are different."

"Tell me how," he said, hoping he sounded patient, like a good teacher.

"The second one looks more like crystals than a solid lump, like the first one."

"Good, yes, yes." He nodded, hoping she would continue her thought, but she didn't. Well, there was no need to go into detail if she wasn't interested. "Which would you rather walk on?"

"The first one. It looks like a solid rock, not like a piece of jewelry."

"Good. Lesson one complete."

"That's it? Don't walk on snow that looks like you shouldn't walk on it?" She dropped the snow on the ground and put her hands on her hips.

"You told me very clearly that snow is just snow. There were no types of snow. Now you've seen two different types, and you know which is safe to walk on and which isn't. That is progress." Karl turned around to head back to the inn, gambling that she would stop him. He hoped she would stop him and ask more questions. This was important, but he didn't want to force the knowledge on her.

"That's it? We're going back inside?" Justine said behind him.

"Do you wish to learn about more snow?" This was his hope, but she was clearly uneasy, and he didn't understand why.

"Yes," she said impatiently.

"Will you tell me what is wrong? You do not seem yourself."

She bent backwards and looked at the sky and groaned. "Why are you like this?"

"Why are you like that?" he shot back. Instead of answering, she glared daggers at him, which he didn't mind at all, because at least she was looking at him.

"I really don't like you," she said, folding her arms again.

He took a step closer to her. "I think you do like me. At least a little."

She sighed. "Lady Rascomb is worried about how appropriate it is that I go on these outdoor excursions that are not exercise-focused without a chaperone of some kind. It is not how a young lady is supposed to behave in England."

"But Fräulein Bridewell disagrees?" Karl asked, thinking back to the whispering trio before Justine agreed to go with him this afternoon.

Justine wobbled her head. "In a way. She has realized that I . . . that I . . ." she trailed off.

Karl could have taken pity on her and changed the subject, but he was far too curious about what she would say.

"I do not admire many men. But I do admire you."

He had been ready to stamp his feet from the cold, but he suddenly felt quite warm. "Admire? Is that a strong word in

English?" As far as he understood, in English, one could admire a horse. Or a nice cake. Or a sunset. Did this mean she liked how he looked?

She scoffed. "Don't let it go to your head. What's the next lesson about snow?"

Chapter Six

IF ANYONE COULD die of embarrassment, it was her. She had told Karl that she admired him, and his response was to ask a translation question. She'd never given an encouraging word to any man in her life, and then when she did, he didn't even understand her.

But she carried on, because what else could she do? Dinner was once again meat and some kind of brined and pickled vegetable. If she never ate another vinegar-based meal in her life, she could be happy.

"What did you learn today while you were out there with Mr. Vogel?" Eleanor asked, because bless her, she was trying to not talk *about* Karl Vogel.

Justine knew the minute they'd left the inn, the entire dining room had glued themselves to the windows to watch her and Karl hike down to the stream.

"I learned about snow," Justine said. The silence of the table, full of her climbing friends and their mates spoke volumes about how little they cared.

"Snow conditions are important to understand," Tristan said slowly, surprising her by being on her side. But then, he'd triggered an avalanche that almost killed his mother and had fallen through a cornice on Ben Nevis.

"I learned about rotten snow," Justine said. "Had I known this sooner, perhaps I could have saved you and Eleanor from falling down into a crevasse."

"It wasn't a crevasse," Tristan said.

"I didn't mind," Eleanor said at the same time.

Given how the two of them had ended up married after their travail on the Scottish mountain, perhaps Eleanor didn't mind not knowing snow conditions.

"Anyhow, it is something we should all know. Just as Eleanor taught us all of our useful knots, we should also learn the snow."

"But we'll be hiking in July," Eleanor said again.

"Snowy conditions stay year-round on larger mountains," Prudence said, piping up for the first time.

"Just so," Ophelia said. "And that is fine thinking, Justine. Perhaps Mr. Vogel could teach you and you could teach us."

Justine sipped the ale they'd been given in lieu of wine. Herr Brunner had explained that the next shipment of food and drink had been scheduled to come in before the cold snap, but had been delayed for some reason or another. He had also told them to not be alarmed, as they had plenty of food for everyone, just not the amenities they might have been accustomed to in London. Like French wine.

"Why would I teach you when Karl is right there?" She gestured towards him, sitting at a table with Lord Rascomb and Mr. Moon. When she looked back at her companions, they all had their eyebrows raised. Her heart dropped into her stomach. Why were they looking at her like that?

"Karl?" Ophelia prodded.

Justine nodded before she caught her mistake. Her dinner stuck in her throat as she choked out, "Mr. Vogel."

"Bad News has found her own bad news," Tristan teased.

Justine wanted to throw a bread roll at him, but she liked them too much to waste one. "A simple slip of the tongue."

"Are we talking about tongues now?" Prudence questioned, as if she were nothing but innocent.

Eleanor laughed. Even Ophelia snickered.

"I don't know what anyone is talking about," Justine grumbled.

"Poor sod," Tristan said, shaking his head and looking over at the other table. "I feel like I should join them, but the conversation here is far too interesting."

"I hate you all." Justine felt the heat from her cheeks as if she were a radiator. She put her hands to her cheeks as if she could leach the redness away.

Ophelia put her hand on her shoulder. "It's all in good fun. We're all astonished that you *like* any man at all. Given your past, it is frightfully new."

"I am here to climb the Matterhorn," Justine complained. "That's all. And I need to be good at everything in order to do it."

"As do we all," Ophelia said, gently tugging her hands away from her face. "We all want the same things."

"I know, but must you tease me?" she asked.

"Yes," Tristan said with a definitive nod. "Unquestionably, yes. And given how rough you made things for me, I will be teasing your irritatingly healthy grandchildren as well to make up for the years of your insults."

"You still managed to catch yourself a wife despite it."

"When shall we do a snow-learning session?" Ophelia asked. "We could start as soon as tomorrow?"

Justine was forever grateful to her best friend for changing the subject. After everyone agreed, and they finished their meal, Ophelia took it upon herself to talk to Karl about the following day's schedule.

Apparently he agreed, and they set a time to meet in the dining room in the late morning, without being bundled up, to talk about what they would learn, and then bundle up and take it out of doors. Justine was relieved that she didn't need to teach anyone anything. And she was relieved that at least for the next outing, she would be surrounded by her friends, so no more embarrassments might befall her.

JUSTINE WAS THE best pupil. He was ashamed that this surprised him, but it did. The others either tried so hard they looked past the obvious, or took too long. Though the experiment where he made Herr Bridewell stride into the trough of rotten snow did manage to make them all laugh.

The man took the ribbing in stride, and his father clapped him on the back after he dug himself out. All of them were shivering inside their coats as they stood around and looked at snow. Taking pity on them, he led them up a mild hike to keep them out of doors and help them acclimate to walking while wearing layers and layers of clothing.

They all needed the exercise. And Karl, most of all, needed to clear his head. The sound of the snow crunching in rhythm calmed him, and he hoped it would do the same for the rest of them. They reached the shoulder's summit, and he let them stare down at Täsch, as he had once let Justine stare down at it.

"I'm winded," Frau Moon said. "That doesn't bode well, does it?"

"We should be hiking daily, regardless of the weather," Fräulein Bridewell agreed. "I apologize to you all for letting our exercise regime go slack."

"As long as Mr. Vogel promises to go easy on us at first," Herr Bridewell said. "Not put us through our paces right away, as he did for Miss Brewer."

"We will begin slowly, as I will allow one of you to lead and test your new snow knowledge." Karl ushered them back towards the trail, indicating that it was time to return. Tante Greta had promised cake and hot coffee. Though Justine preferred tea. He shouldn't know that, but he did.

The clouds were clearing, and the sun shone on them for the first time in two days.

"That feels good," Frau Bridewell said, clutching her arms

around herself.

Karl couldn't help but notice Justine hanging back, letting others go in front of her on the trail. The dry snow crunched beneath all their feet, a cacophony of noise without rhythm. Karl brought up the rear, making sure they all followed the trail and didn't veer off to do something ridiculous. It was surprising how many experienced mountaineers could become unpredictable and step off into rotten snow, or even off a cliff, so entranced in the beauty surrounding them.

Perhaps Justine was letting others go ahead so that she might stay back with him. Tante Greta had told him how they'd teased her at dinner, how she turned red and suffered. Karl didn't care for that at all. While his pride was gratified that she might admire him, he didn't want her to feel that she could not trust him. He needed to remain professional and courteous. Not familiar and flirtatious.

"Do you remember what Mr. Vogel told us, Eleanor?" Frau Moon asked. She was also very good at reading snow. She wasn't quick, mostly because she was distracted by her new husband who had opted to join them today. He typically did not accompany their walks, and his slim build made him appear more fragile than the men of Switzerland. But Karl was pleased to see him glued to his wife's side, for that was what a husband ought to do, wasn't it? If a man pledged himself to a woman, he should be next to her always.

"About what?" Frau Bridewell asked.

"The sun!" Frau Moon said with a laugh. "Clear skies make for cold days, and cloudy days make for warm days."

Frau Bridewell shook her head. "That makes no sense to me at all. The sun feels so good on my face."

Karl smiled. He was happy that they were discussing it at all. Though Frau Moon had said she hailed from a place in America with a very strange name that had harsh winters and lots of snow, but no mountains. More like Augsburg than Zermatt, Karl figured. He wondered if America was a copy of Europe, with matching places to their climates, or if it was something different entirely. But he didn't figure he'd ever find out.

He was tethered to Zermatt, tethered to the Matterhorn and this inn. He would be guiding until he was like Luc, hunched and arthritic, saddled with responsibilities not of his own making. There would be no chance for a marriage or family of his own. He would be mending fences, tending livestock, and climbing mountains for the rest of his days. Which didn't sound like a bad future, but it did sound like a lonely one. What woman would want to be the helpmeet of that man? Not one like Justine Brewer.

Of course, he could take the other path, return to Augsburg and work with his father. But that would mean travel, and he would leave his wife alone in Augsburg, up to her own devices. That didn't sound appealing either.

"Thank you," Justine said, falling into step next to him.

Her soft words pulled him from his cynical daydream. "For what?"

"For taking time to teach us. For making Tristan get stuck in thigh-high snow. I particularly enjoyed that." She laughed and it sounded like silver bells ringing, and dread struck him. He was far past being able to control his emotions. Reining in his desire for her was only going to increase in difficulty.

"I am glad the lesson went so well," he said, his mind racing over ways to protect her from himself. Otherwise, she would become stuck in Zermatt like so many others had over the years. It was beautiful, yes, but it was a town that could only be reached by donkeys. That was no life for a wealthy young woman like her. That she might regret meeting him hurt something deep inside him.

She nodded and kept her eyes forward. He did not like this new way they walked together. Even when they did not speak and he took her on grueling treks at speeds he was sure she could not match, there was a sense of connection, even if it was one of disdain. He shouldn't have tested her so hard, but how could he not when her arrogance seemed so misplaced? How could a man look at such a small woman and wonder that she believed herself to be so strong?

But she demonstrated that to him day after day. The early mornings were brutal, and his requirements stringent. Still, she kept up. But now, as they walked side by side in the expedition group, there was a far bigger distance between them. Both of them had tried to keep space. Karl didn't like it at all.

"Have you and Ophelia found a training mountain you'd like to try first?" Karl asked. This was a safe topic. Something a guide should inquire after, since he would be the one leading them up whichever peak they picked.

"We have a list of mountains we'd like to start with," Justine said, staring at her feet as their boots tamped down the already-crusted surface of snow. "We will narrow them down to two or three and ask your opinion on which would be best."

"Good," he said, feeling rather stupid for not having any follow-up question for her. He was waiting for her like a dog, and he hated that.

"Yes," she said, and he wondered if she felt as flustered as he did.

That was the torture of it—he wanted that camaraderie that they'd had before her friends teased her. Before he began to understand his own attraction to her. But he didn't know how to fix it. And certainly not in a way that would allow them a friendship without tempting him into creating something more than that.

At least with mountain climbing, there was a straightforward purpose. One climbed to the top, using all a man's skill to overcome the obstacles. Endurance was key above all else. But how was one supposed to endure this kind of torture? The kind that dangled laughter and teasing versus the stalwart awkwardness of them denying their easy rapport?

His instinct was to address this head-on, but that hadn't gotten a very good result. He would wait for her to approach him.

Once again, he was the dog waiting at her doorstep, begging for scraps.

"I look forward to you letting me know," he said. And they didn't speak for the rest of the walk back to the inn.

Was it obsession when all she thought about was him? Or was that infatuation? Justine had never been clear on the distinction, having never experienced either. After returning to the inn, Justine and Ophelia opened up all the trunks of gear and the never-ending checklists Ophelia had compiled.

Fortunately, the equipment trunks were delivered to their room in anticipation of Ophelia's incessant need to put eyes on every bit and bob. Besides, Justine knew Ophelia thoroughly enjoyed this cataloguing. She typically hid it from the other people on the expedition, doing these checks with either her father or Justine, assuring others that she was well prepared.

They had no idea how well prepared they were.

"This month's checklist," Ophelia announced, waving about the paper she kept at the ready for each month they would stay in Switzerland.

"Hurrah," Justine said, not bothering to feign enthusiasm, but Ophelia didn't seem to notice. Equipment check was theoretically a two-person job, but Ophelia liked both tasks: checking the item off the paper list as having been completed, and putting hands on the equipment to make sure no repairs or replacements were required.

"Top of the list," Ophelia said, her entire posture straightening with pleasure. The woman really liked her lists. "Ropes."

Justine nodded and opened the first trunk, where the ropes lay on top. They were on top for a number of reasons: so they could not be torn or cut by any other object, but also so that when Ophelia did her checks, they could go in order. It honestly made Justine want to scream. But this was her very closest friend in the entire world, so she endured it, letting her mind wander between items.

Of course, today it only wandered to Karl. She'd had to put distance between them. Lady Rascomb, who was their official chaperone, made a point that while they were in mixed company, they were also out of doors and moving the entire time, which made it tolerable to spend time with Karl. There was no chance for them to become overly familiar. Technically, there had been no violation. But that was a semantic trick. For it was obvious that Justine was mooning over Karl. Obvious to the whole lot of them, and they were not the most observant bunch.

The idea that *Tristan* noticed, of all people, made it clear she was being ridiculous. Tristan might as well have walked through life with his eyes closed for all he spotted.

Ophelia started running the first rope through her hands, and Justine took the second. They looked for any fraying or decay, any pests that might have found a place to nibble, and overall integrity. It was a visceral way to ensure they would all make it down the Matterhorn alive.

The death of Lord Francis Douglas on the first successful Matterhorn ascent haunted Ophelia. Justine was well aware of how the Bridewell family saw the parallels between themselves and Lord Douglas. It had been a rope mishap that caused four members of the expedition to fall off the side of the mountain. The local guides, a father and son that Karl had mentioned once in passing that he knew, were still being harassed by not just newspapers but also by solicitors. Many wanted to believe the guides had murdered the men, regardless of having no reason to do so.

The Bridewells had discussed the case at length amongst themselves, a lecture Justine had been privy to, given how many evenings she stayed at their townhome in London.

After each woman had checked their ropes, they got up to swap piles and check the other's work. "Four eyes are better than two," Ophelia said brightly, which is what she said every time they did this dance.

The Bridewell analysis had been that the original Matterhorn party suffered from too much joy. Overcome by their accomplishment, they did not pay close enough attention to their gear, did not have systems in place to check one another, and thus did not realize that one of the ropes that was supposed to keep the men tied together was in fact a weak supply rope, not meant to hold the weight of several men.

The party had been roped together, which was standard practice for mountaineering, the idea being that if one climber slipped, the others could gain traction and haul the dangling man up. But in the difficult conditions of the Matterhorn, the boulders and icy haze kept the expedition from seeing one another, and the first or second man slipped off the edge, dragging the others along until that weak tether rope snapped around the side of a boulder, saving the last three men from certain death.

The two guides and Edward Whymper, whose journals and sketches permeated every newspaper across the world, survived. Ophelia was determined that would not be their fate. Her belief not in her own hard work, but in her attention to detail, would keep them from harm.

Justine believed in Ophelia. She had no opinions so lofty, and was happy to agree with the Bridewell conclusion. She even endured these equipment verifications so that Ophelia would not be alone in her perseverance.

The ropes inspected and deemed adequate, Ophelia checked the box on her list.

"Do you think it's inappropriate to be friends with a man?" Justine asked before Ophelia could announce the next item, which was always slings.

Ophelia blinked, her mouth still open, ready to continue on with their task. But, in deference to Justine's question, she put down her paper and closed her mouth, thinking.

"No. I think men and women can be friends without physical

attraction being a part of a conversation."

"So there's nothing problematic with me being friends with Mr. Vogel?" Justine asked, not daring to look Ophelia in the eye, because she had a feeling she already knew what her friend was going to say.

"That is not at all what I said." There was Ophelia's frowny silence, when she was thinking, gathering all the facts and data in her head, as if she were her own beautiful machine, whirring and clicking away like the most perfect automaton. "You and Mr. Vogel do seem to have attraction for one another, which changes the dynamics. But I suppose if neither of you acts on such attraction, there is nothing wrong, and a friendship can be pursued, as long as it is kept at a formal remove."

"How far of a remove?" Justine asked, getting out the slings. There were sixteen of them, and three spares. All had been fabricated by the same seamstresses that sewed sailing cloths, and all had been designed originally by Eleanor, with her profound knowledge of knots, and then perfected by Lord and Lady Rascomb, Tristan, and Ophelia. Justine had been grateful to be left out of that project. Her only reasonable input could have been the color, which no one thought was important in the least.

"Not permitting him to use your first name, nor using his," she said pointedly. She took up one harness and began inspecting the seams, the stitching, looking for fraying. After the visual inspection, they pulled on different lengths, as if to mimic a fall, to test their integrity. Each group of slings had initials embroidered, so that each person would not lose them. This was also checked off on Ophelia's list.

"What if I cannot bring myself to return to calling him Mr. Vogel? What if I liked our friendship when it was as familiar as that? I have called Tristan by his first name since we were children."

"You were children," Ophelia pointed out. "Which is entirely different. And there was no amount of tutoring that would have ever made you call Tristan Mr. Bridewell. You invented other clever names instead."

Justine chuckled. She'd had fun inventing new ways to torment him. Which didn't help at all with her new conundrum. She'd never liked Tristan the way she liked Karl. Tristan had been an annoyance, an unwelcome presence to her time with Ophelia. Karl was something different entirely. "But how does one go back? It's like trying to put perfume back into the bottle."

Ophelia opened and closed her mouth several times as she checked Justine's work. "I don't know."

That was as honest as Ophelia could be, Justine supposed. She dropped the subject and they continued the task at hand. After the fabric-related items, they examined the metal hooks and cleats they'd either had made custom for them or scavenged from other uses. Everything was oiled and in working order. Once the list boxes were thoroughly ticked, it was time to dress for dinner.

Wordlessly, they helped each other into their better gowns— nothing as ostentatious as dressing for dinner in London, but they did still keep with the tradition in their own fashion. Justine helped with Ophelia's hair, and then they switched.

Down at dinner, Justine found herself unable to contribute to conversation, which was so unlike her that everyone commented. It was yet another embarrassment, but Justine didn't feel it as keenly as she'd felt the previous night's teasing. Tonight, she was sad. She didn't want to be sad, and indeed, felt foolish for being so, but she had never been good at examining her feelings and keeping them to herself. She just felt them, and they leaked out of her just as easily as tears.

She did her best to not look at Karl, so she didn't know if he was paying any attention to her, which was for the best. She didn't want to make the Ladies' Alpine Society seem foolish, like any one of them was so scandalous as to run away with a foreign mountain guide. Of any of their accomplishments in Switzerland, that would be what London newspapers would choose to print. Never mind being the first women to summit the Matterhorn, one of them had lost her head with a Swiss goatherder.

After dinner was over, Prudence took her aside and apologized for the teasing. "We were just happy to see you infatuated," her friend explained. "You are always so lively, but to see you like this was transcendental. You glowed. And now you don't. I'm sorry." Prudence squeezed her arm. "I know it isn't the same hearing it from me, but I would love to see you happy again."

"Thank you," Justine said, trying a weak smile. Instead of lingering to chat, Justine excused herself to bed. By the time Ophelia came up, Justine was already in her nightrail, on her side, facing the wall, pretending to sleep.

Justine listened as Ophelia crept around the room, changing her clothes and sliding into her own bed. It was much harder to undress without someone to help with the buttons in the back, but not impossible. Should she have waited for her? Gotten up to help? If she were a better person, yes. She would have.

But tonight, she didn't want to talk. She didn't even want anyone to look at her, even Ophelia, who had always been unfazed by her. Justine's mind was churning through thoughts that couldn't be articulated. The emotions were bland colors being mashed and turned by invisible gears, keeping her from any semblance of peace.

What it came down to was that outside of the Ladies' Alpine Society, the only person who had ever seen her as strong and competent as she saw herself was Karl. She might not have an Oxford education or have travelled the world, but she knew enough that this was rare for a woman like her. Like Ophelia, Justine's ambitions were not to be married and have a brood. If that happened, that was fine, but she had bigger dreams than perfecting her mending.

The experiences she'd had in Zermatt, of moving her body, of climbing over cold boulders and punching through soft snow, these almost felt like a fever dream compared to the contained life she was expected to lead in England. Unlike Ophelia, her family had no inherent social cache, and unlike Eleanor's family, they didn't aspire to it either. Her father wouldn't care that much if she married a man without a fortune.

But would he tolerate a foreigner? A mountain guide at that? There was a vast difference between an English working man and a Swiss mountaineer. Justine worried her lip. And why did it matter? She wasn't proposing marriage to Karl. She only wanted to return to their easy banter and teasing friendship. Why did it matter what her father thought about anything? Why was she so upset about this?

The self-loathing surged through her all at once and she threw her feather covers off. She expected to startle Ophelia, but her friend was already well into slumber. Justine couldn't stand it. What a positive ninny she had been. Everything was fine. So she didn't know how to be teased, because she'd never been in this position before. But it was absolutely fine. Everything was fine.

Before she knew it, she'd gotten out of bed, pulled on her slippers and wrapped herself in her shawl. She would just go down to Karl right now and they could talk about it, and then tomorrow would be pleasant and perfect, and she would be able to sleep.

It was frigid cold in the stairwell, and she could feel the thin heat emanating from the dining room stove as she descended. What if he was asleep? A normal person would likely be asleep, since Ophelia was. But hadn't their morning meet-ups proven that the man didn't need rest? Still, she couldn't turn back now, or she'd never sleep.

This was really for the good of the entire expedition, anyway. This way, any awkwardness would be dispelled, and off they would go climbing nearby mountains.

"Karl?" she whispered as she pushed the door open. "Are you awake?"

"Nein," he answered, twisting round on his pallet. His body was limned by the firelight. His blond hair tousled and his bare foot sticking out from under the blanket. He stared at her, his lips parted, shocked. A moment later he recovered enough to say, "You cannot be here, Justine."

"I had to, otherwise I wouldn't be able to sleep." There were so many alarms in her head clanging, telling her to go back upstairs, to wait until daylight, to wait until Lady Rascomb was present as a chaperone, but still Justine stepped forward. The whispering sound of her slipper on the wood floor was loud in the midnight dark.

"What could be so important?" Karl sat up, the blanket falling away from his torso, and the firelight illuminating the outline of his chest through the thin night shirt he wore.

He was beautiful. The way a pine tree was, sturdy and purpose-built. As if Karl could only exist in the mountains, and would melt away like snow in warmer climes. Another whispered step towards him.

"I've been told I need to act more appropriately with you. That we are too friendly. That this needs to be professional." She wanted to look away from him when she said this, as if to hide. She was ashamed in some ways—but not for how she acted, rather, for how the world thought she ought to act.

The world told her to stop talking so much. To stop fidgeting. Stop laughing when she thought something was funny. They wanted her to lose all sense of herself and become an automaton in some curio shop.

But with Karl she'd been free. She could hurl her best insults and he would take them as they were, not dress her down for her lack of decorum. He'd taken her up steep trails where she'd huffed and puffed, and felt the sweat drip down her back in the most glorious of ways, and never once did he turn around and lecture her on her appearance.

And while it was specifically Lady Rascomb who had asked her to keep her distance, she did so because it was the expectation of Justine's family, of a hierarchy back in England that kept her mouth laced tighter than her corset.

But she didn't want this time in Zermatt to submit to that. She wasn't wearing a corset most days, allowing her to breathe deeply as she hiked, sucking in thin air like any man was allowed to.

Karl said nothing in response to her, only watched her, waiting. So she stepped forward again. It wasn't that she was bold, it was that there was something in her body urging her forward, propelling her feet, her knees, and without any resistance left to herself, she sank to her knees in front of Karl.

"You should not be here," he rumbled. His expression was open and vulnerable, as if he might tell her anything. Listen to her without filter and judgment.

"Why not? I don't care what other people think."

"Justine." His voice caught, and she melted at that hitch and the way he said her name. "It isn't other people. It's me. I cannot trust myself."

Her brows furrowed. The words sounded like rejection, but everything about his face and body screamed otherwise. "What is there not to trust?"

He ran his hands across his face and then through his hair, his breathing clearly measured and controlled, as if he were hiking up a steep grade. "I am a man, Justine."

"I am well aware." Oh, she had noticed.

"I want to do . . . man things . . . to you." Karl frowned. "That is not good English, but I am having trouble thinking."

Justine nodded. "I'm sorry. It is the middle of the night and you were sleeping."

Karl scoffed. "I was not sleeping."

"But you said—"

"Justine. I cannot stop thinking of you. It is worse at night. I think of your laugh, the curve of your neck, the curve at your waist." He stopped talking, swallowing another hitch in his voice. "You are . . ."

She cocked her head to the side. "I am what?" She was waiting for the words she'd heard before, the words that other men had said, like *pretty,* or *beautiful,* or even that she was a *firecracker.*

". . . surprisingly good at everything."

Justine rocked back on her heels. "I am?"

"Yes," he said. "And you're quick-thinking, ready to solve problems, always witty and charming, even at the crux of a difficult walk. Still, you can make me laugh when my heart is pounding in my chest."

"You are annoyingly capable too," she said. Was it just her, or was this making her heart beat faster? Her words harder to get out?

"I find you so irritatingly attractive." Karl inched closer, on his knees, matching her. "Especially now, with your hair down. I like that best." He reached up, as if he might pull a lock of hair between his fingers, but he stopped short.

"I like you best." She leaned towards him, her lips inches from his, wondering if she should be doing this, and what Lady Rascomb would say. Oh, she knew exactly what Lady Rascomb would say. And she knew it was a bad idea, but they felt like two magnets, opposites, being pulled together by unseen forces.

"You are my best client," he murmured, leaning down so that his lips gently brushed hers.

The tingle of his rougher lips against hers drove dancing sparks down to her toes. "Is this something you—"

He pressed his lips to hers, shutting off her question, and shutting off her mind. His arms came around her, one cradling the nape of her neck. She'd been kissed before, of course, even passionately so—but this was different. He was bigger, he was respectful, he was what she wanted.

He angled his head, his tongue exploring outward, but she didn't know what she was supposed to do. Soon, he shifted and pressed smaller kisses to her mouth, and then her cheek, and her neck. "Justine, tell me I have to stop."

But she tilted her head back so he could kiss down to her collarbone. "I don't want you to stop."

"I must, because if I don't, it will be more than you want—"

"What if I want everything?" she asked, her eyes blazing open.

"It isn't right. You are—" he stopped nipping and talking and grunted as he slid his tongue across her chest, pushing aside the nightrail that covered her.

His hand moved from her back and the nape of her neck, to squeezing her waist. Then those broad calloused hands inched up her rib cage.

"Tell me to stop," he begged.

"No," she said, her heart pounding, the heat between her legs pulsing.

He groaned again and cupped one breast in his hand, shocking her with the suddenness of his touch. Lifting his head, he recaptured her mouth as he kneaded her breast.

Then she melted against him. This felt better than anything. Better than ascending Ben Nevis. Better than any cake or tea. This was bliss, and she wanted every piece of it.

He tore away from her. "Nein," he panted.

Justine was gulping air as if they were on a mountaintop, and she was pleased to see he was as well. His erection was clear under his night shirt, outlined in the dim glow of the stove. She couldn't help but stare. It was different than she thought it would look, but then, she didn't know exactly what she'd imagined.

"This isn't appropriate." Karl shook his head, getting to his feet. "You are an Englishwoman. I am your guide. Mountain guide."

"What about—"

"It does not matter." He walked in small circles. "If word got out that I ravished you, I would no longer be deemed trustworthy."

"Ravish *me*? I wanted this more than you did."

He barked out a laugh. "Trust me, no."

"Don't tell me what I want."

"You don't know what you speak of, Justine. My desire, my lust for you is too great. If I go past a certain point, I can no longer think. That is why I cannot begin."

This had not been her experience. But her only partner had ever been Annabelle Rivers, and those afternoons were slow and exploratory, nothing like the blaze that roared with Karl. But she'd felt that need, that pull, so strongly. Was there something she was missing about the essentials of intimacy? "But wouldn't it feel good to give in?"

"Of course it would!" Karl threw his hands in the air. "But don't you see? What if I got you with child? What if your chaperones found out? What if your parents found out?" He ran his hands down his face.

"But we wouldn't have to go that far," she insisted. "We could just—"

"—That is what I'm telling you, Justine. I cannot control myself at that point. There are no half measures for me. I cannot. All. Or nothing. And we must choose nothing."

"I don't want nothing," Justine said, getting to her feet. What a confusing situation. He liked her but didn't? He wanted her but wouldn't? "I want everything."

"Of course you do. Who doesn't want everything? Only very foolish people think they get to have everything." Karl paced faster.

"I'm not a foolish person." Justine had heard those words enough, and she was tired of it. She wasn't a fool. Or a dreamer. Or inconstant. She was bigger than all of those things.

"I don't mean you." Karl stopped pacing. "Ich hasse Englisch."

Justine paused. She only caught the word *English* and considering the only other time she'd heard him say it was in relation to her, she could only assume that it was something derogatory about her. "What did you just say?"

"It's English. This stupid language. I don't like it. Not enough precision." He put one hand on end and tapped it into his other, as if mimicking slicing bread.

"What does the language have to do with anything?" She was still suspicious.

"Go to bed, Justine. We will sleep and all will be well." He went from looking furious to exhausted in the span of a minute.

Justine didn't know that she had a balloon in her heart until it deflated as Karl dismissed her. Her head spun with confusion. She turned dumbly away from him, facing the endless dark.

❧ ❧

Chapter Seven

HIS FATHER HAD told him he was a smart one, leaving Augsberg to help Onkel Peter in his venture. That he was listening to his family, listening to his brain, not the lust in his blood to join the Austrian army, where yes, he would find glory for all of a minute before dying horribly on a faraway battlefield for no reason other than some prince's greed.

The morning after he had kissed Justine, had nibbled his way down her beautiful neck, and run his tongue along her elegant clavicle, he had congratulated himself on that same intelligence. He had not been lying that it had taken every ounce of strength he had to tear himself from her. But it was the right thing to do. An honorable man was a man of restraint. Of fortitude and reliability. And lingering in his mind was the threat to his livelihood should it become known that he had strayed too close to his pretty English client.

But as the weeks wore on, Karl did not feel smart. What he had learned were "snubs," *auf Englisch*, were his only direct communication with Justine. She no longer looked at him or spoke to him directly. They had switched from the two outings, one in the morning just the two of them, and then the later, easier group walk, to all-day big climbs of nearby mountains. Monte Rosa, Breithorn, Castor, Pollux.

At first, he could have sworn they were chosen because they were nothing but grueling. Fräulein Bridewell had said she would consult him about which excursions to take, but then, she informed him of her decision, rather than asking his opinion. It was his job to counsel and advise. It made him wonder if Justine had some hand in it, rendering him as useless as a pack mule. She had been upset that he'd turned her away that night, but what else was he to do? Ravish her with no thought to the consequences?

But the long mountain trudges were her penance then. If he had been consulted, he would have counseled towards something more pleasant, with better views.

Indeed, Fräulein Bridewell had insisted that she lead their marches, given that she was the leader of the expedition, and that they should go in their expedition order, which was another thing Karl thought foolish. So regimented and strict in their thinking, the British. As the weeks had stretched, their different abilities and stamina changed. Being able to address this phenomenon seemed prudent, but Fräulein Bridewell would have none of it. She and Justine charged forward at the front, while he was relegated to the back with Lord Rascomb, who seemed to struggle with the steeper climbs.

Karl would have also counseled on eating well in the morning, carrying no meal as to move faster, and then eating when returning to the inn. This was how everyone did it. Every expedition he had worked with operated like this. And by the time those mountaineers reached the inn, Tante Greta's food was nothing short of divine and holy.

But no. The English pushed a bag on Karl to carry, full of thermoses of tea and sandwiches. Sandwiches! Not even a proper cheese and meat and a slice of bread. But sandwiches. Sometimes even little cakes, and it made him frustrated more than he would admit, but he carried the damn pack up the mountain and down the mountain again.

By the time he was carrying an entire meal for the company, he knew this was punishment because he had *spurned* Justine. But hadn't she understood why? He did this for her. He could not control that rutting instinct, and if she had any sense at all, she would understand that. Instead, she held it as a personal insult that he did not ruin her good name and impregnate her. Would her father really want some mountaineer's babe in his daughter's belly? No. This was the obvious, practical approach. But he hadn't meant *never talk to me*, or *treat me like your personal donkey*.

Perhaps he shouldn't feel so aggrieved. Perhaps it was his fault for taking her shunning so personally. This is what he'd advocated, wasn't it? Some distance? She had certainly managed that. He no longer wanted to take her up to private meadows and trails that he alone traversed or take in the stunning views of the Zermatt valley only a local would know.

And then, to make matters worse, last week, her brother showed up. Mr. Francis Brewer was a mop-headed dandy who had no business being in the Alps. Swaying along on the donkeys coming up from Zurich, he heralded English rations that no one in Zermatt could have predicted. There were teapots and horribly stale flattened cakes made of oats, yet even more woolen clothing and extravagant party dresses and metal gadgets he had no idea what use they could be for. But Fräulein Bridewell treated him as if he were an arriving hero, and Justine welcomed her brother with open arms.

Karl wasn't sure why it felt like surveillance, but it did. Her family could not have known how close he and Justine had been, and surely could not have had time to send her brother to interfere. But Karl found himself disliking Francis Brewer from the outset. And then came the late nights in the dining room, which interfered with Karl's sleep, and he liked Mr. Brewer even less.

The cards slapped together as Mr. Brewer shuffled. "What do you say, a pfennig ante? Is that what they're called here? Yes? A pfennig."

"No," Karl said, trying his best to be stern but not too inhospitable. He was tired. Another calf had arrived early this morning, and he'd been there to help things along. And then there were the goats, of course, and bottle-feeding the babies so they might milk the mother goats for the season. And then Tante wanted to make some cheese, even though it wasn't one of the village cheese-making days. She sent him off to beg permission and obtain some rennet from a neighbor, because the English loved their cheese too.

Karl had been pushed and pulled, and all he wanted was to walk up a mountain without a pack laden with ridiculous foods. He wanted to stand on top of a crest or a ridgeline and stare out at the incredible sky and the sharp outlines of the peaks that surrounded him. The air was different there, sweeter somehow, and he wanted it. Alone.

Instead, he was the expedition pack mule, and Mr. Brewer's mark. But Karl had dealt with men like him many a time. One could not be a traveler and not encounter those who could smell another man's card hand. But he had no desire to do so tonight. It was nearing eleven, and he would be up early again for animals, and then a hike where he would carry everyone's midday meal, because heaven forbid any of these British people were hungry for more than a minute or two.

"Come now, we don't even have to play for real money. We could play for pine cones or pebbles or whatever you have around here." Mr. Brewer shared his sister's complexion and shiny brunette locks. On his sister, they cascaded down her shoulders in gentle waves. In Mr. Brewer, they were tightly curled and lay placed like eggs in a hen's nest atop his head.

"You must forgive me, for I am very tired," Karl said, remembering with some satisfaction that this man was not born as an aristocrat, and therefore did not require any deference from him. They were both sons of merchants.

"What do you do around here for fun, then?" Mr. Brewer threw his cards on the table and leaned back in his chair. "Where are the wine, women, and song of Zermatt?"

"We don't have enough leisure time to facilitate such things." Karl put the chairs up on the tables, trying to indicate in another way that he'd very much like Mr. Brewer to leave.

"And I'm stuck here for two months?" Mr. Brewer let out a groan of misery.

Karl could see the resemblance between the siblings once again, in their lack of formality and verbose nature. "Mr. Brewer—"

"Get out, Francis." Justine appeared in the doorway, her robe over her nightrail, her silky brown locks loose and gently curling.

"What are you doing down here like that?" Mr. Brewer demanded of his sister.

"Trying to get you to respect our hosts. Go to bed."

"You go to bed."

"Francis." Justine stepped further into the dining room. "This is where Mr. Vogel sleeps. He cannot go to bed until you leave."

"I had no idea—" At least the man had the decency to look abashed.

"You didn't ask. There is no gambling here, no painted ladies for you to woo, so go on. You'll be hiking with us tomorrow, and you aren't acclimated yet. You'll be exhausted. Let us go up." Her voice was soft, an explanation, not a demand or even a command. Only some gentle information about what was expected of him.

"I say, I am very sorry, Mr. Vogel. I had no idea." He looked contrite as he swept up his cards into his hand and stood. "If I had but known—"

Karl waved away his apology. "All is forgiven, Mr. Brewer. I will see you both tomorrow."

For the first time in weeks, Justine met his eye. She even gave a small apologetic smile. It did strange things to his heart, or maybe his stomach, or maybe both. He finished stowing the chairs on the table and set out his pallet next to the fire. Pleased by Justine's gesture, he fell asleep before he had a moment to pine for her.

"My toenail is coming off," Justine announced, picking at the blackened tile that barely hung on to her foot.

"Mine came off two days ago," Ophelia said. "At least the blister on my little toe has turned into a callous."

"Mine formed weeks ago," Justine countered, pulling off the black shingle that was purportedly once a toenail. It stung a little as she tore the last bit of skin from it. But the nail underneath was already growing, which was something. "So glamourous."

"I had to take in the gowns that Francis brought." Ophelia brushed her hair until it shined. Not that it took very long.

"Mine feels like it was swimming around me, and I remember when I wore it last year it felt tight." She eyed the green dress. It had once been one of her favorites because it was so over the top. Frills and ruffles and pearlescent ribbons with tiny eyelets running through every hem. There were jet spangles running in patterns all over the bodice, and she had fairly jangled as she'd waltzed.

Here, the dress felt foolish. Silly. Not that it was beneath her somehow, to wear the dress she once loved. No, it was more like she'd outgrown it. More akin to requiring a new pinafore at school because last year's no longer fit.

"Does it not feel odd to do this?" Justine asked.

Ophelia twirled one of her strands of shiny gold hair and pinned it in place. Her dress was a new French silk frock, dark blue with white and pink roses climbing up the skirt and the bodice, with cream-colored lace on the sleeves and the low, swooping neckline. "To do what?"

"To pretend to have a formal dinner here. It seems excessive. And I feel bad for Frau Brunner. This isn't what she normally cooks. To dress this way seems—"

"Odd." Ophelia finished her sentence, twirling up another golden strand. "You mentioned. And yes, it is odd, for us to go to other countries and try to make the other places Britain, instead of enjoying the decided not-Englishness they have."

She slid on silk stockings for the first time in months. They were very fine things, and she knew how costly they were. Six months ago, she had drawers and drawers full of them, reveling in the different clocking patterns on the backs. Now, she couldn't bring herself to even miss wearing them, despite their smoothness.

She stepped into the green dress, and without asking, Ophelia stood and helped her with the buttons.

"This is still too big," Ophelia said.

"If I take it in any more, I'll have to start unstitching the bodice designs." Justine lifted her arms, where the spangles scratched the sensitive flesh on the underside of her bicep.

Ophelia considered. "Padding?"

Justine looked at her as if she were suggesting wearing live chickens under her frock. "Maybe we should get Eleanor in here. She's a master at knots, maybe she can think something up?"

"Do you think a ribbon can help that much?" Ophelia's face wrinkled in concern.

"Might as well try. It is a better option than unstitching all those spangles."

Eleanor arrived, cheeks flushed and hair mussed. Ophelia cocked her head to the side, her eyebrows drawing together. "Are you well?"

"Hm?" Eleanor asked, somehow a bit breathless. "Now who needs what?"

Justine stood up, letting the gown sag away from her.

"Oh my. Yes." Eleanor considered the green gown that was now very much tent-like.

"I didn't realize I'd lost so much weight. But the sleeves are tight on my arms." She raised her arm, demonstrating how the sleeves restricted her movement.

"They've always been like that," Ophelia said, slipping ear bobs on.

"Not this bad, surely." Justine raised and lowered her arms again, feeling the pinch of strained fabric around her biceps.

"It never mattered to you before."

Meanwhile, Eleanor had pulled and stretched the fabric of the bodice in different ways, pulling at the waist, and then the loose bodice. "I think our best option is the window shade."

"I beg your pardon?" Justine said.

Eleanor worked her magic with some pins and the longest black velvet ribbon in the room. The three of the working in tandem, they used the extra fabric of the bodice to create an internal channel for the ribbon, then looped it around the front, allowing the skirts to billow out along the ballooned crinoline, but raise the green outer skirt and expose the white underskirt.

"Won't I be uncouth, exposing my underskirt?" Justine asked, already wary of what Lady Rascomb might say.

"They did it all the time in the fashions of yesteryear. I'm sure Mama wore things far more scandalous." Ophelia waved off Justine's concern as she gathered up Justine's jewelry from the table and handed it to her.

"I like this," Justine said, ignoring the jewelry and playing with the ribbon that raised and lowered her skirt, exactly like a window shade. "This is really fun."

Eleanor smiled. "You are welcome. I have been thinking about it for when we climb the Matterhorn."

Ophelia's eyes locked on Eleanor, like a hunting dog realizing he's scented his prey. "How so?"

"I noticed on Breithorn that we often end up holding the front of our skirts up as we walk, to avoid them getting trod under on steep grades. And even as we tramp through snow, the hems get wet and make our woolen skirts very heavy. What about if we implemented something like this for our walking dresses?"

Justine stared. "I think you are the smartest person I've ever met, Eleanor. And that's saying something because I know Ophelia."

Eleanor blushed, and it was easy to see why Tristan had fallen for her. Smart, unassuming, very clever, and her blush made her very pretty indeed. She smiled at her friend, and then realized why Eleanor had been out of breath. And why her hair was an absolute mess. Tristan had been mid-expressing his appreciation for his new bride when they'd summoned her. Because Eleanor was Eleanor, she came right away instead of finishing up and then arriving.

"Do you need help getting ready for dinner?" Justine asked. "There isn't much time left to dress."

Eleanor blanched and looked at the clock sitting on the dressing table. "Oh dear."

"We can help you dress," Ophelia said.

Justine noticed Eleanor's brief hesitation before she invited them back to her room. On they traipsed, and luckily discovered that Tristan had dressed and wandered over to Francis's room.

"Did I not get an invite?" Prudence popped her head in Eleanor's room. "I heard the commotion."

"Look at this!" Justine said as Ophelia waved Prudence in. Justine accordioned up her overskirt as Prudence admired it. "Eleanor thought of it!"

"Phenomenal. But I feel like you all know something I don't," Prudence said. She was already dressed in a scarlet red gown with pink spangles sewn in with white thread. Her skirts were not as wide, but rather made up for the width by the longer train in the back.

"For when we go up the Matterhorn!" Justine said, but Prudence did not seem as impressed as she ought to be.

"Instead of holding up our skirts with our hands," Ophelia explained. She stuck a pin into Eleanor's hair, and then another. "We don't have to worry about stepping on them, or getting the hems soaked and weighing us down."

Prudence made an appreciative noise. "That is clever, Eleanor! Show me again."

Justine pulled the ribbon at her waist that pulled up the skirt and tied it, as if she would keep it that way for a long while. She swanned about the room, the skirt remaining just as she'd left it. She stopped short in front of Prudence and untied her tiny knot at the waist, and the overskirt dropped back down.

Prudence applauded and Justine curtsied.

"Eleanor, that's brilliant. It really is."

"That's what I said," Justine added.

Eleanor blushed in the mirror, and Ophelia finished pinning her hair.

"Let's get down to dinner." Ophelia patted Eleanor on the shoulders, and Justine fell into step beside Ophelia.

"Maybe tomorrow we could make a first run at those for the skirts," Justine said.

Ophelia nodded. "I was thinking after dinner, and then try them out tomorrow."

"What if they don't work? I don't want to be halfway up a mountain and decide the skirts are terrible."

The smells of the dining room wafted up the stairwell. The aroma of beef and roasted potatoes, something with honey in it, made Justine's stomach grumble.

"Good point. Maybe we delay tomorrow's climb in favor of working on our equipment." Ophelia sniffed the air. "My word, that smells like home."

Justine grinned. The best way to Ophelia's heart was through a well-roasted, wine-soaked slab of beef. "Doesn't it? I'm so hungry. I'm always so hungry."

"It's the mountains, it's the exercise," Ophelia listed, before stopping dead in her tracks. "I smell sticky toffee pudding."

"What?" Justine stopped too, sniffing the air. She'd always been jealous of Ophelia's excellent sense of smell. "Impossible."

"I'm going to eat myself unconscious," Ophelia said, almost giggling, which made Justine laugh.

"Race you. First one down gets extra pudding." Justine took off down the stairs, bowling over Prudence and Eleanor, Ophelia shrieking behind her. Justine's feet bounced down the stairs as fast as she could go. The crinoline cage of her skirts swayed, knocking against her knees as she tore down the staircase.

At the bottom of the stairs, Karl stood with his arms folded, nodding as he was in deep conversation with Tristan.

Justine tried to slow down, tried to adjust her speed, but her feet were on a streak of their own, but she stopped as quickly as she could. And Ophelia slammed into her back, throwing her forward on the landing. But she caught herself against the banister, even as the air went out of her lungs.

"Ungh," she managed. "You all right, Fee?"

Ophelia grunted and pushed away from her.

Both of their crinoline cages swung back into shape.

At the bottom of the stairs, the men turned to look up at the commotion. Karl wore tight black trousers that men favored this close to Eastern Europe. His coat was longer, hitting at mid-thighs, with elaborate brass buttons going down the front. He'd clearly freshly bathed and shaved. His shoulders seemed somehow bigger in that coat, and he seemed as if he could pick her up, toss her over his shoulder, and march away.

His blue eyes were magnets for hers, and she was being drawn into a whirlpool that she'd happily drown in.

"My goodness!" came the rushed gasp from Eleanor.

"Are you all right?" Prudence asked, examining both her and Ophelia.

Eleanor straightened Justine's gown, since Justine was just open-mouthed staring at Karl, his straw-colored hair neatly combed back, and not flopping over his eyes.

"Fine," Justine said.

"I suppose that's why they say no racing inside," Ophelia said with a light laugh. The Ladies' Alpine Society descended the rest of the stairway with far more decorum. Eleanor and Prudence went to their husbands and while Ophelia drifted towards her father and mother, Justine stood close enough to Karl that she could smell the fine, clean scent of him. No sweat, or hay, or animal. He wore a light cologne that combined with his tight trousers and flared coat made her want to throw herself at him again.

She opened her mouth to greet him, or say anything at all, but the dining room door swung open, capturing all of their attention.

"Dinner. Is. Served," Herr Brunner announced from the doorway, his English clear, though accented.

The Bavarian man smiled broadly at them, pleased with himself, and no doubt pleased with the rich smells emanating from the kitchen.

"Get straightened up, dears," Lady Rascomb said before entering the dining room with her husband. "We will be taking a photograph this evening."

"I beg your pardon?" Justine said.

"You are welcome," her brother said, dipping down to reach her ear. Every single one of her siblings got to be tall except her. Life wasn't fair.

"You brought a camera here?" Justine asked. "I didn't even know you had one."

"My newest obsession," Francis said. He always seemed steadier than he actually was, but that was because he was always with Tristan. Between the two of them, Francis had been the more level-headed. But since Tristan married Eleanor, Francis had become unmoored and flighty. "Besides, with a photo of you all dressed like you were dining in Mayfair, along with an article from Ophelia about the mountain-climbing aspect, and every journal from here to Boston will want it."

The public did love a photo of rich women dressed in their finery. But would they respect Ophelia's words that went with it? Justine had her doubts. Still, it was worth the effort.

"Then does my dress look good for your camera? I don't want to look rumpled."

He eyed her, making a face. "Did I bring the wrong dress? It looks too big for you. No matter, we'll hide you in the back so no one can tell."

Justine made a face at him. "I'll be front and center, right next to Ophelia, thank you."

"Come on," Francis said, offering his arm.

They may have dressed for dinner like they would in Mayfair, but they did not observe the rules of entering a dining room according to rank. The girl Justine often saw around doing various chores was in the dining room, wearing a traditional Alpine dress. It made Justine think of the children in the cheesemaker's shack, peering down at her from the loft. How old until they took work? How long did childhood last up here in the mountains?

Watching the girl filling wine glasses, Justine realized that just past her gaze was Karl. And he stared back at her. It was so strange to admit that she missed him. How could she miss him? She saw him every day. But she missed the easy conversations, even the drudging walks with him. She missed the freedom that she'd had to be herself.

And she begrudged the limits. She begrudged this English dinner and the confines of her life. Francis would no doubt report back to her parents that she was being a docile, good girl, climbing her silly mountain.

Francis fooled with a tripod, atop which a camera perched. "Everyone! I'd like you to crowd around for a photograph."

The room buzzed with compliance, even though they'd all seen the camera sitting there as they'd entered the dining room. Before Justine realized it, Karl had squeezed in next to her, his thigh flush with hers. She didn't dare look over.

Her hand rested on the table, and his was next to hers. As everyone else squeezed in around them, Francis barking orders of who sat where, Justine raised her pinkie finger off the table. She had no clear purpose in mind, just a hope, a need, a wish. Her exploratory gesture was met with Karl's little finger. His answer to her question. That together they were something more. A force so inviolable and inescapable that fighting against their inevitable collision was a Sisyphean exercise. They didn't speak, just stared straight ahead, their hands hidden from the camera by the array of wine and water glasses.

"This will take a moment, so please remain absolutely still with no talking," Francis said.

Justine couldn't have talked if she'd wanted to. She was frozen in this moment, her finger linked with his. This connection with Karl reciprocated, her pining felt and acknowledged by him in this one small gesture.

"Wonderful, everyone! Thank you so much." Francis applauded them, and everyone moved back to their original seats. Justine looked at her empty bread plate as the heat of Karl dissipated once he'd left her side.

"Justine?" Ophelia asked, noticing her sudden and unlikely quiet.

"I—I'm fine. Sudden dizziness, that's all. It will be over in a moment, I'm sure of it." Justine gave a winning grin, and though Ophelia wasn't convinced, she let her line of questioning rest.

Something burbled inside Justine. Something bigger and more important than anything she'd ever felt before, and she didn't know what it was or what it meant.

Chapter Eight

KARL FOUND HIMSELF wondering which was superior for climbing a mountain—his trousers or their skirts. The trousers did not get caught underfoot, but he noticed he was prone to being colder without the woolen layer trapping the heat of both legs together. But his trousers were dry, tucked into his boots. Their skirts dampened around the hems, and their complaint was the weight of the wet wool.

Karl could attest that hauling more weight up a mountain was almost an exponential problem. Not that he was a mathematician and understood precisely what exponential meant, but he knew that it was more than saying two or three times harder. Certain weights were not much of a burden. But once over five pounds, it changed. An additional ten pounds was significant enough to alter his pace. An additional fifteen or even twenty pounds would slow him down by more than a few minutes.

The women had devised an internal pulley device for their skirts, to hike them up as they hiked. Their hands were free to use a walking stick or catch themselves with both hands. A very smart innovation. He did not know the dry and wet weight of a woolen skirt, but by the pleased noises coming from them, the experiment was a success.

It helped to have all the women on the trail. With the four of them talking, their high-pitched English accents paired with the lower-pitched American one, he could forget about Justine. The past weeks had been agony. And then last night at dinner, what had he been thinking sliding in next to her for the photograph?

She was stunning in her dark green gown, her shoulders bared. He'd never seen her like that. Her hair was pinned up, but the idea of that silky hair brushing against her elegant shoulders was more than he could bear. It was how she looked at home, no doubt, the kind of woman who was accustomed to the ornate dresses, velvet ribbons, and silk stockings. The kind that ran smooth against her shapely calves, and he wondered what it might sound like to hear his hand running up her silk-clad thigh. But it was another reminder that she was not for him. A punch of reality admonishing him to do his job.

But she had smelled so good, powdery and vanilla and night and sex, and he wanted one last sensation of that before putting away his needs forever. So he'd slid next to her for the photograph. And the indescribable relief and heartbreaking want that surged through him when she'd lifted her finger, as if asking for him, asking if he thought about her.

It had given him a hope he shouldn't long for. The hope he himself had tried to grind out of existence. They were only a week away from the Matterhorn climb. They all needed to be solid climbers with excellent stamina. And he needed to evaluate them, as if he hadn't already been watching them on the difficult mountains they'd already climbed.

But Justine made him unable to see straight, unable to trust his own judgment. The joy he felt at the end of a day with a big mountain climb was shockingly close to the joy he'd experienced just being with her, talking with her. And that was impossible. The joy of a mountain climb had been second to none. He'd much rather climb a big mountain than plow a barmaid. He'd made that choice dozens of times.

So why was he unable to see that easy equation with Justine? Why was it different with her? And he wasn't even plowing her! None of it made sense.

"Whoa there, Speedy!" called Frau Moon. "Slow down and

wait for us mortals."

"Who needs to slow down?" Justine called, surging through them, on his heels.

"Nutters," called Frau Bridewell.

"Justine, slow down before you injure yourself. I'm not carrying you down the mountain." Fräulein Bridewell's words made the steps on his heels, which he'd wanted to hear closer and closer, stop short.

"My apologies," he called over his shoulder and slowed back down to his normal pace. His mind had gotten too wrapped up, and he'd forgotten himself. Which was precisely why he kept his distance from Justine. Which was why he wanted to be with her. How proud he was that she wanted him. And how he wanted these two opposite things at the same time! It was so frustrating to have those both of them warring inside him at once. It made no sense.

"Mr. Vogel!" Frau Moon called again.

"Oh, let him go," Justine said behind him.

And so he did. A guide should not abandon his clients, but the trail was obvious and the snow pack was stable. The season was warming up again, and the rotted snow had melted away. He left the four women on the mountain while he went up ahead, pushing himself almost into a run.

He had to clear his head. How could he manage the next weeks with Justine, seeing her every day, talking around her every day, watching her laugh at dinner? He'd tried to ignore her, but she had wedged into him like a grass seed in a woolen sock. He'd have to return to his first strategy: wear himself out so completely that he didn't have the energy to think of her.

The gradual ascent of this hill was not satisfying and the views were subpar. He huffed out his annoyance. Footsteps scrambled behind him, and he turned to see Justine emerge, charging ahead to try to catch up to him. Hope sprang up in his chest, a bloom he'd tried to dig out, but couldn't.

"Karl," she said as she gasped for breath.

But on her heels came the rest of the group. They were loud with their staggering and panting, but they'd kept pace with her, which was impressive.

"You weren't kidding about that," Mrs. Moon said, her hands on her hips. "That was faster than I thought I could go uphill."

"Light feet," Ophelia gasped. "Brilliant image. Very helpful."

Karl shifted, hoping he was able to maintain a placid, helpful expression. But Justine had said his name. She wanted to talk to him, and as much as that was terrible news for one half of him, it was the kind of joy that made climbing mountains look like nothing more than a swipe of honey on one's finger after dinner.

"I CANNOT SAY that was anything but an unmitigated success," Ophelia said in the darkness.

Justine normally adored a midnight chat, the dark being a place where one could say more to one's friends because one didn't gauge the look on their faces, didn't have the walls in place to keep secrets buried.

"I agree," Justine said, because she wanted Ophelia to go to sleep. Justine gritted her teeth to keep from chatting, which was very difficult because Justine *always* had something to say.

There was a silence where Justine could hear Ophelia noting her verbal reticence. "Are you well, Justine?"

"Absolutely brilliant, thank you."

"Are you upset with me?"

"Absolutely not!" Why did she get in trouble for talking and then now get in trouble for *not talking*? "I'm just—it's only that—"

"You can tell me the truth," Ophelia said, her voice small and quiet in a way that Justine hated. It was the sound of her friend doubting herself, questioning what she had done wrong, believing herself to have made a grave social faux pas.

"Ophelia," Justine sighed. She rubbed her hands on her face.

"I don't want to say anything because I don't want you to know."

More silence, and Justine could practically hear Ophelia crawling up inside her shell.

"Not like that. I mean, that I don't want you complicit." Justine gritted her teeth. Might as well say it now, she thought. Since she'd confessed to having a scheme.

"What would I be complicit in?" Ophelia asked, her words dancing on the knife-edge of support and propriety.

"Maybe nothing?" Justine said, not knowing what Karl would even say to her when she snuck down to see him. "But maybe everything?"

"Is this about Mr. Vogel?"

"Yes."

"You like him very much."

"More than I've liked anyone other than you. And well, Prudence and Eleanor. The first time I've liked someone that also came with a fluttery feeling in my throat. Like drinking too much champagne, or laughing so hard I can't breathe."

"I've never felt that." Ophelia sounded sad.

Justine could hear Ophelia's nails clicking as she picked at them. It was her nervous habit. She didn't do it often, typically only in midnight chats like this when she was in deep introspection.

"But if this leads to my ruin—"

Ophelia gasped. "You cannot be serious."

"I don't know what will happen, Fee!" Justine felt as if she could take out all of her insides, hold them in a bubble, and put them aside. All of the bits of her that warned her away from Karl, all the propriety, all the need to obey Lady Rascomb, all of the wariness of ruining the reputation of the Ladies' Alpine Society or Karl's career. It was stupid, and she knew it, to put all of it aside for one night. But the compulsion to do so was irresistible.

"This is a very serious thing."

"It is," Justine agreed. "But I feel like I must. Not that I should or that I want to, but it feels as if I am being pushed by something larger than me."

"God? Fate? The devil himself?"

"I don't know." Lust? Foolishness? Those were just as power-ful.

"You'll go to him when I fall asleep?" Ophelia asked, her words once again careful and precise.

"Yes."

"So it doesn't matter what I say, because this will happen regardless of its folly?"

"Believe me," Justine snorted. "I know it is folly."

"Then consider this a conversation of our dreams. I have been asleep, and I know nothing other than the blissful oblivion of rest."

Justine sat up. "Truly?"

"What could I possibly say? To scold you is to only say what you already know. To tattle is to ruin you, and myself in the process. Why would I not say, be careful with not just your body but with your heart. And his. We need you both."

She swung her feet to the icy floor, already seeking her slip-pers. "I'll try."

"Please don't get pregnant." Ophelia sounded very grave. "You cannot have morning sickness while climbing the Matter-horn. It would slow us down."

Justine barked out a laugh but then covered her mouth from its unexpected volume. "I don't think *that* will happen."

"Many a mother has thought that very thing, I believe."

She'd left her dressing gown and shawl on the chair, which was four paces away. In her planning this evening, she'd done her best to figure out each step so as to not wake Ophelia. "You are right. Good advice as always. Wish me luck."

In the thick darkness of their room, she could hear her best friend smile.

"Good luck, Justine."

"Thank you, Fee. I mean it." Justine cloaked herself in the dressing gown and shawl and left the room as she heard Ophelia turning over in her bed, nestling down for sleep.

Tonight, Justine didn't feel the cold in the stairway. Nor did she note when she could feel a warmer draught emerging from the dining room. She was so focused on talking to Karl, wondering how to start this conversation, that she wasn't entirely sure of what it needed to be herself.

By the time she creaked the dining room door open, her heart was pounding like she'd just ascended their biggest climb. Walking into the brighter room made him almost seem to glow. He sat at a table, staring into the fire. The light caught his hair in a glow, and the blue of his eyes seemed almost transparent.

"You're here." His voice was soft and low. Tired, but not unwelcoming. He still wore his clothes, and not his nightshirt. The pallet was not made up in front of the fire as it typically was.

Justine didn't know what to say. She stepped forward, but then questioned herself again. Should she stay where she was? Should she approach him? What was she supposed to say? Finally frustrated with herself and all of this dancing about in her head, she blurted out, "This is silly."

He raised his eyebrows, clearly amused. "Which part?"

"All of it." Justine stepped forward now, closing the gap between them. "I like you. You like me. We both like climbing mountains. Why is it agony to not speak?"

He looked down, but she was unable to read his face. Unable to see how he felt about her in return. "I have regretted these weeks. I knew it was correct to distance myself from you. But I hated every minute." He looked back up at her, and the vulnerability on his face unmoored her.

She closed the gap between them, coming to sit next to him on the bench behind the dining table. He had a cup of some kind of herbal tea at his elbow, a cup that looked like it had gone cold hours ago. She took his large calloused hand into her lap, letting her fingers trace along his wide, square palm.

He watched her fingers in his hand as if he were a wild animal in a children's book trying to behave. His hand flexed, and for a moment she thought he would hold hers, but he didn't. He relaxed again, and she continued her work.

"I want things to go back to how they were," she said.

"I do not," he said immediately.

Her motions faltered, and then he did grip her hand in return, lightly, caging it rather than taking a firm hold.

"Why?" Her heart hammered away once again, unable to tell the difference between her emotions and a steeply graded mountain switchback.

"Because then I wanted to kiss you and knew that I couldn't. But now I have kissed you, and it is the sweetest nectar I have tasted and I want it again." His blue eyes bored into her, the intensity of his gaze stealing her breath.

"Oh," she managed, unable to take her eyes off his. "I think that would be fine."

A smile crept into his expression. "Would it be fine?"

"Very fine, I expect."

A full grin emerged, and Justine could feel herself being pushed closer, not that she moved of her own volition, but rather that she was drawn in by a force she couldn't—perhaps wouldn't—control.

His hand slipped around her waist, pressing the thick fabric of her dressing gown and her nightrail against her skin, and he gathered her up as if she were an armload of firewood.

"I want you here," he said, pulling her onto his lap, his breath whispering against her neck.

Perched on his legs, supported by his arms encircling her, she felt safe and warm in a way she'd never known. Just as her heart pounded in her own breast, she could feel the fast thump of his heart in his. There wasn't an experience she'd ever had to guide her in this moment. She hadn't a seducer's language or the coyness to be seduced.

As always, the only thing she could do was what she wanted. So she leaned down and brushed her lips to his. It was like baiting a hook, for soon one of his hands cupped her face and pulled her down to him, deepening the kiss as if he were a drowning man and she were the only air.

Clinging tighter to him only enflamed them both. Her fingers explored the stiff stubble along his jaw, the tender, smooth skin under his ear. A low rumble came from his chest, and his kiss turned to shorter nibbles, gasping with need as she continued her movements.

His hair was surprisingly soft, and almost curly underneath. Not knowing why, she fisted a handful of it at the nape of his neck. He stood almost instantly, holding her up, pulling her legs around his waist, growling.

"You can't," he rumbled. "That's . . ."

"You liked it," she said, surprised and delighted by her discovery.

"Too much." He swallowed and worked to slow his breath. Sinking back down to the bench, he pulled her in close, almost as one would tuck a baby animal close to one's body. "I am wanting too much."

Justine felt almost drowsy with the attraction between them. It was a surprising drunkenness, except for the tight concentration of desire between her legs. He brought his hand to her face, dragging his thumb across her cheek.

"I want everything with you."

Justine shook her head. "I'm not sure I know what that means."

He grinned back at her. "I'm not sure I know either."

"Does it mean I get to speak to you whenever I want?"

"Yes."

"And make jokes and tease you?"

He blessed this question with a kiss on her lips. The searing touch of it had her straining to make him stay, even as he pulled away. "Yes."

"And kiss you?" She looked at him, knowing she was crossing into a territory more dangerous than the previous questions.

He kissed her again, more thoroughly this time, pushing his

tongue into her mouth. She responded in kind, which seemed to surprise him by the way he startled but clearly enjoyed as he tangled with her all the same.

His left arm had cradled her legs, but now he slid his hand up so he was cupping her bum. He kneaded and palmed her arse, which was far more pleasant than Justine would have thought. Leaving her mouth to gasp for air, he slid his kisses down to her neck. This desire of his, how it focused on her heightened every sensation.

Her afternoons with Annabelle Rivers were *nothing* like this. They had giggled and kissed and petted, and it was very nice. This tidal wave of lust and need was dizzying and exciting and made her feel good in a way she'd never felt before.

And here was the moment her mother had warned her about. The exact decision that her mother knew she would make when she chastised Justine about her impulsivity. And Karl Vogel's tongue drawing circles across her chest, pulling the nightrail lower and lower drowned out any whisper of caution.

The neckline of the nightrail caught, snagged as low as it could, and Karl could not get to her bare breasts. She knew that was where he was going, that's where she wanted him to go. But he couldn't use the hand he was holding her with, and he clearly did not want to sacrifice the one occupied with her bum. He growled in frustration.

Through the haze of desire, she pulled his face up to hers. "I want more, but this is a sign to stop."

"A sign to get new sleeping clothes."

She threw her head back and laughed, glad that he was as frustrated as she was. "This isn't reasonable. I can't let you ruin me in a dining room. I ate a pork chop just there." She pointed.

He nodded, making a considering sort of expression, looking where she indicated.

"Are you not going to say anything?" she asked, feeling awkward now that they weren't devouring each other.

"Not yet. It's—" he stopped speaking, flexed his thighs, causing her to bounce in the air, which made him groan. "I'm trying—"

His whole body tensed this time. She couldn't figure out what was going on. "Are you ill? Should I leave?"

His eyes squeezed shut and he relaxed. "Yes. Please stand. Not leave."

"Of course." She scurried off his lap, collecting her dressing gown and woolen shawl around herself, as prim and proper as she could manage. "You don't seem well."

Suddenly, Karl stood and strode through the dining room, around the bar and to the back door. Justine followed him, curious now. He got to the door and picked up handfuls of the old, stale snow that lingered in the shadows of the building. Then he clapped one on the back of his neck, and the other he rubbed on his face.

"Are you . . ." She trailed off as he turned around, his face red from the cold and his eyes bright blue.

"The inferno you inspire takes some effort to control, Justine." He stood close to her in the doorway, the midnight hour freeze creeping into the inn. Still, she could feel the heat of him. The inferno that raged inside her as well.

He pushed her against the doorframe and kissed her. She pulled him down to her, holding him with all her strength.

"Warum ist das Zimmer kalt?" came a low voice.

Without speaking, Justine slipped outside as Karl shut the door. "Onkel, warum bist du noch wach?"

"Es ist kalt!"

Justine couldn't hear them as the door shut completely. She stepped further away from the door and caught sight of the night sky. It was teeming with stars that she'd never seen in England. The moon was big and heavy like an expensive pearl. The specks of stars dusting the sky numbered far more than she ever expected. It was a cool night, but she no longer cared. Not when this experience, this sight, had been hidden from her view.

The night sky in the English countryside was beautiful, yes, and far more dense with stars than that in London, but it was nothing compared to this, framed by the white mountain peaks. The stars were in whorls of other colors, and the variety in size and shape astounded her. Why had no one told her this was here the whole time? She'd been here months, and no one had once suggested walking outside when it was dark. Women were ushered up to bed after dinner, never having the opportunity to step outside. The men did so in order to smoke, but a well-bred lady didn't smoke.

Maybe she'd take up the nasty habit if it allowed her this view.

"Justine?" came Karl's whisper.

She startled at his voice and stumbled back towards the door. "The stars—"

"You must be freezing." He pulled her inside, cupping her hands in his and blowing on them as he shut the door behind her. She liked that too.

"I'm fine," she insisted.

"Come sit by the fire," he said, pulling her towards the hulking iron stove. He guided her to the warm spot on the floor and settled behind her.

She extended her legs so that her wet, slippered feet nearly touched the iron grate. That alone was enough to warm her lower extremities. And the gentle embrace of Karl behind her was enough for the rest of her.

"That was a close call with Herr Brunner." Justine couldn't think as he combed his fingers through her unbound hair.

"Indeed. You should go to bed. We have much to do in the next month to prepare. Time is short."

Their lives had revolved around this mountain for years now, taking her focus and attention and time. Sometimes she regretted it, because there were so many things in the world besides one mountain. But she was glad Ophelia kept her focused. "I believe that we are ready. Prepared."

He made a noise that didn't sound like he agreed.

"No? What else must we do?"

Karl sighed, and the heave of his chest rocked her forward like a wave on a boat. "There is much to still learn about the terrain and which routes would be best. It has been grueling, but the Matterhorn is even more so. I think everyone is nearly ready. Nearly."

Justine didn't like the sound of that at all. "Who isn't ready?"

"You are ready, Fräulein Bridewell is ready. I think Frau Moon will do well enough, as she seems to understand snow. But it is Frau Bridewell that concerns me. She has stamina, but she lacks confidence."

"Walking does not require confidence."

"It does." He cleared her hair to one side, leaving her neck bare to him on the other. The whisper of his words along her skin was distracting in a way she didn't anticipate. It made her not want to argue, but agree, so that he would keep talking, letting air dance along that space between her neck and her shoulder.

"How so?" she managed.

"A confident step sinks into the ground. An uncertain one slips. It is simple."

"Ah," she breathed. If he wasn't sitting right there, holding her, stoking the inferno inside of her, she might have argued. They sat in snug, drugged warm silence. There was no place in the world she'd rather be.

"Are you warm enough now?"

She hummed a response because she could not actually open her mouth to use her words.

"Then off to bed with you," he said, his voice rough with forced control. "Or I will lose myself all over again."

His lips brushed against her earlobe as he spoke, and she nodded. "But I don't want to go."

He chuckled, and she thrilled at being able to feel the growl of his chest through her body. "Then we must someday find a way to do this, but perhaps not before the Matterhorn."

She nodded, too drugged on heat and lust to argue. The

climb was soon. Everything was coming together so fast, and *after* was not so far away. "After."

He kissed her neck, as chaste as a kiss could be on one's neck, and pushed her gently to get her to her feet.

"Go on, then," he said when they were both standing. "Liebchen."

What had he said to her? Probably some form of *goodnight*, so she nodded and said, "Goodnight, Karl," and went back up to her room in a daze.

⇶⫷⫷

"WHAT DO YOU think you're on about?" Francis asked, cornering her in the stairwell after breakfast. They had thirty minutes or so until they needed to be back down to start today's cross-valley trek. Karl had explained that he wanted to see the group's endurance, and it was hard for him to see every person while in forested switchbacks. Ophelia had agreed, and they sketched out a cross-country trek. It sounded like an easy day to Justine, and she was more than happy to walk all day. She preferred it, actually.

But then, here was Francis, blocking her path, being a right nuisance. Who would not be joining their expedition, today or otherwise. "I don't know what you mean."

"With our guide, Mr. Vogel." Francis jumped up on the landing of the stairs, barring her way.

"*Our* guide? You aren't going anywhere." Justine walked around him, wishing she were wearing her accordion-pull skirts so she could hike them up and take the stairs three at a time. Well, two at a time. Her legs weren't long enough for three.

Francis heaved a beleaguered sigh that sounded just like their mother. And it was one of those things that had always made her blood boil instantly. "The blond muscle-bound ox down there. Him. What is going on between you?"

Justine turned around, her anger mixing with that horrible need to be obnoxious. How often had her mother counselled her on controlling that? But Mama wasn't here. Francis was. And he was a turd.

"What if I told you I was going to marry him on top of the Matterhorn as a publicity stunt for Ophelia?" She crossed her arms.

His face contorted in that entitled, superior way of his when their parents or governess wasn't around. The face that was hell-bent on controlling her for no other reason than he thought he could.

"Ophelia isn't climbing the Matterhorn for publicity. It's that *guide* that can't stop looking at you, and you, well. The scandal sheets got that part right at least: a harlot looks at men the way you look at him."

"A harlot?" Anger flushed her body. "How dare you, Francis?" For years those accusations had chased her, despite when she behaved or when she didn't. Rejected suitors made up stories and called her names when she didn't allow them a kiss or a fondle. And now here was her own brother, believing the rumors and the gossips that had dogged her. "How. Dare. You." She spun on her heel and ran up the stairs, a hot star in her chest, anger and hurt blooming in a horrible flower.

Ophelia was already there, her blue eyes wide. "What has happened?"

But Justine couldn't speak. Tears, wet and furious, streaked her face. Ophelia took her hands and guided her to her bed. As Justine sobbed in frustration, Ophelia unlaced Justine's shoes and slid them off, tucking them under the bed. Justine curled her legs under herself. Ophelia poured a glass of water from their ewer and handed it to her. It was cold, given the room was chilled from the night air seeping in through the window.

Justine drank and handed over the empty glass. Ophelia put it on her nightstand and sat down next to her, taking her hand. "What is the matter?"

"Francis," Justine said.

And at that moment, a fist pounded on the door. "Justine, it's Francis. You must come out."

Justine had the urge to say a very unpleasant and shocking curse word she learned from Eleanor, given that she'd grown up around sailors, but Ophelia found her voice first.

"Francis, will you please give us a moment? Justine is indisposed."

There was a begrudging grunt outside the door. "Fine. I'll be in my room."

They listened to the footsteps go down the hall and then the door open and shut.

"I hate him," Justine whispered.

Ophelia rubbed her leg. "Only because he reminds you of your mother."

Justine laughed despite herself. "He'd be a terrible mama."

"Yes, so thank goodness no one will let him," Ophelia agreed. "Now what did he say? I can ask Tristan to set him straight."

Justine fell back onto the bed. She might as well tell Ophelia—she did see her sneak out last night, after all. "Francis knows something is going on with Karl and called me a harlot because he's mad that I am an actual human person."

Ophelia nodded. "Then he is more perceptive than I would have thought him to be."

"How could you say that?" Justine demanded, sitting back up.

"I only mean that I am surprised Francis is able to discern that something is decidedly happening with you and Karl."

Justine flopped back down, grunting out her disgust. "I hate your logic. Just be on my side, no matter what."

"I am absolutely always on your side. However, your brother, in this one very particular case, is correct in describing the action, not the person. But the attraction between you and Mr. Vogel is palpable."

"Palpable?"

"Almost as if it had a smell," Ophelia said.

Justine took her pillow and whacked Ophelia in the face with it. Being the good sport she was, Ophelia laughed and let herself be pulled down onto her back as well. They both stared up at the ceiling.

"I tried not being attracted to him, not speaking to him. But that made us both miserable."

Ophelia hummed her agreement.

"So last night we talked about it, and we decided we get to be friends and attracted to one another, and after the Matterhorn, we will be physical."

Ophelia sat bolt upright. "As in . . .?"

Justine turned on her side, surprised at the sudden wave of contentment that flowed through her thinking about their time together last night. It was as if her emotions couldn't figure themselves out this morning. "As in, I'm not sure?"

Ophelia's face grew very serious. "Then there is time to prepare."

"Prepare for what?"

"For all possible outcomes. You will want some kind of anti-pregnancy precaution. We can ask Eleanor what they have been using. She may be able to procure something, given that she's a married woman."

"Procure?"

"And then, of course, we will have to figure out privacy for you, so that we can keep it secret."

"Wait, Fee, this isn't—"

"Our departure dates aren't set, given how our expedition is weather-dependent. But we had planned on leaving shortly after our accomplishment. Perhaps you could persuade Prudence or Eleanor to stay after. I can't, of course, be a chaperone, and my mother would be appalled if this happened on her watch."

"Ophelia." Justine touched her friend's arm, often the only way to get her to stop her excessive catastrophizing. When she stopped speaking, Justine retrieved the empty water glass and filled it again from the ewer and gave it to Ophelia.

The gesture was not lost on her friend, who gave a wry smile and drank it down.

"Hearing you plan for intimacy between me and anyone takes the joy out of it. You are your own anti-pregnancy device."

Ophelia snorted a very unladylike snort. They were silent for a moment. "What was the trouble with Francis again, if it was not the situation with Mr. Vogel?"

Right. That. She'd almost forgotten. "He called me a harlot."

Ophelia was on her feet. "That will not stand."

Before Ophelia could go charging out the door, Justine grabbed her. "He said that a harlot looks at men the way I look at Karl. For all I know, he's correct. But it's still a rather mean thing to say."

"I will not have any of my team slandered in public places. There are too many other climbers in town," Ophelia said. "That is damaging to all of us, and I'll have Francis watch his tongue."

"He said it because he's my brother."

"He said it because he's a twat," Ophelia shot back.

Justine chuckled at her friend's uncharacteristic use of foul language. "You aren't wrong about that."

"I can't sit by on this, Justine. This has bigger implications than just you having a row with your brother."

And off she went. Justine knew she'd hear blow-back from Francis about Ophelia taking him to task, but it was worth it at this point. But it did make her wonder what she was supposed to say to Francis. How to explain to Francis this connection she had with Karl? That he seemed to understand her in a way that no one else did? That their common interest was *mountains*? And specifically, walking up the sides of them? It sounded bizarre at best.

But she knew that he would caution her away from Karl. Honestly, Justine was not flattered by her own behavior either. But there was something heady and intoxicating about him. As if she couldn't speak or think straight when he touched her. Staring at it the way Ophelia would, any relations with Karl were a terrible idea. And Karl himself had said he would lose his reputation as a gentleman's mountain guide if it were found he was deflowering his virginal clients. What a mess.

And of course it was Justine wading into this ridiculous mire. Ophelia would never be so foolish as to conduct herself like this. And Prudence would never be a lovelorn puppy. And Eleanor? Well, Eleanor had been trapped with Tristan. Perhaps she'd thought they would be stuck there on Ben Nevis forever, so might as well experience something before they died. Why else would someone be naked with Tristan Bridewell?

Ugh. She'd still flirt with Karl, especially now that it bothered Francis. That was a given. But perhaps the post-Matterhorn assignation would not happen. It was ridiculous of her. A midnight thought, the kind where consequences didn't exist. But it was morning now.

Should she tell Karl that nothing would happen between them? Or should she keep it all to herself? One never really knew how men handled rejection, so she'd stay quiet and let him think that a night of passion was still happening. That was for the best, wasn't it?

Chapter Nine

K ARL WAS BURSTING to tell someone. Not his Onkel or Tante, of course, they would talk him out of it. Now that summer was here, his guiding compatriots had returned to Zermatt. They would be meeting up in a few days to compare notes, expedition groups, and weather theories in order to discuss routes. It would be unbearable for so many parties to be on the Matterhorn at one time.

He finished splitting the lumber rounds in front of him and kicked them about to separate the pieces. They would need to cure and dry out for another year at least. He still had to pick out the kindling-sized wood and then stack the other logs into their off-season woodpile. It was never-ending work, but he didn't care today, because his heart had wings.

He was going to marry a British girl. Him, married! It would be quite a strange change. They would need their own cottage in Zermatt. He couldn't have her sleeping on the dining room floor with him. Or even the unfinished caretaker's room. His Onkel and Tante had their own cottage just steps away from the inn, but there was a room off the lobby that had yet to be finished that was supposed to be his.

No one thought about Karl marrying—including himself— because he rarely encountered women. But Justine Brewer was a different kind of woman entirely. Would she be content to stay in Zermatt? Would she travel with him if he were hired to be a guide in a different country? Would she return to England to be with her family if he left?

Or he could take his father up on his offer to be a part of his trade. It was an option, but one that would take him out of the mountains. Out of the snow and wilderness. And that's not what he wanted. Nor what Justine seemed to want either.

There were many things to think about. He lined up another round, and it gave easily under the weight of his axe. They would be leaving for a long day's hike in a few more minutes, but he had enough time to split a few more logs. Better to get a few done every day than leave the entire chore never started.

Indeed, the thought of their marriage made him energetic, despite his lack of sleep. He had taken himself in hand after she'd left. He'd gone outside, not wanting to do such a deed in the inn's dining room. But no sooner had he allowed himself to think about her on his lap, moaning into his kisses, than it was over. She was all he could think of, all he *wanted* to think of.

But first, they had to climb the Matterhorn. He could focus on that task without difficulty. He finished with what splitting he had time for, hearing the church bell ring its single bell to mark the quarter hour, and returned to the inn. At the tool storage shed, Karl oiled the axe before stowing it, which was where Mr. Brewer found him.

"I don't know what is happening between you and my sister, but I need to make it clear, nothing *will* happen. Do you understand?" The Englishman spoke the last words slowly, as if Karl didn't speak English.

But Karl couldn't help himself. He knew he couldn't headbutt the man, which was his impulse, given his hands were occupied. "I find it best to not threaten a man who holds a weapon."

Mr. Brewer's brown eyes—the same shade as Justine's— widened as he looked down to see the axe in Karl's hands. Had he not noticed as he approached what Karl was doing? Single-minded to a fault, it seemed. "I am not threatening," Mr. Brewer said, his tone much softened. "I am reassuring you that Miss

Brewer's family will protect her at all costs. As will Lord Rascomb. With the full force of English law."

Karl did not like being threatened. It was cheap, especially in a place like this where *law* and *family* were secondary very much to the forces of weather and nature. Family was important here, yes, of course, but it was a broader sense. The entire community had to function as family, otherwise they would not survive. "I am sure that means something where you come from. But where we stand now, we respect other things more than English law."

This was perhaps the wrong thing to say or, depending on what Karl wanted, exactly the correct thing to say, for Mr. Brewer's face went purple.

"I will have you stay away from my sister, sir. Make no mistake, I will brook no trespass upon her person."

"What if she marries me?" Karl could not resist a taunt.

"Be careful of what slander you speak, sir," Mr. Brewer spat. His face was becoming a rather concerning shade of purple. If he were an older man, Karl would have advised him to sit down.

"I speak no slander." Karl finished with the axe, tucking the metal head inside its leather case and stowing the tool inside the shed. "Excuse me, I need to ready for today's trek."

He smiled and left Mr. Brewer heaving angry breaths behind the inn. It shouldn't please him so much to make his betrothed's brother mad, but it did. He would apologize later, when they were brothers, and could perhaps laugh about this moment.

After that remark, the urge to tell others subsided. Days passed without him wanting to blurt out the news every time he saw Onkel Peter. Even when he met with the other climbing men of Zermatt at the tavern, he felt no urge to speak about his pending nuptials. They drank and ate and joked, and all was as it usually was.

It was night, but warm, and the grass was healthy and green. He swayed as he walked up to the inn, full of beer and camaraderie. His body was warm too, and the smell of the fresh grass that would eventually be reaped into hay at the end of the summer felt like home in the best way possible.

They might even try an early climb, in mid-July rather than late July or early August, as the weather was improving faster than anyone had anticipated. It would make it easier for more teams to have a crack at the mountain this season.

Still. Preparations first, then climb the mountain. Climb the mountain, then marry the girl. Yes. Then bed her. He fumbled with the door latch. The place was dark as it should be at the late hour. He hoped that perhaps his Onkel or Tante had laid out his pallet. He stowed his hat and boots in the closet by the door and entered the dining room to find . . . her.

Delightful, yes, but difficult. He was in no presence of mind to keep his hands to himself, or the rest of his body in control.

"What did you say to my brother?" she demanded.

Oh, her eyes were very angry. He stopped and blinked, trying very hard to clear his mind and focus on her. Hair: down and flying about. Eyes: very passionate, but not in a way that beckoned him. Cheeks: pink. Lips: thin and pressed together.

"You," he declared, very sure of himself, "are mad at me."

She threw her arms in the air. He was fairly certain that was disgust. But should he not be proud to have discovered her anger? He thought it was well done of him, considering his inebriated state.

"You told my brother that we are engaged."

He took a breath to respond, but his English wouldn't come out. Nor would it process her words either. Her words stuck in a circle, running over and over on a loop that he couldn't comprehend.

"Marriage, Mr. Vogel. You told my brother I was marrying you."

Marriage. Yes! He understood that one. "Ja, gut. Das ist richtig."

"I don't know what you are saying. So yes, you told my brother I would marry you?"

Karl decided gestures were better than words, so he nodded

his head, which was largely a mistake. The room tilted and he stepped sideways to keep himself upright. He found the wall and leaned against it for safety.

"Why would you say that? What am I supposed to do?" She began to pace.

"Du bist sehr schön," he said, sighing. It was true. Simple, but true.

"English Karl, English. I don't speak German. Dear God, I wish I did." She put her hands on her hips, which accented the curve of her waist. It made him think of her sitting on his lap, and the feeling of cradling her ass in his palm, and how nicely it fit there.

"Englisch, ja." He would teach her German at some point. Not now. It was night, and he was drunk. "You." Why was his mouth so dry? "You are very pretty."

She looked at him as if he had just said the most outlandish thing possible. But he was quite certain of his conviction.

"It's true." He slid his back down the wall to the floor, which was much safer.

"Get some sleep," she said, shaking her head. She disappeared, and he closed his eyes, not caring if he slept on his pallet or not.

But then she was in front of him again, holding a cup out towards him. "Drink some water first."

He glugged the water down, grateful, watching her as he did so, unable to be ashamed or coy about his love for her. Oh, did he love her? He had not thought of it yet. But perhaps yes? This was also very fun to think about.

When the cup was empty, he handed it back to her.

"I'll get you another, and then I'm leaving. Do you understand? And you go to sleep. We'll speak in the morning."

"Ja," he said, his tongue suddenly feeling very thick in his mouth. His eyes closed, and when he awoke, stiff from sitting upright on the floor, the cup of water was next to him, and his pallet was spread out next to the fire.

JUSTINE WAS EXHAUSTED and confused. She had assiduously avoided her brother for days, which wasn't too hard since he was always down at the other hotels, looking for someone to play cards with. Her mind kept going over that confrontation where Francis had asked if *it* were true.

She didn't know what the *it* was, until he clarified—was she engaged to Karl Vogel? She had been gratified to see how mortified Francis looked at the prospect, and so she had half a mind to let him believe it, but given the speed at which her mother would show up in Zermatt, she told him that she was not engaged to Karl or anyone else.

That was when Francis told her Karl was the one who told him that she'd agreed to marry him. Justine's whole body went cold and then hot. So she waited up for Karl, knowing he was at a mountain guide meeting or something of the sort, since he missed dinner. But he didn't come and didn't come, and then when he did arrive, he was stinking drunk and made no sense whatsoever.

But that softening bit of her wondered if it was a translation issue. When she had said they would begin their torrid affair after the climb, did he then assume marriage because she had money?

Her gut churned with impatience. The idea that men were off making assumptions about her made her want to tear her hair out. How dare they? As if either Karl or Francis had any say over what happened to her. The very idea of it had made her want to smash every piece of glass in the entire inn for the past week. Which, of course, she didn't and wouldn't actually do.

This seemed like something she should talk to Prudence about. Without Mr. Moon lurking around, if she could manage. But Ophelia was right here, and they were reinforcing the window shade pull lines of their skirts to ensure they wouldn't break or snap.

Despite the hikes and climbs, marriage had changed their group. It felt even more divided in halves, Eleanor and Prudence on one side, her and Ophelia on the other. Especially now that those two women were paired up. She would call Prudence and Mr. Moon married, even if officially, they were not, but honestly, it was obvious that they would be in time.

"Justine, are you listening to me?" Ophelia asked, putting down her mending.

"Yes. I am now. I am."

"This is serious."

"I know," Justine said, looking over her last line of stitches. When she got distracted, so did her sewing. "It's fine."

Ophelia looked at her, knowing that she'd done something but not yet understanding Justine's state of mind. She didn't know that Karl had told Francis that she was marrying the mountain guide. And Justine didn't know if Karl had said it to make her brother furious, which honestly, she would have done herself, or if he really believed that she had somehow agreed to marry him.

Was it something he'd said to her when he was speaking German, and she didn't understand? Or was it some cultural context she didn't know about? If a girl danced three dances with the same man, people would assume they were courting. Was it the same here, as if you climbed three mountains with a man, you were engaged? Well then, Karl was engaged to the whole pack of them.

"Fee." Justine looked up at her best friend in the entire world, hoping she would not yell at her. She loved Ophelia more than her parents, but right now, she couldn't handle Ophelia's nervous chatter. Justine leaned back and rested herself against the bed. She wasn't wearing a corset—she was wearing the jumps they wore when they took their exercise—and she might never go back. The feeling of her spine slightly rounded and resting against the bed felt good. Easy. Free.

"You're so pretty," Justine said, sincerely meaning it, even if the comment had no bearing on the situation at hand. It was true, and Justine didn't even feel envious about it. Her golden hair was braided and pinned up—the braids kept the hair from tangling further, and would be better suited for sleeping on the side of a mountain. She was like an illustration for women's mountaineering.

But Ophelia was used to Justine's aesthetic non-sequiturs. "What's wrong?"

"Everything," Justine said, groaning. She both wanted to talk about Karl and wanted to forget him entirely and go climb a fucking mountain. "Nothing."

Ophelia sank to the ground, her big blue eyes trained on Justine. Some strange man would fall in love with her someday, and if Ophelia could let him love her, she would be so happy. But that day might never come, and she might marry for convenience, or perhaps not at all. Justine could be a spinster with her, living in their own townhouse, having adventures together. Ophelia would write her papers and give lectures, and Justine would bully places into allowing her to do so.

"Something happened?" Ophelia guessed, slipping her hand into Justine's.

"No. Well, yes, but really no."

Ophelia hummed appreciatively, as if this answer told her anything at all.

Justine sighed. "Karl told Francis we were getting married."

Ophelia was silent a moment. Then she asked, "Who is the we? You and me? You and Francis? Or you and Karl?"

Justine laughed, because only Ophelia would ever be confused about a sentence like that. "Me and Karl, of course."

"Ah." Ophelia nodded. "Why would he say that?"

Justine could tell Ophelia was doing her best to step carefully in the conversation.

"I don't know, and I tried to ask him, but there hasn't been a good time." Justine squeezed her eyes shut. "I know I shouldn't care, I know I should be focused on the Matterhorn, but every time I try to shut out the memory of Francis demanding why I'm marrying Karl, it just swirls around in me, and I can't focus on anything at all."

Ophelia nodded and straightened her back: Expedition Leader Time. Justine would bet Ophelia didn't even know her posture changed when she switched from being Justine's best friend to Ladies' Alpine Society Expedition Leader. "What can we do to resolve the situation with Francis and Mr. Vogel? Because we should resolve it before we start up the mountain. I can't have your attention divided."

"I know, but I don't know."

"You haven't been able to speak with Mr. Vogel, correct?"

Justine unstitched her last bit of seam and redid it straighter this time. "Correct."

Ophelia nodded and then stood, dusting off her skirts out of habit. "Who else knows about this?"

"As far as I know just you, me, Karl, and Francis." Justine put down the skirt. "I thought I might talk to Prudence about this."

Ophelia nodded. "Excellent idea. We shall call an emergency meeting of the Ladies' Alpine Society. I'll meet you downstairs."

In true Ophelia form, she swirled out the door to make preparations. Justine smiled and tucked away the mending. She gathered up the other two women from their rooms and herded them down to the corner of the dining room, nearest to the stove that still churned out a delightfully low heat, despite the declaration of *summer* by the calendar.

Mrs. Brunner brought out a tea pot and cups early for them, along with leftover plum cake, which none of them minded. And when Mr. Moon came round, Prudence shooed him away with both hands.

"Away with you. Go play with the other men."

"I don't know where they are," Mr. Moon protested.

"Then go find them," Eleanor chastised. "I think mine is in the barn, pretending to know about livestock."

Mr. Moon sighed, but dutifully trudged out of the dining

room.

"I've a problem," Justine said in a low voice, once Mr. Moon cleared out.

Ophelia made a sound halfway between a grunt and a sigh.

"Is what your brother said true?" Eleanor asked.

"Ooh, what did he say?" Prudence's eyes were wide with curiosity.

"Apparently—"

Mrs. Brunner walked over to their table, and to be safe, Justine stopped talking. She didn't think the woman knew too many words in English, but she certainly didn't want to chance it when talking about the woman's nephew.

"Good, yes?" Mrs. Brunner asked, wiping her hands on her apron.

"Delicious," Prudence answered with a wide smile that the Swiss woman returned in kind.

"More?" Mrs. Brunner pointed to the tea pot.

"Oh, we wouldn't want to trouble you," Ophelia said, displaying that knack for sounding kind while also asking for more. Justine also knew Ophelia well enough to know that she copied her mother's mannerisms down to the crinkle of an eyebrow and the exact pitch of the opening *oh*.

Mrs. Brunner waved her hand and picked up the pot. "Hot water," she said and bustled off to the kitchen. As soon as she was out of the room, the Ladies' Alpine Society huddled together again.

"Apparently," Justine continued, "Francis confronted Karl about what's been going on between us—"

Eleanor's eyes went wide and Prudence's smile grew wider. "What has been going on?" Prudence asked with a saucy tone that Justine wasn't sure she appreciated.

"Nothing much," Justine protested.

"Kissing," Ophelia supplied. "Clandestine midnight meetings."

"And lots of walking in the woods without speaking," Justine protested.

Eleanor and Prudence exchanged looks, as if this was the obvious path to becoming one of them: *married*.

"Anyhow," Justine said, wresting their attention back. "Karl told Francis that we are engaged to be married."

Eleanor gasped. Prudence gushed.

Justine held up her hand. "But he never asked me if I wanted to marry him."

That stopped short Prudence's tumbling congratulations.

"Do you want to marry him?" Eleanor asked.

"I would like to have been consulted," Justine said.

"Of course," Ophelia said. "But that's not the question, is it? Nor is this the whole truth."

Justine rolled her eyes at Ophelia. She didn't feel like laying the entire midnight conversation with Karl bare in the dining room. Even if, technically, it had happened in this very room only a few feet away from where she now sat. This room was different at night. As if they were in another world entirely, made for just the two of them, where nothing else mattered.

"I had suggested that we, er," Justine struggled. Was she going to blush? Was this the fate of Bad News Brewer? Brought to blushing maiden status by a Bavarian mountain climber. "I suggested that we let our passions go after we climb the Matterhorn."

"Passions?" Prudence asked with raised eyebrows.

"That seems better than before the mountain?" Eleanor squeaked.

"It's no way to judge a time frame," Ophelia said. "For that might be a day, a week, or never, depending on what the weather does."

Tristan burst into the room. "Just got word from another guide coming down from Monte Rosa. The clouds have shifted. We're climbing the Matterhorn tomorrow!"

The Ladies' Alpine Society sat in shock.

"Didn't you hear me?" Tristan asked, clearly put out by their reaction. "I wanted to be the one who told you."

"This is wonderful!" Prudence clapped.

"I have so much to do—" Ophelia said, a smile creeping onto her face.

"Tomorrow?" Eleanor asked.

The excitement boiled in Justine's stomach, the joy becoming almost intolerable. She had to stand. Had to walk. Had to move.

As she stood, Prudence leaned over and whispered, "Better get your passions ready."

The rest of the ladies heard her and they all giggled, moving to ready the hours of preparation it would take.

"What did you say?" Tristan asked. When Prudence didn't answer, he looked to his wife. "What did she say?"

"Not to worry, love," Eleanor said, taking his arm. "Let's go pack."

Ophelia was giddy with excitement as they checked the equipment. This time though, they were packing it up on donkeys. The next day, they would hike up the Matterhorn as far as the start of the Hörnli Ridge and make camp early. They would need their sleep, as they would awaken at three in the morning to start their climb. The climb that had defined their lives. That perhaps would always define their lives.

"This is it, Justine! Aren't you excited?" Ophelia was fairly quivering. "We should be able to pack fairly quickly since we've been so organized," Ophelia said, waiting on Justine to finish her task so that she could then double-check her work, as Justine would double-check hers.

"I know," Justine said.

"It should be no problem to leave exactly on time."

"I'm aware."

"Some of the others have asked to walk us to the church, which is kind of them."

"Yes." Justine gritted her teeth. She'd been there at breakfast when Mr. Moon and Francis had asked to accompany them. It had been a given that Lady Rascomb would accompany them, but on a donkey due to her leg injury.

They finished the equipment check, and Tristan brought in the canvas satchel that would lay over the back of the donkey, like modified saddlebags. Together, they packed the ropes and harnesses, metal pitons, and other carefully designed gadgets they may or may not use on the adventure.

"It seems as though—" Justine said, just to fill the silence, when Ophelia interrupted.

"Tristan, have you seen Mr. Vogel this morning?" Ophelia asked.

"I believe he is fetching Luc Meynet. The cheese maker has agreed to help us as far as the Hörnli Ridge. But they may have returned by now. Should I tell him you are looking for him?" Tristan hefted the canvas bag and groaned under the weight.

"No, I'm sure I'll see him." Ophelia looked sympathetically at Tristan as he staggered out their door.

"Do you think we need all those things?" Justine asked.

Ophelia nodded. "Unfortunately, yes. We've made everything as light as possible. I don't know how we could shed any more weight. But, distributed amongst the eight of us, it should be a bearable load for one day."

Tomorrow. Tomorrow they would go where no woman had ever stepped foot. A thrill went through her. They were really climbing the Matterhorn. A mountain that had already killed many men. Hopefully, it felt more positively about women.

KARL WATCHED AS the Englishman weighed down the donkey. Even Luc, who normally resisted commenting on anything, seemed surprised.

"Do they need all of these things?" Luc asked in Swiss German.

"Apparently. They have all sorts of gadgets I have never seen before, but Fräulein Bridewell assures me it is all necessary." Karl answered back in the same language, and noted that a few of the other mountain guides arrived to see them off. No doubt they wanted to see these ladies in their climbing gear to take their measure.

Marco, Francois, and Hans came to stand next to him, also watching the loading of the equipment.

"How many people are going on this venture?" Marco asked in Tyrolian, a language that sounded very much like German, but with significant differences, even more than the Swiss dialect.

"Seven," Karl answered back. "Eight if you count Luc, but he will stay at the Hörnli camp."

Francois swore gently in French but then asked in German, "Who is the one who is insisting on bringing her paints?"

Karl gave his friend a look of incomprehension. "Not one of this group paints."

"They are English ladies, do they not all paint?" Francois asked, switching now to French.

"Not these English ladies," Karl said.

Hans watched, not commenting, because Hans was not a man who spoke often.

"You are going, too, Luc?" Marco asked the older man.

"Only to the first camp at the base of the mountain. I will cook for their return, take care of the donkey." Luc was not the most obvious touchstone of mountaineering in the Alps, but he had been on many expeditions. He stayed at the base of the mountains, maintaining camp, tending to animals, helping with set-up and return packing.

"Will you be able to accompany my expedition next week?" Marco asked.

"Of course," Luc said with an easy shrug that looked painful to Karl, given the twist and hunch of his back. But the gesture didn't hurt Luc, and it reminded Karl that he was as capable as any of them standing there. He was a valuable member of their community, raising children he did not father, donating excess milk from his goats during the cheese-making days, and working harder than anyone else at the public ovens on bread-making days.

The realization made Karl feel useless and selfish. He did not know how to make cheese or bread. He could milk cows and goats, and did so when needed. But he spent so much time caring for the inn or guiding expeditions that he did not have time to give back to the community. Which bothered him. Luc was able to do much more with much less. Another change he would have to make for himself. Find ways to give back, to be a part of something, not always on the periphery, up a mountain instead of helping his neighbors.

Fräulein Bridewell and Justine exited the inn, squinting against the bright summer sun. Karl knew the group planned to leave soon after the ascent, but he hoped they would stay on. They had been here for the worst of the Alps, the freeze-thaw cycle of spring, and not the glorious warmth of the summer, with the endless green grass and meadow flowers.

He wanted to show Justine the high, hanging meadows filled with tall grasses dotted with tiny yellow buds and the short spread of the white, starry-shaped edelweiss.

"Mr. Vogel." Fräulein Bridewell nodded her greeting, and then extended it to the rest of the guides who stood by him. "Mr. Meynet, gentlemen."

They all doffed their caps and gave shallow bows in acknowledgment. Karl clutched his hat in his hand, feeling as if he were a schoolboy about to be admonished. She had that air about her. "Fräulein Bridewell. Is all well?"

"Yes, very much so. However, I would appreciate if you and Miss Brewer scouted ahead for weather conditions. Between me and Mr. Meynet, I think we should be able to lead the donkey and the rest of our team once we are finished with our preparations."

Karl frowned. "As your guide, I should be with the bulk of the team. It is my duty to ensure that—"

"Between myself and Mr. Meynet, we shall find the way. I

have excellent map-reading skills, and I'm certain Mr. Meynet's memory will serve him well. Miss Brewer is ready."

Karl gritted his teeth. He didn't need this sort of dressing down in front of his colleagues. They'd already mocked him for accepting this job, called him a nursemaid and worse. But to have this girl, who looked more suited to reading French fairy stories to children than climbing the most dangerous mountain in Europe, dictate how to conduct himself in front of his guiding colleagues was a blow to his pride.

But she paid his wage. And she had proven herself over the last months as being thoughtful, precise, well prepared, and well informed. He glanced over to where Justine stood, straight as an arrow, her hands slipping on woolen half-gloves. Fräulein Bridewell's face didn't give any clue to an ulterior motive, but Karl had his suspicions.

Mr. Brewer exited the inn and stared Karl down, his arms folded across his chest. Well, off he went then, by order of the expedition leader.

"I am ready. I will see you all at the church. Should there be any barriers, we will remove them in time for the rest of you." Karl nodded his farewells to his friends, who all looked vaguely shocked to be in the presence of a woman like Fräulein Bridewell. Marco, who considered himself a connoisseur of women, couldn't seem to speak, which made Karl want to laugh.

"Close your mouth," he murmured to Marco, in German, and the man seemed to come back to himself.

Justine had not yet spotted her brother, and Karl hoped they could escape without his censure. "Güete n'Abu," he greeted Justine. He put his hat back on, snugging it down against any unexpected wind.

"Good morning." Her greeting was terse, and there were small lines on the sides of her mouth, gentle curves in a hard set.

"Fräulein Bridewell bid me to take you ahead of the rest of the team. We will clear the path of any debris on the way to the church. Did she tell you this?" His palms were sweating, he realized. He had never been nervous to talk to her before, but yet now his heart pounded as hard as it did on a steep ascent. Perhaps it was the clearing out of the alcohol in his system. He had imbibed too much the night before.

"Let's go," she said, and there was no warmth in her voice, no sparkle of mischief in her eye.

Warning bells went off in his head. Typically on this day, the preparation day before the Matterhorn, he felt clear-headed and powerful. Today felt as if he were traversing a snow-covered glacier, unable to see the fatal crevasses cleaving around his feet.

"Justine," hissed Mr. Brewer, coming up behind them.

"Francis, I'm embarking on our climb. What do you want?" Justine stopped and turned towards her brother.

Karl likewise stopped but couldn't help feel like all the eyes were on them. His mountain guide friends, the members of the expedition, Tante Greta who had come outside with foodstuffs wrapped and ready to pack.

"We need to talk," Francis said to his sister, but he looked at Karl.

Karl looked over to Fräulein Bridewell, who made a shooing gesture with her hand.

"And we must go. You may walk along with us as long as you are able. Yes?" Karl looked to Justine for approval.

Thankfully, she smiled. She understood what Karl meant. That with his thin-soled shoes and lack of physical conditioning, there was no way he would be able to keep up with them, nor harangue them. He'd be lucky if he kept up for the first kilometer.

"That's fine. Come along, Francis," she said, and Karl began to wonder which of them was older. Francis certainly seemed like the older one, but now he was not so sure, the way she spoke to him.

They started walking, Mr. Brewer maneuvering between them. "I'm glad both of you are here."

Karl let Justine set the pace, and she was quick. He fell easily into her rhythm, reminding him of those first marches he'd taken her on, determined to see her break. But she didn't. She kept up, didn't complain, kept going, no matter how fast he went. She was impressive.

Mr. Brewer, however, already began flagging. His dance-floor-ready shoes slipped on the dirt path, making it harder for him to keep to his sister's speed.

"I was hoping to speak with Mr. Vogel myself," Justine said, glancing over at him.

Karl winced. He was back to the honorific, or perhaps that was just for her brother's sake.

"I am here, let us speak." Karl did not want to have any kind of conversation in front of Mr. Brewer, at least not by the look that was on her face.

"I feel Mr. Vogel and I need to speak again as well, for I need to understand what he intends," Mr. Brewer panted.

"My intentions are clear," Karl said. Out of everything everyone had said, he felt he had the clearest position. He wanted to make Justine his wife. He had lustful feelings, but since he was a good man and she a good woman, they would marry and sate themselves within the bonds of marriage. She would be Frau Vogel, his wife and companion. What could be clearer?

"I'm not clear on them," Justine chirped, giving Karl a pointed stare.

"But we agreed," Karl insisted. "You were there. We said after the Matterhorn—"

Mr. Brewer tumbled into the dirt with a yelp.

"Francis!" Justine stopped, but did not go to help him stand up or brush the dirt off his coat.

Mr. Brewer stood up, his dark curls falling into his eyes as he tried to catch his breath. "After the Matterhorn, you said Mr. Vogel?"

"Yes, our agreement was for after the Matterhorn, we would—"

"Why does this concern you, Francis?" Justine put her hands on her hips, a gesture that highlighted her slim waist and ample bosom. Karl was an ardent admirer of this pose.

"Because I am your brother. I am your guardian—"

"No." Justine shook her head. "You are not. Father is. You have no legal rights, and nor will you. Go back to the inn, Francis. I will speak with you in two days, after we've climbed this mountain."

"How dare you—" Mr. Brewer's cheeks splotched red, almost as if he'd been struck across the face.

"Go. Home," Justine announced, not yelling nor angry. Karl was impressed. She and Fräulein Bridewell were a formidable pair and spoke to men without the deference most women did. No wonder both he and Mr. Brewer chafed at it.

"I will write to our parents," Mr. Brewer threatened.

"I will speak to you after the Matterhorn." Justine turned on her heel and took off down the trail.

"I must go. Auf wiedersehn." Karl left Mr. Brewer to find his way back to the inn, the few meters they'd gone. He did want to stay cordial to the man he hoped to be his brother-in-law, though he felt like his chances of that were somehow diminishing the more steps they took.

He caught up to Justine in a few strides, opening up his gait and exceeding her pace. Her steps were so small.

"Do you really believe I agreed to marry you?" Her voice exploded out of her body, and the birds in the nearby trees took flight in surprise. She didn't seem to notice.

Karl glanced behind him to see if Mr. Brewer had heard and was running to keep up, but he wasn't. He couldn't even see the man anymore. "Yes, I do, because you did."

"When?" She was angry. He may not always understand the complexities of others, but this he could see very easily.

The best he could do was appease her, remind her, and not argue. Which he was not good at. "The night by the fire. When your feet were cold, and I held you there because you'd stood out in the snow. Do you not remember?"

"I remember kissing you." Her cheeks blotched red just as her brother's had as she said it. He liked the sight of it, proud to see that the memory affected her, because it very much affected him. "I remember standing in the snow, looking at the stars while you sent your uncle back to bed. And I remember you holding me in front of the fire to warm me." Her voice softened as she recounted that night.

The satisfaction he felt in that moment was not one he could have described. He was outside, on one of his favorite walks, with the dark forest trees on either side of them, the cows lowing, their bells clanking as they moved slowly from meadow to meadow. And here was a woman impressive enough to out-hike her older brother and send him back home with her stern words, despite their notable height difference.

"But you never asked me to marry you," she said in a low tone that he was starting to realize meant that she wanted to scream the words at him but didn't want to lose control.

"But it was understood," he said. Thinking back to the conversation. "We said that after the Matterhorn, we would have time to ourselves to . . ." he trailed off. He did not want to be a man who spoke so crassly to a woman. Or a man, for that matter. It was not how he wanted to speak to anyone.

"I thought you meant an assignation."

He tested out the word in his mouth. "I do not know this word. Assignation."

"A tryst. A night of passion. You know. What we've been doing, but more." Justine's cheeks flamed again.

His mind blanked out for a moment, his body wanting to take over, but he wrested control back. He very much wanted an assignation. "Yes, that is what we said. But you are no barmaid. Loose woman? To have this night, we must marry. And then we have many, many assignations."

Justine looked at the sky, and with a big gesture of her arms open wide she screamed and groaned at the same time. He'd never heard a person make that sound before, and it startled him. Why was he wrong? He was not wrong, he was sure of that.

"You are from a respectable family." He put his hand out, as if that represented her family. "I am also from a respectable family." He put his other hand out. "To be together, we marry." He clapped his hands together. "Why is this bad? Why is this wrong?"

"You don't know anything about me, Karl. Nor my family. How do you know we could have a successful marriage?"

"Because we are both stubborn," he answered immediately because he had no doubt in his mind. "To stay married is a matter of will. If you can climb the Matterhorn, you can have a marriage."

"But I want to be happy," she said, looking at him as if he had suddenly sprung goat horns.

"Then you will be happy," he said, still very much bewildered as to why they were arguing.

"You don't understand." She kicked a stone off the path, sending it tumbling down the side of the hill. The gradual incline of the trail was why Karl liked this one so much. It was an easy walk, beautiful, and felt more like a rolling stroll than the hard climb of the mountain that stood so tall and so striking that they could not see the summit from where they stood.

The mountain's weather contained many small areas of different climates, of which the fog was the most hazardous. It was hard to see what was coming, as the white of the snow seemed to blend with the white of the air surrounding them.

But here they were surrounded by lush greenery, and Justine's extravagant frustration was no hindrance. Only confusing.

"So you think that lust is a solid foundation to marriage."

"As good as any, yes." Karl kicked a stone just as she had, watching it shoot out across her path before tumbling down the hill as hers had. "But why only lust? We have far more in common than only this. It is fun, yes, but there are other things."

"Like what?" she demanded. "You are from Bavaria."

"Yes. What does this matter? We met in Zermatt."

"I don't want to live in Bavaria."

"Have you been?" The self-centered nature of Londoners was

famous throughout the world, so he should not hold it against her. He had likewise never been to London. It was probably an amazing city, full of wonderful parks and palaces. But he didn't want to live in any city, let alone London.

"No, I have not been to Bavaria."

"Ach, so you don't know if you like it or not." Karl did his best to shrug and seem unbothered by her bias.

"I've also never drowned, but I know I don't want to do it."

The comparison stung him, and he chanced a look at her. The muscle of her jaw flexed, and he saw her annoyance. She had no idea the wound she'd inflicted. "That is perhaps a bold comparison. I would not say my hometown is akin to death."

"I didn't mean that," she said, though the contrition in her voice was not obvious. "I mean that I know my own mind, and I don't like being told what to do."

"That is clear." Karl picked up his pace. She had made an idea that he found beautiful—a marriage that had both a physical component and a spiritual component—and turned it into something small and tired and degrading. A night of deflowerment. A single event, where they sated themselves and walked away. Something he had done before, yes, true. But he had not felt this way before.

Why was this different? He didn't know, but it was unmistakable. She was wrong, but she couldn't admit it. He would have to show her, but he didn't know how.

SHE COULDN'T BELIEVE that in the end, Karl was just like every other man she'd ever met. Wanting to trap her like a butterfly, pin her to a board and keep her quiet and beautiful and most of all, contained.

From their talks and walking from one end of the Zermatt valley to the other, she thought he understood that she craved movement, fresh air, outdoors. She wasn't ready now—maybe never—to be the little wife who stayed home mending his shirts and pushing out squalling babies. A woman who was tired, red-faced, sagging from her unnoticed exhaustion. She didn't want to have a world that small. If Ophelia managed to stay unmarried, then she and Justine could adventure the world together!

Perhaps while they were young, they had to keep themselves purer, but as they aged and society and newspapers found them less conventional, they would stop caring if they took lovers as long as there were no children. And didn't that sound exciting?

There were no guarantees that the beautiful, rich, aristocratic Ophelia would stay unmarried. In fact, it seemed a rather slim chance. And it would leave Justine alone in a world that would ridicule her for her choices. And the idea of hiking with Karl every day wasn't a bad one. In fact, she rather liked the idea.

"What is in this for you?" Justine asked, trudging next to him on the wide dirt path. This was more than a footpath, rather a dirt road large enough and well-traveled enough to host full carts if needed.

Karl huffed out a laugh. "You must ask this?"

"Yes, I must ask this. What do you get out of marrying a woman like me?" Her limbs felt jittery, as if she wasn't walking fast enough, like she needed to run or skip or jump to expel the energy.

"I don't wish to marry a woman like you. I think marrying you would be . . . fun."

"I think your translation of the word *fun* is suspect."

"Why would it not be fun? You and I can have fun together, that is proven."

"Yes, but when I'm your wife, I'm supposed to be at your house cleaning and cooking and having babies and mending shirts and—"

"Why could you not hike up mountains? That is what I do."

"I hate to shatter your worldview, Karl, but I am, in fact, a woman."

He gave her an irritated look, and she smiled brightly at him. "There is no one more aware of this fact than me."

"Besides, we couldn't suit. We aren't even the same religion. And Anglicans and Catholics do not mix."

"I would not know. I am not Catholic."

Justine stopped short. "Excuse me? But everyone here is Catholic. The church—"

"I am not from here, Justine." Karl sighed and gestured for her to keep walking. "You say that I do not know you, but you do not know me. I pay very close attention to you. I know you do not like the sweet white wine. I know that you prefer berries to apples. I know that you prefer cheese instead of cake after a meal."

Justine's mouth dropped open. "But—"

"You favor your right side to your left. You believe you can do anything, even if you don't know anything about it. This one is perhaps the most concerning, for I fear you do not understand your own limits, but given how you were raised, I am not surprised."

Her hackles went up and instead of stopping, she sped up. "You don't know anything of how I was raised."

"No," he agreed, which was more infuriating than if he'd argued. "But I know you are the youngest sibling, and that you have rebelled."

"I don't know what Francis has told you—"

"Francis has told me nothing," Karl said, but it was him who stopped this time. He grabbed her arm to stop her, and his touch melted through her sleeve. She loved bickering with him on these nature walks. It made her forget to worry about the Matterhorn tomorrow. It made her forget that Francis was being an arse and would likely bring down the full force of her mother onto her head when they returned to Zermatt. "You are not wanting to be trapped. I am saying I would not trap you."

She couldn't bear shaking off his grip, so she stayed stock still. "Said the hunter to the rabbit."

He sighed, let her go, and continued walking. It was a disappointing feeling, like he'd given up. She knew, of course she knew, that if she pushed him far enough, he'd stop pursuing. Because that was the point, wasn't it? But it seemed that if he didn't want to marry her, then he wouldn't want to talk to her either. And she would lose the teasing friendship they'd built.

But she didn't want to think about that. She ran after him, catching up easily.

"How do I know this isn't a ploy to get my family's money?" she challenged him.

Again, he laughed. "I do not want your money."

"Everybody wants money," she said.

He gestured to the mountains and trees and the absolutely stunning mountains that surrounded them. "This doesn't need money. And this is what I love."

Justine sighed. "Me too."

"Then . . ." Karl blew out a disgusted breath. "I do not want to talk about this any further."

"You don't want to talk about this? So we aren't getting married anymore?" She was teasing, but as the words came out, she saw the emotions flit across Karl's face. He was done. She'd pushed too far.

"I will not make you do something you do not wish to. Consider this my sincere apology." He sped up, outpacing her faster than he'd ever done before.

She tried to keep up at first, out of anger, but then realized she didn't want to talk anymore either. Embarrassment flooded her. He had every right to be upset, but didn't she as well? She'd been informed by her brother that she was engaged. This whole thing had been Karl's fault. His mistake.

But she hadn't let him make it gracefully. She'd teased and shamed and blown up at him. It was not well done of her. Not at all. And this felt worse than any other time a man had walked away from her. She let him get far out of range, knowing there were no turns or ways to get lost on along the way to the church. She walked alone on the ridge, the looming slopes of the mountains comforting her, as if they were her confidantes.

Chapter Ten

J USTINE COULD HEAR the rest of the expedition before she could see them. She remained perched on an exposed rock face outside of the squat, white-washed walls of the church, not wanting to go inside where Karl was, chatting with whoever was in there. The slate-roofed building was modest—not near what she pictured when Ophelia marked it as a waypoint on their journey. The lake in front of the church was crystal clear, reflecting the rocks and grass and blue, blue sky. The illusion was so complete, one could easily wander into the lake, believing it to be a continuation of the trail.

The rest of the team arrived: the Ladies' Alpine Society, Luc, and the pack donkey, with Lady Rascomb riding primly sidesaddle on another creature, her cane tucked across her lap. After them came a crowd, with Francis sulking in the back of the group. Even Frau and Herr Brunner came to wish them luck. She enjoyed them so very much during the months they'd stayed there. Herr Brunner's brötli-offering kindness would forever lodge in her heart.

The crowd felt almost like a party. Karl emerged from the church, his face bland and expressionless. Was this a Bavarian sort of thing, or was this only Karl, keeping himself bottled up so she couldn't read him this way or that? She wondered if he would tell Francis about retracting his proposal.

Mr. Moon shook Karl's hand. Lord Rascomb helped his wife

off the donkey. Tristan and Eleanor untied the ropes lashing the cargo to the donkey. Luc smiled at everyone, seeming happy to be amongst them.

Their spirits buoyed Justine. She wouldn't let Karl take this from her. No, she couldn't think of it like that—he wasn't taking anything from her. She was letting her feelings interfere with what would be an accomplishment of a lifetime. Something that would put them in history books and newspapers worldwide. They even might help the burgeoning women's rights movements, the push for suffrage. The Ladies' Alpine Society would prove to the world that women were capable of so much more than Queen Victoria believed.

The sunshine was warm on her face, and she closed her eyes and tilted her face to the sun. This was her path. Her earth-shattering, world-shaking path. Ophelia's telltale purposeful steps approached, and Justine didn't bother opening her eyes. Her friend sat down on the rock next to her and threaded her arm through Justine's. This was right. This was true. She and Ophelia would take over the world.

"All is well?" Ophelia asked, her voice low so the others wouldn't overhear.

Justine opened her eyes and looked at her friend. She didn't need to even say anything. Ophelia nodded her head and gave a slight shrug. "We tried?"

Justine nodded. "I tried."

"Are we still letting him guide us up the mountain?"

Justine laughed. As if they could get a replacement guide at this moment! But Ophelia's loyalty warmed her. "Yes. We are still letting him guide us."

Ophelia sighed with relief. "Oh good. That makes logistics much easier."

Justine snorted.

Tristan looked over and smiled, his face brilliant with happiness. Justine returned the expression, and he acted as if he were falling over from shock. She could only imagine the level of happiness Eleanor and Prudence had experienced in the last few months. They were tucked away in a gorgeous part of the world, sharing a room with the men they loved.

And Justine was sort of envious. She looked at Ophelia. At least they had each other?

"Oh, I must help sort. That bag needs to stay at the church." Ophelia hurried over to the donkey.

Lady Rascomb came to stand next to Justine, out of the way of the packing and unpacking that was happening now that Ophelia was involved. A man came out of the church, and Justine didn't know if he was a man of God or a caretaker, but he offered a flask to Luc, who was more than happy to wander over to a wooden bench and chat.

"Is all well in your world, Justine?" Lady Rascomb surveyed their troupe but asked in the same low tones that Ophelia had used.

"Yes, my lady."

The older woman tsked. Despite her bonnet, bits of her shiny blonde hair caught the summer sun, showcasing the telltale trait of the Bridewell children. "Then I know something is amiss. I can't remember the last time you remembered to use my honorific."

"We're in mixed company," Justine protested. The *my lady* had rolled off her tongue without thinking. Well, not thinking about Ophelia's mother anyway. She was still roiling, and it would be good to feel her body, let her mind go blank for the next hour or two it took to hike up to the shoulder called Hörnli where they would make camp for the night. Karl had teased her about her pronunciation until she gave up entirely.

But he wouldn't be teasing her anymore. Correcting her terrible pronunciation. Running ahead on a trail to see if she could keep up.

"It seems Mr. Vogel is out of sorts as well," she said, nodding towards Karl, who frowned at the packing and unpacking antics. Then she looked over to the other side, where Francis was sitting down on a rock, picking grass strands up and shredding them. "Not to mention Francis."

"There was a misunderstanding," Justine said.

"Is this a misunderstanding that your mother will snub me over?" To her credit, Lady Rascomb didn't sound the least bit bothered by it.

"No," Justine said hurriedly. "At least, not if I get to share my point of view. Francis is very judgmental."

"He only wants to keep you safe."

Justine harrumphed at that. Francis wanted to control her, just like every other man in her life, excepting her father and Karl. They understood she needed to run and chatter and be unfettered.

"Well," Lady Rascomb said, turning towards her. "I'm going to say the same thing to you that I said to Ophelia. Be safe. Mountains are unpredictable. Be alert, stay roped up, and enjoy your misery."

Justine took her hand, feeling for the first time something like uncertainty. Lady Rascomb used a cane because of an avalanche on a mountain. Tristan had dug her out, but her leg was so badly fractured that it never healed quite right. She'd never climbed another mountain afterwards. On some days, she knew that it pained Lady Rascomb, causing her back to spasm, and leading to days in bed.

Hers was a cautionary tale. As were the six failed ascents by Edward Whymper. Justine looked up past the Hörnli Ridge where the Matterhorn's iconic scooped-out peak hid in afternoon clouds. They had done everything they could to stack the odds in their favor. They were more well prepared than any other expedition, according to Karl. They'd trained. They'd developed their own tools and devices to help themselves.

But weather was unpredictable. Misty fog obscured routes. Avalanches were possible. Rock falls were guaranteed. Cliffs abounded and crevasses gaped beneath snowfields. Wind and cold would blister them. And what could they do? Nothing but try.

"We'll come back safe and sound. You watch." Justine put her hands on her hips, trying to feel more certain of their attempt.

"You are all very capable young women. I know you'll do your best." Lady Rascomb placed her hand on Justine's shoulder, towering over her as all the Bridewells did.

Lord Rascomb collected his wife, escorting her to the recently vacated wooden bench in front of the church, assuredly a more comfortable seat. Karl approached the man with the flask and Luc, no doubt discussing where their post-mountain bags would be stashed. While it was merely extra rations and changes of clothing, it was still more than they wanted to carry up to their campsite.

After they sorted everything and retied the lighter luggage to the donkey, the other women gathered with Justine. Luc waved at them and headed up the trail. It was a gradual incline ahead of them, and soon they would catch and pass by him.

Mr. Moon and Lady Rascomb said their goodbyes. Francis loitered a ways away from Justine, but when it became clear that the others were leaving, he apparently got over his qualms.

He hugged her close. "Stay safe."

Justine nodded, her throat closing as she remembered what Lady Rascomb said: *he only wants to protect you.* And she was doing something that no one could protect her from. But she was proud of that. She wanted that.

Francis walked over to Tristan and clapped him on the shoulder, and Tristan did the same in return. Then he followed Mr. Moon and Lady Rascomb. Herr and Frau Brunner stood side by side, tanned and slightly plump, smiling and waving them off. Perhaps they had the same affection for them as Justine had for the couple. She hoped so.

"Skirts?" Ophelia suggested. They all pulled at their strings to raise up their skirts far enough to allow a good stride and tied them off. Justine grinned at how they all had slightly different lengths, given their different strides. Eleanor was so clever.

Justine felt a burst of pride to be amongst these brilliant people. Her friends.

Tristan, Lord Rascomb, and Karl joined their cluster. With Luc up ahead, they made eight on this two-day trail to the summit.

They couldn't see the top from where they stood, mists obscuring their path. But Justine could almost see that red line Ophelia had slashed onto their maps, the route that she deemed their best bet. She and Karl had debated it day after day in the last months, looking at almanacs and adjusting for the temperatures and weather patterns that emerged from the weeks they'd spent in Zermatt.

Still Karl had warned them that the mountain did what it wanted and adhered to no man's—or woman's—wishes.

"Is everyone prepared?" Lord Rascomb asked in his commanding voice. A voice that led their family, sat in Parliament, and encouraged the dreams of his youngest daughter.

Justine scanned their group as they all looked at each other as well.

"Then off we go," Ophelia said, taking the lead from her father.

They easily fell into their walking order, something that was second nature to them now. Karl in the lead, then Ophelia, then Justine.

With the gentle incline ahead of them, they would not need ropes or spikes or any of the other aid devices Eleanor and Tristan had dreamed up. At least, not today. Today was a rolling walk, one that kept the blood pumping, but allowed conversation. Justine didn't feel like chatting, but she listened to Prudence and Eleanor talk about the desserts they were looking forward to when they returned. Frau Brunner had promised chocolates arriving from Zurich and an apple cake from a recipe she'd learned as a girl.

She glanced up at Karl, his broad shoulders hunched as he walked. Rarely did Karl hunch over like that. Typically when he hiked, he was so upright he could be mistaken for a weathervane. She felt a pang of guilt. This was her fault. She'd made him feel not only rejected, which was true, yes, but likely also a fool.

The part of hiking that she adored was moving her body, partly because it helped her think. Sitting still made it infinitely harder. But here she was, with the fresh air, the sun shining, on the path she had so longed for—wishing she weren't thinking.

Instead of lingering over her own feelings, she listened to the scuff of her boots on the pebbled dirt trail. She listened to her friends' chatter. Ophelia was too in her own head to speak, Justine knew that. Even towards the back, she could hear the low tones of Tristan speaking with his father. They all sounded happy, spirits buoyed by their imminent accomplishment, by how beautiful the weather was, how certain that by tomorrow at this time they would be shouting out from the summit.

They skirted around Luc and the donkey, giving the animal cheerful pats as they passed. The walk became steep enough that the conversations ceased and they shuffled on over the rocky ridge in silence. Justine's feet slipped on the piles of rock, sending pebbles down one side of the ridge, while lush, green Alpine meadows stretched out on the other. The wind was strong, and it battered their woolen skirts between their legs as they walked. Justine was grateful for the curtain-lifting ingenuity from Eleanor, as it helped keep her balance.

They reached the Hörnli peak in early afternoon. It wasn't much to look at: a scree field with patches of snow still lingering in certain shadows, but directly in front of them loomed their goal. The massive, almost fifteen-thousand-foot-tall Matterhorn. Killer of men.

"It is majestic," Ophelia said, breathless.

It took longer than normal for Justine's heart to quit hammering. The winds picked up, battering them, but Ophelia didn't seem daunted. Karl was surveying the land, no doubt looking for the ideal spot to set up camp.

Justine walked closer to the sharp descent into the saddle

between their wide spot on the Hörnli Ridge and the Matterhorn. It was that line they would take to the top. That ridge would bring them success. The wind pushed her one direction, and then the next, and she stumbled.

"Careful." A voice in her ear said, big hands closing around her shoulders. Karl stood next to her, closer than he'd been in a week. The warmth of him was startling, and she appreciated his willingness to block the wind from one side.

"It seems so daunting," Justine said, finally saying what she never wanted to say to Ophelia. And it did. That pyramid-shaped peak was so far away. So high up in the sky. The tallest peak in Europe. And, if one listened to any of the Zermatt locals, the highest in the world, even though she knew that wasn't true.

"Some people say there is a city of the gods up there on the peak," Karl said. "That to arrive there is to disturb their ruins and invite their displeasure."

"Is there?" Justine asked, doubting every moment of the story.

"No, just more rocks."

She nodded. "How disappointing."

"I would not call the view disappointing. But you shall see for yourself, perhaps tomorrow."

He left her then, going to help Ophelia set up and organize camp. His conversation made it feel like he forgave her for her meanness, her insults. She needed to make peace with herself. To ask herself if she was lying when she said she didn't want to marry someone like Karl. All right, not someone like him, but rather him exactly. It was definitely an unknown adventure. And he knew her strengths. Knew them better than anyone.

By the time Justine tore her eyes away from the mountain, Karl and Tristan were moving what rocks they could into a wind barrier. She returned to the group. Everyone huddled down inside the short rock wall, hoping to speak and be heard over the constant wind.

"Is everyone still feeling well enough for this venture?" Ophelia asked, looking around at the group. Luc was not a part of the circle, but rather was returning the donkey back down to the lake by the church, where the creature would be more comfortable. Luc would return the next morning to maintain camp and fix them food whenever they returned from their summit.

Every single member of the circle had the rosy cheeks of wind burn, the wild hair of gusts, and the bright gleam of anticipation in their eyes.

"I'm hungry," said Tristan.

"I don't doubt it," Eleanor said to her husband, squeezing his hand.

"We have plenty of food to eat tonight, but first let's talk about tomorrow's plan." Ophelia smiled. This was her project to lead, and everyone respected it, even her father and her brother. Perhaps especially so. It wasn't the first time Justine was envious of her friend's family. While it was all fine and good for an aristocratic family to be eccentric, Justine's mother wanted her only daughter to be better behaved. More daughter-like, and not the ruffian she got at the end of four boys. But here she was. Her father and brothers nowhere in sight, unwilling or unable to take up this journey. Even Francis.

"Tomorrow we will try to take the summit in one day. However, I want to make sure you understand that most ascent attempts took several days, and many got close to the top before having to turn back due to weather. So far, we've only spoken of other expeditions' experiences, but we are here now, and you can see exactly where we mean to go." She gestured to the ridge that Justine had gazed at earlier.

"I hope to make it past the first camp of Whymper's, which is just under four thousand meters. In order to do that, we must awake at three in the morning. We will be descending this ridge, traversing the saddle in the dark. We will rope up here and maintain that rope contact until we return here tomorrow night. We have been told the descent is more dangerous than the ascent, which is why we are leaving so early in the morning. We do not want to descend in the dark."

They all nodded, and Eleanor again looked to Tristan. During their ascent of Ben Nevis, they'd gotten arrogant about their success and not maintained their rope tether. Eleanor and Tristan had tumbled off a cornice because of it.

"We all have our equipment and our packs, which have our emergency gear. I want us to be more prepared than other teams. We must make it to the top."

Their murmurings of agreement took only a wordless shape of encouragement. When Ophelia seemed done talking, Karl looked to her for permission to speak.

"This will likely be the hardest thing you have ever done," Karl said.

Gooseflesh prickled along Justine's arms. There was something about this that felt wrong suddenly. Felt like the mountain didn't want them on it. But she was likely catastrophizing in her head. Nerves were to be expected at a juncture like this. She could see the glaciers, the cliffs, all the hazards that lay between them and their goal.

"The descent is harder than the ascent. I know you will feel like celebrating at the top. As you should. But concentration needs to be maintained on the way down as well. Remember, that is where the deaths most often occur."

They nodded, somber in their reflection of the lives lost on this rock.

"Lovely mood, excellent speeches, let's eat." Tristan looked at the group brightly, pulling one of the bags over.

Justine laughed, joined by a few others. The anticipation was palpable amongst all of them. Knowing they would not be able to pitch a tent here, as the winds were far too strong, they created their own nests next to the short rock wall Tristan and Karl had hastily dragged together.

Karl built a fire, difficult as it was, but given the rock wall, it smoldered on, heating the kettle full of melted snow, meat and vegetables. It wasn't the tastiest meal Justine had ever eaten, but it was somehow the best she'd had so far, warming her from the inside out.

After dinner, they lazed about on their blanket bags, ignoring the wind. Ophelia sorted gear; Tristan smoked, one arm around Eleanor. Prudence pulled out a small pocket-sized sketch pad. When Justine looked at her in curiosity, since she had never before sketched anything, Prudence's cheeks colored.

"Leo's teaching me to draw." She flipped open to a blank page. "I'm not very good, but he asked to me to capture what I could."

Justine wished she had something to fiddle with, but she didn't, so she watched everyone else, pointedly not looking at Karl, who cleaned and packed away the dinner utensils. Surprisingly, Luc reappeared at camp, carrying a pack of tobacco and spirits. He said something to Karl that the rest of them couldn't understand. But Karl looked around as Luc made himself at home, asking, "Would anyone like a nip of brandy?"

Tristan reached for it, as did Prudence, which surprised Justine. And while normally Justine would say yes, something about this felt so off and wrong to her that she abstained. She wanted to be as clear-headed as possible. Not long after dark, they smothered the fire and tried to sleep. Luc seemed very much put out, no doubt hoping the English would stay up and drink and smoke, carouse into the wee hours. Perhaps other expeditions did. But not theirs. For them, too much was at stake.

To fail, at worst, was to be openly ridiculed. At best, it allowed them time to recover and try again. But as she was dropping off to sleep, Justine realized that failing was far more likely. And the worst of that would not be open ridicule. It would be death.

⌲ ◆ ⌁

Chapter Eleven

K ARL DID NOT know why his eyes popped open at the correct hour, only that they did. It was not his place to question the gifts of the world, and one of them was an impeccably accurate internal clock. It was pitch-dark, icy cold, and extremely windy.

He sat up, his head above the windbreak they'd built the night before, and immediately the freezing gusts made his eyes water. He saw Fräulein Bridewell awake, already rolling up her blanket bag, her boots tied.

The others began to stir as well.

"Is it time?" Frau Moon asked, rubbing her eyes.

He watched as Justine rose, her eyes only on Ophelia, as if garnering strength from her friend.

Herr and Frau Bridewell crawled out of their double blanket bag, likely the most snug out of all of them, given they'd had body heat to keep each other warm all night. There was something inherently more restful with another person right there, sharing the air. He'd only ever shared a bag with another man, inside a snow cave, certain they would be dead by morning. It was surprisingly not as harrowing as it sounded. Mostly boring.

Lord Rascomb was the last awake, but the next person to be readied. Karl admired him. He was a practiced mountaineer, steady and strong. He watched over his daughter and every other member of their team constantly, quietly. This was a man who did his duty by his family. It touched Karl this early morning in a

169

way that it hadn't before. Because he hadn't been able to see that the man was not only physically caring for his children, but valuing them in ways not many fathers did.

Lord Rascomb made a place for his daughter in a world that didn't want her to have this dream. To climb a mountain was a feat of perseverance and inner strength as much as outer strength. Neither of those were named as part of the feminine spirit. Years ago, and perhaps still, an aristocratic daughter was supposed to be used to raise up the family with alliances and bring connections to strengthen their social standing. But this man could see the world had changed.

From what Karl had understood from Herr Bridewell, this was far from the first big mountain they'd climbed with Lord Rascomb. If Karl was going to be a father someday, he hoped he would be able to be as clear-eyed as this man. To see his children for what good they could do in the world, not what good they could bring to their family.

In some ways, it reminded him of his Onkel Peter. Yes, he needed help in Zermatt. The inn required so much labor, but he could have hired men for it, even if it might be difficult to get some parts of the year. Knowing Karl's love of mountaineering, he'd offered it to him specifically. Not because he had a nephew in need. But because it was Karl who needed to be in the mountains.

After securing his own gear, Karl helped Ophelia lay out their rope, organize their packs, and attach the spikes they'd crafted to the front of their boots. It was an interesting design, and he was flattered they'd made a set for him as well. The thick leather straps fit over his boots with a buckle to the side, on the outside of the shoe.

Perhaps this would make the climb easier. Perhaps it was just another thing to weigh them down.

They all worked quickly in the dark, and it was not long until he was tying himself into the rope. The rope that held all of their lives, a daisy-chain of hearts, pounding their way up the side of a cliff.

He gave one sharp tug on the rope, a signal that he was prepared. He felt the rest do so as well, one by one down the chain, and then back up again. He started forward, slow shuffles as he took them down the path, scree rocks yielding beneath his boots and tumbling down the sides of the ridge.

While there was a part of him screaming with nerves, given the dark and the knife's-edge terrain, he had done this particular climb several times. He'd already been to this summit—twice—but each time was different. The snowfields were different, the rock falls were different, the weather was different, the clients were different.

He had faith in all of them, even Frau Bridewell, who had made an effort in the last weeks to become more confident with her footwork. Still, there were things one encountered on these attempts that one couldn't predict. And he needed to keep himself alert and open to all of them and their needs.

Behind him, he heard the scree scrape under their boots. Above him, he could hear a cracking boom, signaling an expansion of ice that broke rock away from the mountain. He stopped and listened. There was no rock fall now, but in the morning, when the temperature warmed and the ice melted, there would be.

Speed would be helpful, but he didn't dare chance it in the dark with six people behind him and a ridge barely wider than his shoulders. A smaller team, or one that had traversed this saddle before, he might. But not today. He picked his way on, grateful when they reached the trough of the saddle and began to ascend again. They would keep at it, slow and steady, until they returned to the Hörnli Ridge tonight. He would see them through, usher them as quietly and gracefully as Lord Rascomb had thus far.

JUSTINE WAS NOT afraid. Her father and brothers had often lamented that she barreled through situations with a sincere lack of fear that was meant to protect a person. She had always interpreted their worries as she lacked the type of fear a *lady* would have. Because had she been another boy, they would have shaken their heads with amazed pride.

But now, shuffling in the dark, hugging a rock as a steep scree field backed into a gaping glacier, she did feel a snag of fear. Which was normal, she supposed. The glacier field glowed white and bright in the starlight. She couldn't decide if the glacier was taunting them with its cold illumination or if it was aiding their climb by providing an extra bit of light to help them navigate the decidedly difficult terrain.

Behind her was a long scrape of a boot missing its ledge. Justine froze, suddenly terrified that one of her teammates had fallen. She braced, but no tug on her tether rope came.

"All is well," came Eleanor's voice.

Justine relaxed and continued on. A glance at what she could see of the horizon told her that sunrise was near. The sky was moving from inky midnight to the deep purple of dawn. The knot of fear in her stomach loosened, and Justine decided she did not like this feeling at all. It didn't seem helpful, or instructional. This feeling was a hindrance, a vestigial part of her that begged her to sit down and stop.

How was this fear helpful? She'd have to ask Francis when they got back, if she decided she would speak to him again. The triumph of ascending the Matterhorn would prove her point of how this fear was utterly useless. She pushed the feeling down, and urged that knot in her stomach to dissolve itself. It was decidedly not needed today.

After skirting around the rock formation, the area opened up into a snow field. As they all stepped onto the familiar crunch, each of them exhaled in contentment. This felt easy and safe compared to the long slog that dark morning, but she kept her mind from noticing the sharp cliffs that bounded the field on both sides. Behind her, she heard Prudence laugh in relief. In front of her, Ophelia turned around.

"Check in," Ophelia announced, her voice quiet, but the air carried it clear as if she were saying it directly in Justine's ear.

"All is well," Karl rumbled.

Ophelia repeated the words. Then Justine. Then Lord Rascomb, Prudence, Eleanor, and Tristan. They all breathed heavily, but controlled. The cold nipped at her ears, and she was grateful for the orange-yellow light that was warming the rock they climbed.

"Good," Ophelia said, and Justine could hear the smile in her voice, even if she couldn't quite make out her friend's face. "Onward."

Their boots scraped against the old snow and they fell into line, walking in silence. Before long, the incline tilted so steep with no perceivable trail that Ophelia called a halt so they could hitch their skirts up as high as they would go.

"Use the boot spike," she advised. "And go on all fours if need be."

Justine dutifully rucked up her skirt as best she could, grateful that the sunrise seemed slow, bathing everything in the gentle light. The snowfield covered everything, making it nearly impossible to tell where to go. She was glad Karl was there to guide them. Glad that she trusted Karl so completely. Did she? At least with her life, she did. He was competent to a fault.

"Onward," Ophelia said, and up ahead, Karl walked.

He stubbed his boots in the snow hard with each step, assuring he would not fall. Occasionally, he needed to fall to his hands to help him climb, but not always. Ophelia did the same with her boots, but she kept her hands out. Ophelia was not one for chances.

So Justine followed Ophelia's advice, and while her woolen gloves protected her hands from the cold for a few minutes, soon snow stuck between the weft of the fibers.

A female voice cried out.

"Brace!" Tristan bellowed.

Without thinking, Justine pressed her weight into her hands, hoping her boots had dug into the snow without issue. There was the sound of snow sliding; the rope at her waist tugged hard, pulling her flat to her belly in the snow. Someone had fallen. Justine squeezed her eyes shut. *Everyone is safe, everyone is safe,* she chanted in her mind, wondering if Ophelia and Karl were thinking the same thing.

Behind her, she could hear movement, but she didn't dare look, didn't dare shift her weight.

"Time, please," Tristan called.

It was the phrase they'd agreed upon to ask for a pause in action. It could be for injury assessment, or if someone needed to rest. Justine looked ahead, watching as Ophelia carefully turned to look behind them.

More murmurs behind her, and she could vaguely hear Lord Rascomb's voice, carried away by the winds. Her woolen gloves were wet now, sodden with the snow that melted in the heat from her hands. So far, her woolen coat kept the rest of her dry.

Then came the words they all waited for: "All is well," Tristan said. Then came Eleanor's voice, and Prudence's. Prudence didn't sound herself, so it must have been her that fell. Lord Rascomb turned his head and said it so Justine could understand him once again. She said it, then Ophelia and Karl.

"Onward," Ophelia said, and they picked themselves up off the snow.

The sunrise was eerie—not because of the sun or the light, but because of the way the snow reflected it into her eyes. She squinted against its brightness as they climbed. They came to a formation that they would have to climb up like some kind of unusual ladder. They waited as Karl pounded a fresh piton—a metal spike—into the rock.

He used that as the first stepping stone, using the ledges of the rock for the rest. Once he ascended, he called for time, adjusted a second rope, tied it to the top of the ledge, and let it down for Ophelia.

Now was the time for their new device. It was a buckle with a spike in it, meant to slide onto their belts and then pass the rope through to hold it in place, allowing the person above to haul them up the side of the rock if need be. The buckle allowed the person who was climbing to not be jerked by the natural give of the rope. The idea was Lord Rascomb's, and they all wanted to give him credit for it, but he wanted to try out the device before he took any accolades. Well, here was the moment of truth.

Ophelia buckled herself in, the rope attached as it should be to the spiked holder. She looked up at Karl, who was braced against the rocks with his feet, his hands on the rope.

This was the absolute wrong time for her to think him utterly handsome, attractive, capable and . . . some kind of word that she didn't know yet. His face was set in determination, the light stubble on his cheeks highlighting the primitive masculine cut of his face. He would keep Ophelia safe on this fifteen-foot-high wall. She knew that.

Ophelia stepped onto the piton, and then followed Karl's same route up. She lifted herself up and over the ledge with no difficulty. Even here, in layers of wool, Ophelia was graceful. She stood and looked down at them, grinning from ear to ear.

But now it was Justine's turn. Ophelia undid Lord Rascomb's device, the rope still in place, and tossed it down. Justine let it fall in the snow and then took her turn, fumbling with her own belt, and having trouble buckling in. Her fingers were so cold. She had another set of gloves in her pack. After she got to the top, she would get them out. But for now, she just needed to get through this.

Once the device was in place, she went to put her foot on the piton, only to realize it was quite high off the ground. Still, she hauled herself up and looked over to the ledge that Karl and Ophelia had both used. But her foot wouldn't reach.

"You must be joking," Justine said to herself. The rock wall was cold against her. She was too short to climb this. She hopped back down, and with the only thing she could think to do, she slipped off her boots, tied the laces together, and hung them from her belt.

"What are you doing?" Ophelia demanded, clearly alarmed at what she was seeing.

Tristan took that as his cue to pay attention and came charging up.

"I'm not tall enough to make the same moves," Justine explained. "So I'm trying something."

And then she worked off her woolen stockings. Was she cold? Absolutely. But skin stuck to cold rock. And she was about to prove it. As long as she moved quickly, everything would be fine, and she could get out every piece of extra clothing in her and Ophelia's pack and warm up. But she had to get up this wall, and this was the only thing she could think of.

"I can haul you up. You don't need to—" Karl called down.

"Too late," she said, swinging her woolen stockings at him. She tied them around her waist and stepped onto the piton. Which was so cold, it seared the bottom of her feet. But she'd looked at that rock. Really looked at it. There were smaller ledges that she could reach. And while it took her twice as many steps, she hopped as fast as she could from ledge to ledge, grateful for the failed dance lessons and pointed toes of her youth. Because it was her big toe that balanced on this ledge, and the inner edge of her knee as she pressed herself tight against the wall, that allowed her to monkey up the side just as quickly as Ophelia had done. And when she pulled herself up and over that ledge, the looks on Karl's and Ophelia's faces were priceless.

It was a look she delighted in. Her ability to surprise people was one of her most treasured talents. But she couldn't bask too long, as freezing as it was. She pulled off the device and tossed it down for Lord Rascomb and pulled on her stockings and boots, already picturing where her dry pair of gloves was in her pack.

KARL HAD CLIMBED many a mountain. But never in his life had he seen anyone do what Justine had just done. He had not known that legs could raise at that high of an angle, and he had to admit, that while this was a most inappropriate time to consider it, he was very, very attracted to this woman. And he wondered how high her legs could go.

He was glad that Lord Rascomb took as long as he did to buckle himself into the contraption he'd devised, because Karl needed a moment to clear his head and focus. But it didn't keep him from watching as Justine pulled on her woolen stockings again. He didn't have words for how impressive she was. It would have never even occurred to Karl to do something like that.

If he hadn't been able to reach, he would have had his comrades haul him up like a cow mired in a mudhole. He would like to try what she'd done, just not in these freezing conditions on the side of the Matterhorn. In fact, he knew just the rock, as it wasn't far from the inn, perhaps a few kilometers or so away. And it was warm there.

Fräulein Bridewell embraced Justine, warming her up and rubbing her arms. Jealousy flared. It was irrational and silly, but Justine loved Fräulein Bridewell, and it was clearly reciprocated. And because of that, they were able to express it. Karl did not like that while he hauled Lord Rascomb up the rock, Fräulein Bridewell warmed Justine with an embrace. But it was for the best. Justine had made it clear that she did not think much of him. Thought him controlling and oppressive, and not worthy of marrying. To think she accused him of wanting her family's money.

But he had to focus on this task ahead of him. Justine was a distraction. He was responsible for this team, both on the ascent and the descent. The court cases and the slander against both the senior and junior Peter Tauber, the father and son guides from the Whymper expedition, were a cautionary tale. They continued to guide, but what could have been an absolute triumph became a scandal accusing them of severing the rope out of cowardice, sending those other men to their deaths.

But rock falls, ice fog, glacier fields, cliffs, all of these things sent men to their deaths. A well-placed rock fall would cut the rope for them. There was no need to plot murder or even a possibility to be cowardly on this mountain. If one was cowardly, one would have never made it to the top.

He held the rope steady as Lord Rascomb ascended, but the man was agile and didn't require any help. The lord pulled himself over the edge, looking pleased with himself. He undid the buckle and surveyed it, as if looking for flaws or perhaps marveling at it instead. "It works well," he said, congratulating himself before he flung it down to Frau Moon.

The man chatted with his daughter and Justine, while Karl focused on the rest of the team. It was a slow process, but given how much ground they'd already covered, he was impressed. Between Frau Moon and Frau Bridewell, he checked his pocket watch and then the sky. They were right on time, and his internal clock was just as accurate as the mechanical one.

Part of the hurry was that while they all carried packs with extra clothing, they did not carry much in the way of rations. They would ascend and descend the same day, even though previous expeditions took a week to do the same. Given the extensive writings of Whymper and his own experience, Karl believed they could accomplish it in a single, very long day.

But it was possible to get stuck on the side of the mountain and have to bivouac overnight. It was not a pleasant way to spend a night—cold, hungry, exhausted. He'd done it himself on more than one occasion, and would do it again however many more times were necessary, but it was not an experience he wanted to inflict on Justine. Or any of them.

Once Herr Bridewell—Tristan, as he'd asked Karl to call him numerous times—ascended, they packed up the extra rope and climbing device, checked in with each other, and checked their tethering line. All was in good order, so they again carried on, falling into their prescribed order.

Karl was impressed with how well-trained they were. There was no bickering or jostling for position. While he did miss the good-natured ribbing that was common among other expeditions—the joking insults were humorous—he could honestly say that this was the most well-oiled machine he'd ever worked with.

They climbed the blocky rock formation, its ledges and easy handholds making individual rope support unnecessary. Yet, the security of the climb didn't stop him from discreetly peeking over his shoulder every once in a while to check on them. There was still a part of him that didn't believe that this group of women could climb this fast without complaint or trouble.

When he'd guided other tourists on other mountains—those who fancied themselves to be in better shape than they actually were—the men would tough it out despite terrible shoes and blisters. The women were typically so poorly prepared, their dresses too restrictive, corsets too tight, shoes too thin, that they could not manage to go very far without needing to stop and be escorted back down. One woman insisted that he carry her down, which he did, hunched over, with her perched atop him not unlike how Lady Rascomb perched on that donkey the day before.

It had been humiliating, yes, and his back hurt for a week. But they paid well, and bought him an excellent bottle of brandy besides, which had helped with his sore muscles.

The snow thinned and scree took over the path. The scree fields made climbing tiring. The give of all those millions of rocks sank their boots with each step, requiring more energy to take the next one, keeping a person always slightly off-balance. At the top of the scree field scramble, the cracking sound that Karl had been dreading boomed above them.

"Rock fall!" he called down to them. They all crouched down, covering their heads with their arms. At the speed with which the pebbles rained down on them, even a small stone could sever their ropes or kill them with a knock to the temple.

The rain of rocks covered them like a second-long shower, the preamble to the larger chunk the size of two fists fit together that tumbled down around them. Karl hoped that was it, and when the debris stopped, he took a moment to look around, listening carefully.

It was as if they all held their breath, terrified that something larger was coming. But nothing happened, and the world was still. They exhaled. It was then that a small boulder tumbled down to their right, dislodging the carefully balanced scree, and causing a slide off a cliff. Karl sat down abruptly, bracing himself in case the ripple effect took one of them with it.

It stopped a meter or so from where their line braced. He saw every one of their wide eyes stare up at him, shocked that they were that close to what would no doubt be a painful death. He scanned them. Overall in good shape, their eyes wet from the wind, lips dry from the same, and scared. Except, he noticed Justine. She looked defiant. And Fräulein Bridewell who looked grim but determined.

He wasn't sure if he admired them or thought them foolish. But he was convinced that these two could do anything they put their minds to, and hopefully, this mountain would let them.

At the back, Tristan held his shoulder. Karl called him on it.

"Naught but a scratch," Tristan said.

"There's blood," his wife called up. She slid down to his position to help tend it. Each of them had two clean rags rolled up exactly for this purpose. It was a jagged climb, and one never knew what would come in handy.

They rested until Frau Bridewell climbed back to her position, letting the tether loosen between her and Frau Moon. And then Tristan said the magic words.

"All is well."

They called it one at a time until it got to Karl, when he repeated the phrase. It had never occurred to him before to do such a check-in, but he liked it. He wasn't sure how other expeditions would handle it, wondering if the men who had so much to prove would think it a weakness to say such a thing. But it was helpful. Karl then knew that they were all ready, with injuries taken care of. It helped him set the pace.

"Onward," said Fräulein Bridewell, and he obeyed.

This was a climb that was slow-going, but in that context, they were ahead of where they'd hoped to be. He looked up at the sky. He could carry a pocket watch to seem more professional, but his internal clock was just as accurate. They would not be making the summit today and would have to bivouac on the mountain somewhere.

They were very near where Whymper was turned around on his first attempt to ascend. It was a common place to turn around, given the chimneys that came next.

"Fräulein Bridewell," he said as they were narrowing back onto a ridge. He wanted to talk before the ridge, so as not to promote distraction for anyone.

"I can hear you," Fräulein Bridewell said.

"We are nearing Whymper's first turn-around point."

"Good," she said, her voice steady between her shallow breaths.

"I believe we will make his chimney, but that typically takes time, especially with a party this large."

"We will stay overnight on the mountain," she said, no question in her voice. So she had already foreseen this.

"Yes. There are some more welcoming spots above us. And we are nearer to the top than to the bottom."

"That is some comfort. Let us finish the chimney and stay overnight above that mark. Then we finish the ascent tomorrow morning and descend completely to the church by evening."

This would have been Karl's suggestion as well. Staying overnight in the sanctuary of the Schwarzsee church, where they had shelter, food, and warm, dry clothes, was far preferable to another night on the windy Hörnli Ridge. If they could manage to drag themselves all down there. "Good," he said, and stepped out onto the rocky ridge, using his hands to balance against the boulder that sat off to the right.

He didn't bother reminding her that descent was as strenuous, if not more so than ascent. That on the descent, the snow-covered ridges could make a person think they would slip and fall at any second. That no amount of rope could save them in a rockslide.

The cold was starting to bother even him, so he wondered how the rest of them were doing. He'd always had trouble with circulation in his fourth toes. Not his smallest toes, but the fourth ones, and they were numb and cold. He would check them tonight for frostbite, though he was certain it had not progressed so far.

The rhythm of his boots kept his pace steady, and before long, they were at Whymper's chimney. It was covered in snow and ice, meaning there were no handholds or ledges to climb. There was no place to pound in a piton. He would have the most difficult job, using the heavy pickaxe he'd hauled all this way, for this area specifically. The rest of the expedition folded in around him, all of them careful with the ropes in a way that should make any leader proud.

If he could describe this moment, of how it felt, he would say it was tense optimism. As he slung off his pack and retrieved the axe, Fräulein Bridewell took their attention.

"We are making excellent time. However, this section will likely take longer than the previous climbing section."

"They were all climbing sections," Justine huffed.

Karl glanced up to see her expression. But he watched her exchange smiles with Frau Moon, and he dismissed it. Her mood was still good. Excellent. A poor outlook definitely affected a climber's physical ability, and he worried that as the day had worn on, so had their optimism.

"Both Mr. Vogel and I anticipate sleeping on the mountain tonight. While this is not what any of us wanted, we are close to the summit. The plan is to climb until nightfall, and then find what shelter we can. Tomorrow morning, as the sun rises, we will finish our ascent, and then use the rest of the day to descend all the way to the church at Schwarzsee. There, we have shelter, dry clothes, and most importantly, excellent rations."

Karl closed up his pack and secured it, listening to the contented murmurs that the discussion of warm rations elicited. Hunger was the best spice. He looked up at the narrowing wall of ice. It was wide enough that at the beginning, he would have to trust his axe and the spikes on his shoes. Then he could drop the axe to his belt and use his arms and legs to spider walk the rest of the way up.

He had no idea what Justine would do. Perhaps here was where they would haul her up like cargo. Or maybe she would surprise him again. His chest ached with a cold, sharp spike. It wasn't the air that made that feeling. No, that was pure Justine Brewer. He had to distance himself from her, that was clear. He was their guide, and no more.

Still, his pride was intact once he managed the wall. At the top, he was relieved to see the piton with the ring secured on the end still anchored into the boulder. One thing to help them today. He threaded the rope through the metal ring and tossed one half down to Fräulein Bridewell below. He pulled on his leather gloves that helped his grip over his woolen ones, and planted his feet as wide as he could against the boulder.

"All is well," he called down, not sure if that was exactly what he was supposed to say in this moment. But Fräulein Bridewell would undoubtedly know what he meant by it. Moments later, he felt the line go taut and then the tug as her weight loaded onto the rope. He couldn't see them down below, could only hear the scrape and scuffle of her boots.

The cold seeped into him, surprising him that there was anywhere left that wasn't already blisteringly cold. This was no doubt some form of insanity to do this. To pursue these heights, to push oneself over and over again. But if he didn't have this, what did he have?

An expectation that seemed as dreary and monotonous as the Greek man who pushed a boulder up a hill all day, only for it to roll all the way down once again.

JUSTINE PICKED UP the buckle that Ophelia had just thrown down. She peered upward again, stealing one last glance of Karl's boot and brown leather glove. It was all she could see of him from where she stood. Once again, this was going to be impossible for her. The chimney wasn't a chimney so much as a sheer wall of ice.

She looked at the sides, thinking it might be easier for her to climb up that instead, but they looked equally impossible. Even taking her stockings off again to climb barefooted wouldn't work, and she really didn't want to do it again. She was freezing, and being tucked in these shadows was even colder than walking out on the windy ridgeline that they'd trudged up.

She had the spikes on her boots. And she had a single piton in her pack. They all did. She got it out, not entirely sure what she would do, but she would do something. She couldn't stand the idea of Karl pulling her up like livestock.

In practice, he'd put them all out on a boulder and climbed to the top himself. From his anchor above, he had pulled the rope taut for each of them, and they had practiced walking up a wall as he pulled them. She could do that, of course. But she wanted to impress him.

"What are you planning?" Lord Rascomb asked, his voice dry and gravelly.

She flashed him as much of a smile as she could muster. Her whole body was already tired, just not entirely spent. She had more to give. "Using the piton to anchor my hand and then the spikes on the boots to haul me up."

He looked at the wall thoughtfully. "I think if you do, it might backfire and cause the whole wall of snow to come tumbling down. Why not just walk up it? You are the lightest of all of us."

She licked her lips out of habit, immediately regretting it as the cold air seemed almost to stick to her, freezing her further.

"Preserve your strength. We have much longer to go." Ophelia's father put his hand on her shoulder, gentling his advice.

She nodded and put the piton back in her pack. "Walk up," she called to Karl.

"Go," came the gruff call back.

The tension on the rope pulled even further, and she planted her feet wide onto the wall, one at a time, doing her best not to slide off one way or the other. The worst would be to sway on the rope, crashing from one side to another. It didn't take long until she was at the top, rolling over the side like a great hog on a sunny day.

She grunted getting up just like one, too. It was not the graceful exit she'd hoped for. She unbuckled the device and tossed it down to Lord Rascomb, who would be up next. Would he walk up as he'd advised her to do, or would he attempt the same climb Karl and Ophelia had done?

She slumped against one of the other boulders, feeling wrung out now that she was at a standstill. Ophelia came over and leaned next to her, her body warmth cutting through the chill. They heard the commands from Lord Rascomb below, and Karl's response. She let herself admire him. Even if he wasn't an option for a life ahead of her, she still enjoyed the sight of him. Even under the layers of wool, his broad shoulders were evident. The bits of frost on his hat and his woolen trousers highlighted the strain. There was something so very attractive about watching him pull the rope up. He was competent and strong, and those leather gloves he wore to keep the rope from causing rope burns were strangely enticing.

Without meaning to, she pushed away from the cold rock and took a few steps, watching as Lord Rascomb stretched out his legs and arms, the same spidery wall-walking move that both Karl and Ophelia had managed. One that she was laughably too short to even attempt.

Below, Prudence, Eleanor, and Tristan waited, watching Lord Rascomb's ascent. They didn't chat, no doubt feeling as cold and tired and stoic as Justine herself felt.

She heard the scrape of his boot before she understood what she saw. Lord Rascomb cried out as he slipped and fell. Karl braced instantly, catching the weight. Lord Rascomb didn't fall straight down—he fell a few feet, stretching the rope, and swung like a pendulum into the chimney's side.

Lord Rascomb's head clipped the side of the chimney with a sickening hollow sound. Justine gasped. The lord went limp, his body swaying, hitting the other side of the rock with a thud like heavy fabric hitting the ground.

Justine felt sick. Ophelia was at her side, her fingers digging into Justine's arm.

"Get him down, get him down!" Tristan bellowed from below.

It was clear that Lord Rascomb had lost consciousness.

"I need help with the rope," Karl said, his voice strained. "We have to unweight it so I can adjust the rope to let him down."

Justine came around to where the extra rope was, trying to take up the slack.

"It's not enough. Someone must guide him down so he doesn't swing into the sides."

Ophelia seemed to shake out of her stupor. "Tristan. Climb up and guide him down. Keep him safe."

The wait seemed interminable. Justine put the rope around her back, hoping the extra friction would help slow the rope from sliding through Karl's hands. Then she sat on it, to help take the weight from him. Finally, she heard a male grunt, and then heard Eleanor cry, "Go now!"

Karl glanced over at her. She slid her bottom off the rope, and let it slide around her slowly. Next to her, Karl let the rope slide little by little, with Ophelia guiding them with her voice. Justine watched her friend, stoic and in charge. My God, how this changed everything.

Justine hoped that Lord Rascomb would wake up, and perhaps Tristan and Eleanor could aid him back down while Karl, Ophelia, Justine, and Prudence made their way to the summit. But if he didn't wake up? How were they to get him down this mountain? They certainly couldn't do it with only half their party. It would take all of them. And it would be very slow. But if they didn't, Lord Rascomb would die.

If he wasn't already dead.

Chapter Twelve

O UT OF EVERY scenario he'd run about possible pitfalls, this scenario had oddly not been one of them. Injury, yes, but in each of those, Karl had envisioned either death or injury but while conscious. Not this catatonic state. His mind ran all options available, but the only thing he could come to was that they had to abort their mission.

The rope slid through his hands, and he was careful to go smoothly and slowly. Fräulein Bridewell was surprisingly calm and capable, and Justine had aided him with no questions asked, and no instructions needed. She was a miracle.

But there was no possibility of him taking anyone to the summit. All of them would be required to figure out a way to get a body down the mountain. This would require complex rope skills, strength, wayfinding, and the only thing mountaineering truly required: an inability to stop no matter what.

Fräulein Bridewell would be lowered down next, he thought, then Justine, then he would have to rappel down himself. Not his favorite, given how the rope jerked and halted, but it wasn't far. Amazing how of all the places things could have turned them around, it was in this protected chimney that the mountain punished them. Not the rock fall. Not the knife's-edge cliffs in the dark. Not foot slips or even the cold. Proof that again, there were a hundred ways to die on the Matterhorn. No one needed to cut a rope to do it.

"They're on the ground." Fräulein Bridewell wrung her hands together.

"Tie in," he instructed, hauling up the rope after a tug from below.

Between them, they made quick work of it, and Justine helped again with lowering smoothly and slowly. Once Fräulein Bridewell reached the bottom, she tugged the line to signal she was no longer tied in.

"Now you," Karl said, looking at Justine.

Her big brown eyes were full of concern and sorrow and anxiety. But Karl did not detect fear. There was longing in there, and for a moment, Karl felt like he could have folded himself up in her, abandoned all he'd ever wanted just for her. But then she stood, and the moment was gone. She tied in, and with a glance and a nod, she disappeared over the edge.

Once she was down, he again hauled up the rope, this time to let himself down the icy face. It was then that he was glad for so many other expeditions treading this trail. The metal piton pounded into the rock had a ring on the end, through which he had tied them. He rearranged the rope, doubling it over so that he could let himself down, and then pull the rope down after. He gripped the rope tightly, and with a pounding heart, stepped backwards over the ledge.

Once down, he concentrated on taking care of equipment. The others crowded around the body of the viscount. Lord Rascomb's pack had carried the medical supplies, as he was located in the middle of their team. His pack was already emptied, and no doubt they were tending to him, all better prepared medically than he.

But Karl had to figure out not how to care for the man, but how to transport him. If this were open snow fields, he could use all of their extra clothing to create a sled, and they could guide him down. But they'd used the ridge to get them up. How would they manage him on the ridge?

This was the type of problem he hadn't wanted to consider. It would be painstaking and slow, but his plan was the only option.

"How is he?" Karl asked, stepping towards them.

They'd spread out their extra clothing, quickly stitching them together to create an insulating layer between the man and the ground. What Karl saw was the beginning of a sled, or perhaps a sling.

Frau Moon moved away to make room for him. And when he saw the injury, his mouth went dry. He sunk to his knees. The blood was slowly leaching from his temple, slowed by the freezing temperatures. But the injury might prove fatal.

"It's not just there," Justine said quietly. "There's also one on the back of his head. We've already bound it."

Everyone was quiet, awaiting instruction. He waited for Fräulein Bridewell, but her face was drawn, her eyes distant. This was her expedition. And this was her father.

"We need to go," Justine said quietly.

Karl stood up. "We need to move carefully more than we need to move quickly." As he tried to make eye contact with everyone, he realized how dark it had gotten. Descending in the dark would be treacherous. Slow. Another way for a million things to go wrong.

"Every single one of us will be a part of this. We have to. Weight distribution amongst this many should not be a problem. We will create a rotation, just as we have an order of climbing."

He scanned them again, mentally pairing them by height. It might not be the best idea, since it would pair him and Tristan, which would mean the majority of strength would be there at one time. Not a good idea. "It doesn't matter what order, other than we maintain it. Four people on him at all times, two people per side. As we traverse down, the top moves to the bottom, and we shuffle Rascomb down this way."

"That's going to take too long," Tristan objected.

Karl zeroed in on him. "Do you have a better idea?"

Tristan opened his mouth and closed it several times before he shook his head. Karl was grateful that there were no tears, no sobbing. Everyone was in control.

"We must remain focused. We cannot afford a misstep."

"I'll start here at the shoulders," Justine said, staking her claim. Fräulein Bridewell stood opposite her, nodding her head, but not speaking.

"I'll take feet," Tristan said, standing next to his sister.

Frau Bridewell moved opposite her husband. "I'm here."

Karl nodded to Frau Moon, who nodded back, her face pale and expression grave. Karl tidied up the lord's pack, tucking the unused items into his own pack and handing the empty one to Tristan, asking him to stuff it into his.

"Then let us begin." Karl motioned Frau Moon to take her position next to Tristan, and Karl took his next to Frau Bridewell.

They passed the body forward to Karl and Frau Moon, with Fräulein Bridewell and Justine letting go of the viscount's shoulders as they were passed to Frau Bridewell and Tristan. Fortunately, whoever had done the hasty stitching of the barrier had made the fabric tight enough that the man's head didn't fall back, but was rather still supported.

Karl had the man's thighs, and passed the body on to Justine, moving then to holding shoulders. Frau Bridewell and Tristan scurried to the feet. It was excruciating. But they were moving. Down and down they went, slow step by slow step. Down the rocky formations. More than once they had to stop and readjust and reinforce the sling they'd made under him.

Instead of taking the ridgeline all the way down, Karl took a risk and moved them off to the eastern face of the mountain, at least for a little while. It was dangerous, but what choice did he have? The sunset was almost over. At least once in the snow field, they were able to pad out the sled and slide him down.

Fatigue and despair showed on all their faces. But it was dark now, and they needed to return to the ridge. How were they going to traverse the narrow crest? It wasn't big enough for the width of two people on either side of a body, let alone people having to go around each other to continue the train they made.

The only thing he could think of was suspending the sling, and tying it between him and Tristan, around their waists.

"Halt, please," he said. The group stopped, and it was dark enough that when they turned their faces towards him, he couldn't make out their features. He explained his idea, and thankfully Frau Bridewell knew precisely what to do. She asked for all the rope they had that wasn't their main tether.

In what seemed to be a short time, she'd created a webbing to lay the viscount on, complete with tie-in. Her knot structures were inventive and included ties that he was unfamiliar with. But on each end of the webbing was enough length for Karl to tie the webbing to his tether line around his waist. He shifted the rope so that he faced away from the man's feet. The women lifted the body, and Tristan tied in on the other side.

Karl had wanted to make sure Tristan would be able to watch over his father.

"You may choose to go in front, to get down to the church quicker," Karl said over his shoulder.

"I'm not leaving my father," Fräulein Bridewell said.

"We'll stay together," Justine said firmly. "We will follow behind, tethered to each other, while you and Tristan carry Lord Rascomb."

Karl nodded.

"We will return to the ridge and take it all the way back. The same traverse as this morning. Except we will pick up Luc at the camp and continue on to the church."

"Onward," Fräulein Bridewell said, her voice pitched higher than before, somehow questioning, not as sure as she'd been hours previous. Karl put everything out of his mind. This was his worst-case scenario. For he didn't believe the viscount would live until they got to the church. He may have tied himself to an injured man, but he believed he would be putting down a dead one at Schwarzsee.

Justine put herself in the back of the line. Ophelia took the lead, as she should. She kept close to Tristan, no doubt able to see her father as the impromptu swing lurched with every uneven step of the snowy ridge.

Behind Ophelia was Eleanor, then Prudence, then Justine. There wasn't anything Justine had ever experienced worse than this. The nighttime descent was terrifying. But Justine pushed that fear aside, just as she had earlier this morning. The snow was old and tamped from their morning footsteps, which her boots gripped better than the icy slicks of sun-damaged snow on the face. Still, the ridge couldn't be much wider than her arm span, and that made her heart pound even faster. Worse, she could see them all in front of her, which only allowed her to worry about each of their steps more than she worried about her own.

What would even happen for Ophelia? For Tristan? Right now, it was clear that they needed to get back to Zermatt. The thought of Frau and Herr Brunner comforted her. The inn, cozy, with the smells of roasting meat and beer and wine. It kept her steps more sure, her mind calmer.

It was dark enough that she could no longer see Karl ahead of her. The shapes of her friends obscured most of the view, but even so. The snow kept the path somewhat illuminated. It wasn't pitch black, but far darker than what was safe. Yet all seemed well within their capabilities, and she was lulled into the familiar rhythm—slower than normal, but familiar all the same. One step in front of the other. Until it happened.

She heard the slip. Instinctively, she threw herself onto the ridge, clinging to a nearby jagged boulder for all she was worth. The cries of her friends were swallowed and muted by the wind. The rope around her waist yanked hard, pulling her off the ridge. She scrambled for purchase, and her boots dug into another boulder.

"Who is with me?" she cried, not daring to look up. But when she heard nothing but wind, she turned her head.

Ophelia struggled on the ledge of the ridge. Oh God. Ophelia was slipping under the weight of both Eleanor and Prudence, swinging down below.

"Karl!" Justine shouted. "Karl!" They needed help. They needed more strength, more bodies, otherwise the four of them would disappear down into the glacier below.

"Hang on," Tristan called.

Justine couldn't hear anything more as her mind clouded over with the hammering of her heart, her blood. When would they get help? She looked over to Ophelia, who had stopped struggling. She was still bent over the edge, but she had found footing, and she was braced. Ophelia looked at Justine, her expression not fearful, not shocked. Of course not. Ophelia was determined, her mouth set in a firm line that even in this darkness Justine could recognize. They were all surviving. That was what was happening, and Ophelia wouldn't hear of any alternative.

No doubt Ophelia had found a braced position and was waiting it out until Karl and Tristan could help.

Then the weight of the rope at her waist loosened. Prudence must have found some purchase down on the wall of the ridgeline. Using her foot, Justine pulled the slack of the rope up and around another rock and held it there with the weight of her leg. It wasn't much, but would hopefully provide more friction if Prudence fell again.

It felt like an eternity until Karl reached her. Not saying anything, he took the slack she'd gathered and tied into it, bracing himself next to her. "I've got it." His voice was low in the darkness, and she had never felt more relief in her life. But Justine was still there, still focused, still tied into her friends, a part of the tether that would save the lives of both Prudence and Eleanor as well as Ophelia and herself.

Careful not to disturb any debris, Justine turned around and peered over the edge, still on her belly. She could make out the figure of Prudence below, clinging to the rock. At least, she thought that was Prudence.

"Prudence? What's happening?" Justine asked, hoping the wind and the darkness would carry her words to her friend. A swell of gratitude hit her when she heard her friend's voice.

"Climbing," Prudence said. "I'm hurt, but not badly. Eleanor is also climbing. She is worse off than I am."

"Do you want us to try to haul you up?"

A sob came. "Yes. Yes please."

Justine looked over to the hunched dark figures of Ophelia and Tristan. "Haul them both up?"

"Yes," came Ophelia's crystal-clear reply.

"On my mark," Justine said, scrambling around the rock to reconfigure the rope. She sat next to Karl, seeing the fatigue in his face. "Can you?"

"Of course," Karl said, his voice clear, not betraying any hint of exhaustion. They'd been climbing this mountain for well over fifteen hours in the cold. None of them had eaten, and all had performed feats of strength. What were a few more?

The rewards of civilization taunted her: roasted beef that fell apart in her mouth. Potatoes smothered in butter and cream. Soft bread smothered in dripping honey. Sharp, tangy cheddar cheese, the kind that crumbled on her tongue. Big hunks of—

"Ready," came Ophelia's voice.

"Mark. Pull!" Justine's mind went utterly still with the exception of this task. "Pull." They heaved the rope. Justine gathered the slack that pooled between her and Karl, tying off knots, in case his hands slipped. "Pull." All four of them heaved again, and again she gathered slack. She could hear the scrambling of hands and feet. They were close. So close. One more. "Pull."

And then Prudence was pulling herself up over the edge. Justine surged forward, grabbing Prudence under her arms, hauling her onto the narrow ridge. Prudence laid half in Justine's lap, her chest heaving. As her breath calmed, Justine realized that Prudence was shaking.

Justine tightened her grip around her friend, holding her tight. "I've got you." And Justine meant it.

They regrouped, and with Prudence's assistance they retrieved Eleanor as well. Tristan held her as Karl examined her arm and shoulder. Justine gripped Ophelia and Prudence as tight as she could manage. She had all of them. Small, but determined. She would save them all.

KARL HAD A plan. It wasn't a great one, but it was the only one available to him. Minutes ticked away from them, becoming hours lost. The only hope he had was that the cold somehow helped the viscount, preventing a loss of blood that would have killed him otherwise.

Tying into the rope sling had been far more challenging in the dark, his hands less dexterous after hauling a climber up the side of the Hörnli Ridge. The only good thing was that they were closer to Schwarzsee. Closer to shelter and food and help.

When they finally found camp, Karl kicked Luc awake, hoping the man would forgive him.

"Go as fast as you can to Schwarzsee. Get the donkey. The viscount is gravely injured. Send word to Zermatt to bring a healer to Schwarzsee. I don't care who. Get the midwife if she's the only one. Have my Onkel send word to Zurich for a physician if there isn't one in Zermatt. Go fast. He's dying."

Luc, bless the man, did not question, did not rub his eyes, did nothing but take off in the direction of the church.

Karl's back ached from the weight of the sling, but he didn't dare put down his burden. It would be faster for them to continue carrying him like this rather than trying the caterpillar method they'd done on the mountain.

The trail ahead was well-worn, dirt, and wide. These were the easy Alpine trails anyone could traverse. Over his shoulder, he asked Tristan, "We can go faster now. Are you able to keep going?"

"Yes," came the firm reply.

"We'll break camp and meet you down there," came a woman's voice in the darkness. Justine. It was Justine. And he wanted to praise her, but didn't dare.

"Good," he said, and he was already walking. They made the descent quickly, given both their long strides and easy terrain. The church had a lamp in the window, and Karl exhaled in relief. Luc was already here.

It was that same hunched man who opened the door at their approach. "I sent Bernhard down to fetch the physician. I've made you some rations and a bed for *monsieur*."

They went inside the small white-washed building—which practically glowed in the dark, starry landscape. The clear water of Schwarzsee reflected all of this, a sanctuary far warmer than the day they'd spent on the mountain.

Karl walked them over to the cot—Bernhard's cot—padded with blankets. He and Tristan carefully unloaded the weight of Lord Rascomb onto it. Karl sank to his knees on the stone floor, the pressure biting into his very tired legs, to make untying from the sling easier. He wanted to lie flat on this floor, letting his back relax from the strain it had endured, but there was more to be done.

"Luc, please fix us whatever you have." Karl looked down at the viscount, whose pallor was not good. But he could see the subtle rise of the man's chest, so he was at least still breathing. "Tristan, we will gently roll him to the side to remove the webbing."

Tristan looked at him with wide blue eyes, his face drawn and finally now terrified. Though they were likely the same age, he looked like a child in this light, worried for his father. "Should we move him?" Tristan asked.

"The webbing cannot be comfortable." Karl gave a grim smile, hoping that would comfort the other man. "And we've already moved him down a mountain." Karl coaxed him through the steps, moving the body on one side, pushing the webbing as far to the center as he could, and then moving to the other side, pulling it out without disturbing the unconscious man.

Karl didn't dare pull the bindings away from his head wounds, afraid that it might spark bleeding now that they were in a warmer temperature. Tristan slid down to the floor and gripped his father's hand, staring at the viscount's face. Luc arrived with two bowls of some kind of soup, but Karl shook his head.

He touched Tristan on the shoulder and said, "Food is ready when you are."

But Tristan refused to look away from his father. "I'm not hungry."

Karl guided Luc back to the entrance, which was colder than the nave where Lord Rascomb lay. Karl took the bowl. The soup was greasy and barely warm. But Karl didn't care.

"Where did you warm this?" Karl asked Luc, wanting to know where the campfire must be, as it wasn't in this rectangular ice box of a structure.

"Outside. It's quite small, I don't think it will last much longer." Luc looked embarrassed, as if he were somehow less of a help.

"Good work," Karl said, downing the rest of the bowl's contents. He dug through the other items they'd left here, finding his change of clothes. Dry clothing. Warm clothing. He didn't relish the idea of disrobing in a church, but he was certain Mother Mary wouldn't mind at the moment.

JUSTINE HAD NEVER been more focused in her life. She packed up the bag blankets and the cookware while Eleanor wrapped her ankle.

"I think it's broken," Eleanor said quietly. "It's very swollen."

"We'll take care of it at Schwarzsee," Ophelia said. Her voice was tinged with urgency. Justine redoubled her efforts to finish packing up the campsite, making sure Eleanor's and Prudence's packs were far lighter than hers or Ophelia's.

"Prudence?" Justine asked. "What's your injury?" Since hauling them back on the ridge, Prudence had not volunteered anything, had not said anything. Ophelia had been focused on Eleanor, whose injured ankle had apparently caused the tumble over the side, pulling Prudence along with her.

"It's nothing," Prudence said, but her voice was strained. As Justine got closer, she could tell that Prudence cradled her arm in her lap.

"Tell me now, and I can help," Justine whispered.

Prudence bit back the sob that escaped. "Too much has happened, I don't want to make it worse."

"It will be worse if we don't fix it." Justine reached out to touch her but Prudence flinched. "Is it your arm or your shoulder?"

"Both? I don't know anymore."

"That's perfectly fine. I'd like to make a sling for your arm. We still have at least another hour down to Schwarzsee. Can you make it?"

"Of course," Prudence said, sniffing. But she seemed calmer.

Justine dug in Prudence's pack, which was closer, and found the only bit of rag left. Thank goodness. All their extra clothing had gone with Lord Rascomb, and most of their clean rags, too. It wasn't the best, but it was the best Justine could manage right now. She carefully threaded Prudence's very light pack onto her back, and then created a sling for Prudence.

"All is well," Justine said, hoping that her calm declaration would help them. She slid into her heavy pack as the other two women did as well. Ophelia smiled, the hope in her face returning.

"All is well," Prudence said, her voice careful. Justine knew she was trying not to betray her pain.

"All is well," Eleanor said, equally steady.

"All is well," Ophelia repeated. A heavy exhale came from her. "Onward."

And so they walked in the dark, in silence. Justine staggered under the weight of her pack, but she had little choice. She certainly couldn't leave their camp littered all over the mountain, and she would not be coming back up to clean it.

They descended slower than Justine would have thought, but given that Eleanor could barely walk, Prudence was in prodigious amounts of pain, and Ophelia and Justine were weighted down, their pace was understandable.

A small campfire blazed next to the church, and the windows were lit with lamps. It was a welcome sight. Justine no longer cared about food. She wanted dry socks more than anything. She wanted her ears to be warm. Sleep would be nice, but not entirely necessary.

This level of exhaustion exceeded even the early conditioning treks Karl used to take Justine on. She could feel every joint in her body. Her hips ached. Her shoulders burned with the weight of the pack. Even though they were no longer tethered together, she felt the ghost of the rope around her waist. Every so often, she felt a phantom tug that filled her with fear.

Ophelia opened the door of the small church, and Justine felt the urge to cry from relief. They filed inside. Ophelia strode over to the cot in the nave, where all the candles were lit. Tristan looked up at her as she dumped the pack on the stone floor. The expressions they exchanged stopped the rest of the women in their tracks.

"Let me," Karl said, lifting the pack Justine carried.

She closed her eyes and let him unthread the straps from her, taking the weight of her burden. She let out a shaky breath, the fatigue clouding her mind. Was the danger over? Could they relax?

"Change into dry clothes first," Karl said, gesturing to piles set on the short wooden benches that were this church's pews. "No one will look."

Justine nodded. She didn't even care if someone looked. She was beyond modesty, beyond caring about trivial things like that. The other women stepped forward. Eleanor's hands were shaking. And Justine had no idea how Prudence could change one-handed.

"I'll go prepare some food," Karl said, stepping out of the low-ceilinged church.

"Sit down," Justine instructed both Prudence and Eleanor. Methodically, she pulled the boots off them both, being more careful and slow with Eleanor, considering her ankle. It had swollen to an abnormal size, but Justine couldn't tell what was bandage and woolen stockings, and what was actually Eleanor.

"We'll have to take this off," Justine said, and Eleanor nodded. Justine worked on the bandage while Eleanor pulled down her shredded woolen stockings. Once everything was off, and Justine could see the bare skin, she was appalled to see the marks in Eleanor's shin where the binding had kept the swelling down, and the rest of her flesh ballooned out around it. Deep, angry red scrapes laced around Eleanor's legs. Wool fibers had stuck to the dried blood.

Justine frowned, unsure what steps to take next.

"Bind it first, then put the fresh stockings on," Prudence suggested, pulling her own stockings off, one-handed. "We can clean it when we get to Zermatt."

Justine bound Eleanor's foot as best she could.

"I can handle the rest," Eleanor said. "Help Prudence."

Justine looked over as Prudence eased off the sling, pain causing silent tears to run down her cheeks. It was then that Justine realized how badly Prudence's clothes were torn. She was probably as scraped up as Eleanor. "We'll get you to rights in no time," Justine said, hoping that helped.

She aided Prudence with her blouse and skirt, helping her change into a dry shift, and then the rest of her layers, doing her best to avoid the angry bloody wounds that she found peppering her friend's shoulders. Once Eleanor and Prudence were taken care of, Justine looked to Ophelia.

"I'll get her to come change," Eleanor said, limping over to where Lord Rascomb lay resting on a cot. With the candles surrounding him, he almost seemed dead, like a saint that had martyred himself to a cause.

It wasn't far from the truth. If he did die, was he a martyr? A martyr to the cause of Alpine climbing? The urge to push oneself to the very edge of human endurance? For Justine felt that way now. She'd thought she'd known it before, but it was nothing compared to how she felt this moment, staring down at her dry clothes, knowing she would feel better if she could change.

She needed to get her boots off. Her toes were numb, and if she didn't do something, there was a real possibility of frostbite. But she was so tired.

"I'll go see what we can eat." Prudence laid her hand on Justine's shoulder. That human contact felt so warm and precious. It spurred Justine into movement, and she sat down to unknot her boots.

It wasn't long before Ophelia joined her on the bench. They exchanged a look of exhaustion and despair. It took all of Justine's strength to find Ophelia's hand. But she did, and she held her best friend's fingers as long as she dared. This was only part of their strength. They were together. And together, Justine Brewer and Ophelia Bridewell could do anything. Anything. Even this.

Finally, Ophelia gave a shallow nod, and they both bent over to untie their boots. Justine felt the sharp sting of open wounds on her own body, but ignored it. She would get to that in Zermatt. They would fix everything later. She wondered if Ophelia was feeling the same way.

When they finished changing, Prudence came in with two bowls of steaming soup, followed by Karl. Luc hobbled in with warmed bread and cold butter, slices of cheese and a pocket overflowing with apples.

"Tea is coming soon," Karl said as he handed bowls first to

Justine and Ophelia.

Justine glanced over to Prudence and Eleanor, ensuring that they were taken care of.

"I'm going back over to my father." Ophelia stood.

Justine watched her friend go, her gait hobbled and raw. Something hurt Ophelia, whether it was a blister on her foot or a hitch in her hip from stiffness, she didn't know.

Karl watched Justine eat for a moment, but she couldn't be bothered to feel self-conscious. "I will watch over them, Justine. Eat. Take care of yourself. There are pallets over there—" he pointed to a nest of blankets on the other wall. "Help is coming from Zermatt. Rest now so you can help later."

She swallowed hard. There was no flavor in the soup or stew or whatever it was. But it was hot going down into her chilled body, and that was worth it. Her teeth began to chatter. There was comfort from him, even if he didn't touch her. She wanted him to, wanted to curl up in his arms, hear the rumble of his voice in his chest.

But she'd thrown that opportunity away. Not because she wouldn't marry him, but because she'd made him feel a fool for thinking it. Her whole body wanted to shiver, but she clamped down, willing herself to be still. "Thank you," she managed, her voice scratchy.

"You are welcome." Those were formal words. Words that he'd protested about in one of his English language rants. In his language there was a formal and an informal way to speak. In modern English, there were formal terms of address, but that was it. How was a person to know when respectful distance was given and when the informal, friendly words connected them?

But Justine felt that respectful distance in his tone. She heard his formality, accepting it as what she had forced him to use. He ducked outside once again. To check on food, to see if help was close? Justine didn't know. She ate her bowl of soup, took a bite of cheese, and found that chewing an apple or a piece of bread took far more work than she could manage.

She took off the slippers she'd packed and bedded down, certain she wouldn't sleep, but needing the rest.

The next moment, everything changed.

It felt as if she'd blinked, but hours had passed. The sun was fully in the sky. Prudence was curled up next to her, breathing deep and rhythmically in her heavy slumber.

Justine sat up. Her head hurt. Her back twinged, as if to contest her head's priority in pain. There was an ewer of water and two cups sitting on the short bench in front of her and Prudence. She poured a cup and drank, downing it in seconds. Her stomach rebelled at the cold temperature, but she didn't care. She poured another cup. Looking around, she saw more people.

Mr. Moon leaned against the wall on the other side of Prudence, his arms crossed, his hat clutched in his hand. Justine followed his gaze over to the nave, where there was a crowd around the cot where Lord Rascomb lay.

She didn't recognize some of them—healers from Zermatt, perhaps? But Tristan and Ophelia both stood there, clearly not having slept. Justine got to her feet, swaying with fatigue. Her feet were swollen, feeling as if the bottoms of them were rounded like a wheel rather than flat. She stumbled as she disengaged from the blankets.

Mr. Moon pushed off the wall, stepping over Prudence to provide aid.

Justine waved him off. "Thank you, I'm fine." She leaned on the wall, scanning the room again. She couldn't help but notice that there was no one watching over her. No Karl. No Francis. She was on her own. Isn't that what she'd asked for? Her independence? "Where's Karl? I mean, Mr. Vogel?"

Mr. Moon nodded towards the door. "Outside. Securing the cart."

A cart. Definitely one for Lord Rascomb. Justine did not look forward to hiking back down to Zermatt, but needs must. A cup of tea would help her uncontrollable shivering. She didn't bother putting on her slippers or her boots, not sure her feet would fit in either covering, and padded outside.

Karl held the reins of a donkey, attached to a cart, discussing something with his uncle. Herr Brunner broke into a smile when he saw her.

"Fräulein Brewer!" he said.

Justine shielded her eyes against the blinding sun. The air was warm with a chilly undercurrent she had come to associate with the Alps. "Herr Brunner," she croaked. She cleared her throat.

The older man said something to her that she couldn't understand. Hopefully, she couldn't understand it because it was another language, but she couldn't be sure right now.

"He says that he is glad you are safe," Karl said. The look in his eye made her think that perhaps Karl was glad too. Of their seven-member expedition, Karl, Tristan, Ophelia, and she were the only ones unscathed. Lord Rascomb might die. Eleanor had either a twisted ankle or a broken ankle. Prudence likely had a broken arm. They were lucky.

"Is my brother here?" Justine asked.

Karl shook his head, and Herr Brunner spoke again.

"Your brother was sent to Zurich to fetch a physician," Karl translated. Herr Brunner said something again, to which Karl nodded along. "It will take some time for him to return. We will likely arrive at the same time, our donkey cart and your brother."

Justine hugged herself. That was a good use for Francis. He did well when he had a task, and fetching a physician from Zurich was important. Lord Rascomb deserved the best care possible.

"Another cart is coming," Karl said after a moment. "This one is for Lord Rascomb. I didn't think you all should have to hike down to Zermatt. I know Frau Bridewell is having trouble walking, and Frau Moon is likewise injured."

Justine nodded, biting her lip so she would not cry with relief. "Thank you."

She hobbled over to the edge of the slate porch, where Mr. Luc Meynet sat next to the campfire, a half-smile on his face as he blew smoke rings into the air.

"Pardon me, but I was wondering—"

"Té?" he asked, cutting her off.

Justine nodded.

The man hopped off his seat and busied himself, taking a moment to shoo her back inside. Karl wandered over, asking the other man something in German.

"He'll bring it to you," Karl said after the conversation was over. "He says he knows how the English like their tea."

The day passed in a blur. Eventually, they loaded Lord Rascomb into the cart with Ophelia and Tristan and the stranger who was some kind of healer. Herr Brunner and Luc passed out food, begging them all to eat. Justine stared at the mountain and the blue sky that surrounded it. She felt betrayed.

It was silly to think she'd been betrayed by a mountain, but still. They'd worked so hard. All of the training and time—not to mention the humiliation they'd suffered at the hands of the gossip columns and members of the English Alpine Society. There had only been fourteen successful ascents in total in history, but she knew the men of London's Alpine Society would pin this on them being women, even if it had been Lord Rascomb's accident that caused them to turn around.

They'd wanted to be the fifteenth. To log their names in history. To prove to the world that women were strong, capable, *worthy*. Tears stung Justine's eyes. She was furious. Furious at the Matterhorn for existing, for turning them around, for hurting Ophelia's father. If she could kick it, she would. Her hands balled into fists.

"Justine," Prudence called.

She turned around, seeing the other cart. They were already loading it with their packs. Herr Brunner helped Eleanor and Prudence up into the cart. She wiped a hot angry tear from her cheek and joined them.

Chapter Thirteen

A T THE INN, the dining room was converted into a makeshift hospital. Prudence and Eleanor were ushered in. There was an older woman, round and wrinkled, with an apron tied so far up her stomach the strings were practically tucked under her pendulous breasts. Justine watched as the woman assessed Prudence and Eleanor as they entered the dining room.

A bed identical to the guest beds upstairs was in the room, where Lord Rascomb was ensconced. Tristan and Ophelia looked awful, but they remained at his bedside. Lady Rascomb looked as stylish and alert as ever, sitting beside Lord Rascomb, holding his hand.

For a moment, Justine wondered why Lady Rascomb hadn't followed the donkey cart out to Schwarzsee. Why did she not look as much of a wreck as Tristan and Ophelia?

There was a small knot in her stomach she didn't want to acknowledge that wondered why Francis hadn't come in that donkey cart either. Yes, she knew he was fetching a doctor. And he had not yet returned with said doctor from Zurich either. But still. Wasn't anyone worried for her? Didn't anyone need to check on her? Prudence had Mr. Moon, and Eleanor was part of the cluster with Tristan and Ophelia. Karl was out being Karl. And she was just . . . here. But she pushed all those thoughts down. It didn't matter. She didn't have an injury. Her family was fine in faraway England. She was being selfish and ridiculous. Better to focus on what needed to be done.

The older woman, a healer? A midwife? gestured to Prudence to sit down. Frau Brunner tried to push Tristan out of the room, but he refused to budge from his father's bedside. Then she tried to push Mr. Moon out, but he likewise refused. Karl and Herr Brunner were still outside, dealing with the cart. The two older women conversed and then shrugged.

Gently, the older woman had Prudence take off the sling. Ophelia stepped over closer, frowning as she listened. But then she started translating for Prudence, which surprised Justine. When had Ophelia picked up this language so fluently?

"She is going to check your shoulder, Prudence."

Prudence frowned up at Ophelia, clearly thinking the same thing as Justine. "When did you—ow!" Prudence sucked in a sudden breath and turned deathly pale as the healer woman manipulated her arm.

The older woman gestured at Justine, and then spoke to Ophelia.

"Come over here, Justine. To catch? I think?" Ophelia shook her head. "I think she is afraid Prudence might faint."

"I'm not going to faint," Prudence said.

Mr. Moon strode over. "I'll catch her."

The older woman spoke again.

"No," Ophelia said, "Mr. Moon, you are to stand in front of her and hold her hand."

The older woman continued, and Ophelia blushed. "She says you are to tell her, er, tell her that you love her. You are to distract her with love words."

Justine grinned. "That's not really what she said, is it?"

"More or less," Ophelia said. "My German isn't perfect."

"I'm surprised you have any at all." Justine let Frau Brunner push her hard flush against Prudence, bracing her body against Prudence's back.

"We've been here for months, Justine. What was I supposed to do? Knit a hat?" Ophelia frowned.

They argued and then Prudence screamed as a wet sucking sound shut them all up. Justine stared at the older woman. Everyone in the room was still, staring at Prudence. No one had heard a noise like that in their lives.

"Oh my," Prudence said, regaining her composure. "I do feel much better."

The healer spoke to Ophelia, and Ophelia asked some questions back, before she said to the room, "Prudence's shoulder was out of place. But it is now back in. She will be sore, but will recover fully."

Mr. Moon dropped his face, kissing Prudence's hands.

"I hope they are all that easy to fix," Justine said. Ophelia shot her a warning glance to keep quiet. Right. Lord Rascomb was clearly not that easy to fix.

Prudence stood, and Ophelia caught her. "She wants you to have syrup of Althea. There's some in my room. Justine?"

"I'll bring it to your room," Justine said, noting the dark circles under both their eyes.

"Eleanor?" Ophelia asked, gesturing.

Eleanor glanced at the healer woman, clearly wary. Tristan helped her over. Justine glanced out the window. It looked like late afternoon, which meant it was even later. She calculated in her head how long it would take to get to Zurich, find a doctor, and return. Francis would be here soon.

She followed Prudence and Mr. Moon out of the dining room and up the steps. She peered out the front window of the inn, seeing movement at the donkey carts. Karl was outside tending them, no doubt. As she climbed the steps, her feet heavy, she tried to remember to not be selfish. To help and not wish someone would come to check on her. To be thankful that she was fine. Everything was fine.

KARL FELT AS if he were already sleeping while he worked, his body screaming out for rest, but the day was far from over. He stowed the carts in the barns, and penned the donkeys, brushing them and giving them extra food for working so hard. With the dining room taken over as the hospital, Onkel Peter told him he was allowed to take a guest room. A real bed for the first time in months. It sounded like heaven.

And then Mr. Brewer showed up with a Zurich physician. More donkeys to care for. He'd have to find a room for the physician, and attend those needs. He was hungry enough that his stomach felt turned inside out, despite the feast he'd had back at the church. The rest of them had gone to sleep, so Karl had managed to eat the rest of the soup, half of the cheese, and three apples. He left the bread for the morning. No one had complained about their rations.

Still, he had to attend that task which fell in front of him, and then whatever awaited him inside the inn. Fresh linens, or fetching more food from the village. Did they have the medications they needed? The apothecary in town had things for basic needs, but not all that might be required for someone in Lord Rascomb's position. Was Kara still on staff? If she could run those errands, perhaps he could sleep.

He wondered if Frau Erhart was capable of dealing with Frau Moon and Frau Bridewell. She had healed mountaineering injuries he'd had in the past—but those had all been some form of bone setting. He'd heard the moan of agony earlier, which he'd assumed was from Frau Moon. Despite the sling, her arm had not hung correctly. He would check on them before he rested. But not until after the donkeys were seen to.

Onkel Peter clapped him on the back. "I will take care of the guests and their mounts. Get some sleep. Greta will bring you a tray. We'll need you at full strength tomorrow."

He'd never been so grateful.

Onkel Peter shooed him away with his hand. "Go rest. You've been brave and strong. Be proud of what you accomplished. You brought everyone home."

He may have brought everyone back, but one was still more than halfway to death, and two were injured. He'd set out with six clients, and half were worse off than when they started. It wasn't a good ratio.

Despite his Onkel's bidding, he peeked into the dining room to see how things were going, and to see if a translator was needed.

Frau Erhart was tending to Frau Bridewell. The Zurich doctor was peering over Lord Rascomb. Ophelia and Lady Rascomb looked at him with heartbreaking hope in their faces. Tristan stood with his hand on his wife's shoulder, but stared back at the bed where his father lay. His allegiance torn.

Karl raised his eyebrows at Tante Greta, whose serious expression morphed, and she mouthed the words *apple cake* at him, in case he was hungry. Yes, he was, and he could eat an entire apple cake on his own, probably two. Instead, he shook his head. Tante Greta needed to focus on the guests there, keeping them fed and warm.

But as he looked around, he didn't see Justine. Nor Herr and Frau Moon. Even if she hadn't wished for his honorable attention, he wanted to lay eyes on Justine to make sure she was well. After all, as a guide, it was his responsibility to check on his client. And perhaps she would tell him how the climb had felt from her perspective. How the ascent felt, what she saw, the downclimb, and how the rest of the way from Hörnli to Schwarzsee had been.

He backed out of the dining room and picked out the key to room number four from behind the desk. It was upstairs, and there was a bathing room down the hall. It only had cold water and a drain, but it was enough for him. That was all he wanted before he allowed himself to fall into oblivion. The last image in his mind was Justine's face as they hauled Frau Moon up and over the ridge. Her expression set in absolute belief of their abilities. Of his.

JUSTINE AWOKE, HEART pounding. She'd been falling down into a bergschrund—the gap between the rock of a mountain and a glacier. There was a knocking at the door. Perhaps that had woken her, and not the fear of hitting the icy ground and dying a miserable cold death, all alone.

The bed next to hers—Ophelia's—was empty. The bed was still made up from before they'd left for the Matterhorn. It had only been three days, but it felt like a lifetime. Justine staggered to her feet and threw on her dressing gown. When she opened the door, the young maid stood there, holding a breakfast tray.

"Good morning?" Justine croaked out, blinking hard to adjust to being awake.

"Guete Morge," the girl said, making a gesture with her head that took Justine a moment to realize she was asking to be let into Justine's room. She lifted the tray. "Z'Morge?"

Belatedly, Justine moved aside to let the girl pass. But no further attempts of conversation were made as she placed the tray on Justine's bed and left. Justine looked at the time—already nine in the morning. She'd slept over twelve hours. Her stomach growled, as if to protest the time she'd wasted sleeping instead of eating. There hadn't even been dinner last night—at least, she didn't think there had been. She'd cleaned herself up, and then gone straight to bed after delivering the syrup of Althea to Prudence.

After she ate breakfast in her room and dressed alone, she wandered downstairs. The sun was bright and cheerful. Peering outside, she saw the crisp green grass, the endless blue sky and the mountains, standing guard as they'd always done. A murmur of voices came from the dining room.

Cots had been laid out on either side of the bed that housed Lord Rascomb. He looked peaceful now. Smaller, sunken, though his color was looking better. Ophelia sat on one side of the bed in a chair. She had cleaned up and was wearing a fresh dress. So at least she'd taken care of herself in some ways. Lady Rascomb sat in the chair next to her, her portable writing desk on the table. The viscountess had a stack of sealed envelopes and was penning yet another.

Tristan napped against the wall, and Eleanor sat beside him, sipping at a cup of tea. At a table farther away were the remnants of their breakfasts, empty plates and silverware, stacked up and ready to be whisked into the kitchen.

They were quite the scene. She assumed Prudence was upstairs in her room with Mr. Moon. Frau Brunner bustled out with a pot of tea on a tray, complete with cake, ready to be sliced. She set it on the table, gesturing and saying a halting, "Please."

She picked up the stack of dirty dishes and hurried back into the kitchen. The young girl came in, carrying a stack of trays from upstairs. Justine felt very much in the way. So after greeting everyone, she slipped outdoors.

The air made her feel better, and the sun on her skin even more so. She wasn't made for a sickbed vigil. But she wondered about Francis, and where he was. Karl was likely around here some place. Probably just as busy as the maid and Frau Brunner. She swallowed hard, once again ignoring the lump in her throat when she thought about how easily ignored she was.

It was a silly thing to feel anyway. Because out of everyone, she was fine. Absolutely fine. And she would figure out something to do to occupy herself. Somehow.

Later in the afternoon, after a short walk around the village, she returned to the inn and tried to offer to help Frau Brunner. It didn't work. She was waved away. Visiting Prudence wasn't any fun, as Mr. Moon refused to leave her side and frowned at Justine the entire time, as if she were somehow leaching all the healing energy from the room.

The dining room was awful, and no one spoke. So she ate dinner in her room alone. The next day was the same, but this time, she found Francis outside the front door of the inn, smoking. He said nothing other than awkward inquiries into her general health. Justine suggested he join her on a walk in town. As they meandered, he told her about running around Zurich trying to find the doctor. Justine gave him a halting story of their time on the Matterhorn, but when she got to the part of how Lord Rascomb got injured, he shuddered and stopped her, saying he couldn't stand the idea of it.

But as days passed, her dreams replayed that moment of Lord Rascomb's head hitting the rock, the sound turning her stomach every time, and also the sound of Eleanor's feet scrambling as she slowly slipped off the ridge, pulling Prudence with her. Sometimes, the dreams made up new versions of the experiences she'd had. That the rock fall that had hurt Tristan's arm was a boulder and knocked him down the mountain, tumbling head over feet. Sometimes, she was hauling Karl up on the rope, but just as he got to the ledge, he let go on purpose, falling deep into an unending chasm.

Every morning, she awoke gasping in fear, wanting to scream, but not wanting to alarm anyone. Her feet were back to normal size, and she no longer felt the lingering fatigue of their attempt. She hadn't seen Karl anywhere, but she also hadn't dared search for him in the barns or along the fence line. She didn't know where he would be.

It was lonely. She sat with Ophelia and tried to comfort her, but all the Bridewells had walled themselves up together, all grim and stoic and strong, never moving from Lord Rascomb's side. Even Francis had a purpose that did not include her. He travelled between the inn and Zurich, the messenger and go-between. He took letters, conducted business via telegraph, returning with new concoctions and advice from other doctors.

So Justine wandered in the hills around Zermatt. She tried to read, but couldn't concentrate. She visited with Prudence and Eleanor, taking afternoon tea with them, and tried to join an impromptu sketching class taught by Mr. Moon, who, it turned out, was a gifted artist.

They were returning to the inn from an out of doors session when Prudence stopped her. Mr. Moon carried all their sketchbooks and pencils.

"We are making plans to travel," Prudence said. It had been a week since the healer-woman had made Prudence's shoulder make that wet, sucking pop noise.

"Travel?" Justine asked.

"Return to England," Mr. Moon clarified. "There's no use for us to stay here. We'd be happy to have you along, if you like."

Justine frowned. "But Lord Rascomb—"

"Doesn't need us," Prudence said, putting her hand on Justine's arm. "Ophelia doesn't need us. She has her family, and they are more than capable."

"But—" They had a point. But while Justine prioritized independence, she didn't relish the idea of travelling alone. Her shorter stature made her all the more attractive to uncouth gentlemen. She stared at the walls of the inn, as if she could see inside the dining room that still functioned as a sick room. The building didn't have another room that could accommodate all of the bedside caregivers. "Shouldn't we have an expedition team meeting? Or at least a Ladies' Alpine Society meeting first?"

Prudence's frown was full of sympathy. "Normally, I would say yes, but Ophelia is overwhelmed with grief and guilt."

Justine felt the criticism as if Prudence were saying it about herself. "That is to be very much expected—"

Prudence's hands lifted in a defensive gesture. "It isn't harshly meant. I only mean to say that Ophelia cannot manage a meeting. And Eleanor is consumed by comforting all of them. Which is fine. Reasonable. But you and I have no reason to stay. We do not add, and we cannot help."

Justine's head dropped. Prudence had a point. But she wasn't ready to leave Ophelia. Or Zermatt. Or anything. She wanted to stay in this chrysalis of time, where the world didn't know of their failure, and hope for the best was still a viable ember. "May I think about it?"

Prudence gave a tight smile. "Of course. We plan to make arrangements in the morning. Perhaps you can come by our room directly after breakfast and tell us what you'd like to do?"

Justine nodded and let them head back in. She wasn't ready to be inside quite yet. She wasn't ready for anything other than staying here in Zermatt. She didn't want to return to England where she would go back to her structured dresses and lady's maid. The indoor life of a well-bred woman was awaiting her, and it sounded terrible.

It was then that she finally saw Karl. After a week without seeing even a wisp of him, she was happy to at least catch a glimpse. He was behind the inn, once again with his hatchet. She ran between the inn and the animal pens, reaching him as he turned to see what the noise was.

"You're here," she said in between breaths. Thank goodness he smiled at her. She would have broken if he had been upset with her.

"Yes, of course. Where else would I be?"

"I haven't seen you all week."

He nodded and gestured for her to walk with him as he continued on the goat path. But his eyes were on the ground. "It has been a very busy week."

She swallowed hard. For everyone else. For people who had a purpose or a person. "Yes, a very busy week."

"Are you well?" He scrutinized her face as he asked, and it made her think this was not polite banter, but rather a guide checking in with his client.

"My scratches and bruises have been healing up nicely." That part was true. She'd had impressive purple marks on her thighs from where she hit the ground as Prudence and Eleanor had gone over the edge. Prudence and Eleanor both sported impressive cuts and bruises on their faces, shoulders, arms, and hands, as they'd both swung against the jagged wall of the Hörnli Ridge. "Nothing like Mrs. Moon or Mrs. Bridewell's injuries."

"Good," he grunted.

"And you?" she asked. He carried a hatchet and was dressed in his usual work attire. He seemed extremely hale. The straight lines of his jaw and the bright flower-blue of his eyes once again sang their siren song. She wanted him. It made her think she had been the most ridiculous person in the world. Here was a man who promised not to cage her. Who had led her onto the most dangerous mountain in the world. Of course he would not try to stifle her. And at the most basic levels, everyone else here had someone to care for and care for them in return. It was Justine who had pushed everyone away, who had insisted that she could care for herself in every way possible, who was lonely.

He looked at her strangely and then looked down at himself. "All is well," he said, echoing what they said on the mountain.

"Of course," she said, feeling very stupid, but still glad to be with him. It was her turn to stare at the trail unfurling in front of them. "Where are you going?"

"Another fence is down. A cow knocked it over."

"May I come with you?" Justine asked, looking across the valley. How was she supposed to return to England when this existed in the world?

"If you like."

She did. She missed the company of another person. They just could exist together. Talk about nothing or something. They found the broken fence, and Justine sat in the grass and chatted aimlessly about her week: the sketches—terrible—Lord Rascomb's prognosis—not good—eating alone in her room—it had its moments.

She picked at the grass and the clover buds that studded the ground.

Karl hauled over the log he was about to split for the rail. "Justine," he said, his voice airy as he caught his breath. He put his hands on his hips, showcasing those wide, capable shoulders. "What do you want?"

She looked up at him, all brawny and strong. She bet he was warm. Her skin had taken on the chill that ran underneath the sunny afternoon. "What do you mean?"

"Why are you out here? With me?"

Her brows knitted together, and if she could have torn every blade of grass to shreds she would have. Instead of forcing her to answer, he turned to hacking at the log, splitting it. The crack of the metal hitting wood gave her time to think. He finished, and then looked at her expectantly.

What she didn't want to admit came flying out of her mouth. "We went through something terrible, and no one will talk about it. We almost died, Karl. And we still didn't get up that damn mountain. Everything we wanted has evaporated, and Lord Rascomb still hasn't woken up, and Prudence and Mr. Moon want to leave, and nothing feels right!"

Karl put his hatchet axe-head down and leaned on the handle. "I cannot fix any of those things."

All those things piled up over and over, taller and taller, and made her head feel hot, like she would explode skyward. "I know that!"

A coy smile played across his lips. It made her want to kiss him and slap him all at once.

"So you've come to be with me because you like my company?"

"No!" she insisted. "I mean, yes. I mean—" She let out a frustrated burst of air.

Suddenly, he gripped her hand. "Justine, I—"

"Herr Vogel!" cried a man's voice from below.

Justine snatched her hand back. She didn't want to make small talk with someone she couldn't even speak the same language as. Before she could change her mind, she whispered, "Come to my room tonight?"

He nodded, his expression grave. And she fled.

CLIMBING THE STAIRS, the last bits of evening summer sun in the windows, Karl felt more nervous than he had on the last traverse of Hörnli Ridge. His hands were actually sweating. He wiped them on his pants. He was reading into her invitation to come to her room. He had to be. There was no other place for them to meet, as the dining room was still occupied with Lord Rascomb.

This was merely a climber who'd experienced a hard and failed expedition who wanted to talk through what had happened. He'd seen it before. In fact, he'd been the climber needing to go over the failure points. That's what this was. He was the guide, she was the client. This was a one-on-one expedition debrief, nothing more.

Still, when he stood at her door, he wiped his hands on his trousers and gently tapped the wood with his knuckle.

The door swung open in moments.

Waves of chestnut brown hair cascaded down her shoulders. Karl's breath caught. He didn't know why in this moment she looked so beautiful, perhaps because the other times he had seen her with her hair down, it was in the low light of the dining hall. Here, with the lamps blazing, he could see her fully. Her pert, upturned nose. Her lips pink and full. And her eyes filled with relief at his presence.

"I didn't think you'd come." She stared at him, her chest rising in shallow breaths, as if she were as nervous as he was.

"May I enter?" Karl balled one hand into a fist. Was he doing the worst possible thing? Was entering her room, alone, dishonorable? Yes. And he knew it. If she initiated any physical act, he was vulnerable to it all. He wouldn't be able to stop himself.

Before, she'd been pretty and capable, funny and energetic. But now he knew the truth of her, having been on the mountain with her, having faced disaster with her. She was calm in a crisis. She was loyal to her friends, willing to risk her safety for theirs. Before she'd slept at Schwarzsee, she'd checked on everyone to insure their health and comfort. Tante Greta had told him about how she'd tried to help here at the inn, even though she was a guest. This was a woman he wanted to make a life with. She was more than a pretty girl from England. This was Justine Brewer, vulnerable, needing him.

"Please come in," Justine said, moving aside.

Her dress was a plain whitish color, but the pop of dark red buttons down the top seemed to call to his fingers. Around her waist was a plain ribbon, the same color as the buttons. The waist ribbon was finished in a bow that seemed so easy to undo. As if he only needed to simply touch it, and it would unravel. He shook his head. No, he was here to listen. To speak with his client about the failed expedition.

"Tea?" she asked, her voice sounding hopeful.

He looked around, then noticed her unfinished dinner tray, with a teapot arranged on it. Tante Greta had been so proud to order those teapots last autumn, as if those dishes proved she had English guests arriving. "No, thank you."

She sighed with relief. "Oh good. It's cold, anyway."

They stood staring at each other. Where was he supposed to sit? Or stand? There were two beds in here and a high-backed wooden chair. The chair was the obvious choice, but it was on the other side of the room, and covered with what was likely her dressing gown. He certainly didn't want to be so presumptuous as to touch her night things.

"Justine, if I may call you that—"

"I want to kiss you." She wrung her hands together, as if she were unsure of his answer.

"Pardon?" Surely, she didn't say what he thought she had said.

"I do. Because I miss you, and I want comfort, but the only comfort I want is from you."

Karl blinked. He had never thought of himself as the comforting sort of man, but he could adjust. "That . . . is fine."

"Good." She stepped forward. "Do you want to kiss me, or are you only letting me kiss you out of pity? Because if it's pity, I don't want to."

Karl stepped forward. "I feel many things for you, but never has it been pity."

"Good." Another step towards him. Almost touching him. Almost.

"I dream of you," he said, not knowing what else to say to draw her closer. Nothing but the truth. "Ever since I met you. I think of nothing else but the mountains and you."

"I dream of falling off the Matterhorn. I lose all my friends every night. I lose you. Sometimes myself. I don't want those anymore."

"Of course not," he said, finally close enough to put his hand on her face, cradling her cheek. Her skin was so soft.

"Make me dream of something else." Her brown eyes were liquid and pleading.

"I can try," he whispered, his lips so close to hers. Their noses brushed against each other. His whole body was flush and warm and greedy. He wanted her in whatever way she'd give.

"Please try," she whispered back, ending the distance between them.

She tasted of honey and walnuts, the dessert Tante Greta sent only to her, after Karl had told her of Justine's preferences. Her lips were soft and lush, and he lost time as well as all sense of himself kissing her. He dropped his hand from her face and instead pulled her closer, crushing her breasts against his chest. It felt good and right. As if there was nothing else in the world that fit together better than the two of them.

She threaded her fingers through his hair, and his knees almost buckled. The sensation of her gently tugging, dragging her hand down to his neck, sent shivers through him. Before he knew what he was doing, he pulled at the satin ribbon at her waist. It didn't budge. He tried the other side, and it flowed like water through his hand.

In return, she began picking at the top button of his coat. He broke away from her, panting, longing, gasping. "Justine."

Her face was flushed, her lips cherry red from his, her dress gaping wide at the waist, and that dark red ribbon lay piled on the floor, taunting him. "Karl."

"If we start this, I do not believe—"

"I want to finish this."

He shook his head. "I don't understand."

She stepped closer to him, an echo of their dance earlier. "I want it all."

His mind blinked out, as if two invisible fingers pinched the wick of a lamp, extinguishing the light. And he pulled her into his arms as he sat down on the edge of the bed. She sat on his lap as he kissed her, letting his hands roam the decadent curve of her hips.

Far from the blushing maid, she grabbed back at him, clutching his shoulders as if she were falling. He was lost in her. Mad for her. Soon, her clever fingers resumed their work on his coat. He helped her, and as soon as he could, he shucked off the garment. He'd only worn it to seem more appropriate, more formal. He'd wanted distance between them, and that coat could not stop him now.

His waistcoat was just as frustrating, and he peeled that off as soon as he could. "Your turn," he gasped. His prick strained against his trousers, begging for the friction of her bottom and her hips squirming against him. But he ignored the whine of its insistence.

"Only if you help," she said with a grin.

His hands were shaking, but he attacked her first red button, standing out in sharp contrast to the cream-colored dress. There weren't that many of them, but the buttons were large and ornate, mocking him with the difficulty of the tight fabric.

"I, I cannot—" His hands shook with effort. He kissed her again, not able to keep control of himself, needing to taste her, be a part of her, be nearer than he was at that moment. Clothes were instruments of the devil.

"ARE YOU NERVOUS?" she asked, hoping she sounded coy, and not terrified with the amount of wanting she felt. He'd kissed her senseless, and she didn't know what to do next. Her entire body was aflame with desire and feelings that were heady and new, and delightful. This is what she wanted, this was what she chased when she went up the mountains. But here, she could have it with someone, share it with someone, be nearer to someone.

But she didn't have any other someone in mind at this moment. Only the man who helped her pull her friends from safety. Who believed in her, challenged her, wanted her.

He grunted at her, pressing small kisses along her jaw and onto her neck. The skin was so sensitive, and his lips were soft compared to the rasp of his stubbled chin. She shivered. He pulled her tight to him again, and she felt hardness press against her leg. This was what Eleanor had told her about, in those whispered sessions when Ophelia left the room to consult with her father, or a map, or something important. Because Justine had wanted to *know*.

His hand moved to her breast, and a moan came out of her mouth. Also a new sensation. "Buttons," he said, trailing kisses up and down her neck.

"Buttons," she sighed, her fingers happily making quick work of the large, slick satin-covered fasteners. As soon as the top three were undone, he slipped his hand inside, his warm palm on the flat expanse of her chest.

"Justine," he said, and that smooth way he pronounced her name made her want to swoon.

She finished undoing her buttons, letting the top half of her dress gape open. But his hand didn't move. He looked at her in a way that seemed to worm into her mind, pulling her out of her experiences and into this shared one here, this moment.

His chest was heaving, as if he were going up a hill. She

opened his shirt the rest of the way and placed her hand on his, warm underneath her palm. "Karl," she said. There were a thousand things whizzing through her mind, all whistling with speed and fury, but here, his heartbeat strong and steady, she felt calmer and closer to him than she'd ever felt to anyone in her life.

"I need you," he said, his voice thick, his brows drawn. "I need more in life than guiding, than Zermatt, and you are the more."

For once, she was silent. There was nothing for her to say, nothing she could manage, as her mind was full of light and color and for once, no other thoughts. Surging forward, she kissed him, wrapping him fully in her arms. He tipped her over onto the bed and let them fall to their sides.

He pulled at the straps to her shift, pushing everything down until the top half of her was bare. His calloused hands were skating all over her skin, raising gooseflesh everywhere he touched. Then he palmed her breast with a reverence that made her feel like a precious gem. As if she were valuable, venerable. But when he moved his kisses downward, sparks danced in her mind, and she felt desire rush in as he licked and sucked her breasts, thumbing the nipple his mouth wasn't covering.

She clutched his shoulders, pushing the shirt off, wanting skin, more skin. He came up and kissed her mouth again, and she unbuttoned the rest of his shirt and he shucked it off. He pulled at her waist and heard fabric tear. She giggled, but he seemed incensed by the sound, yanking the pile of clothing even harder, baring her to the air. She was vulnerable, open, lying there in stockings and nothing else.

His face was intent and focused as he whipped her dress onto the floor. He stared down at her body in a way that she couldn't decipher. He said something in German that sounded like a song. The only thing she could do was take it as a compliment, for he unbuttoned the top of his trousers only to hold himself still, closing his eyes, calming his breath.

"I am trying to slow down," he said, just before opening his eyes.

Justine didn't know what to say. "That's fine."

He opened his eyes and grinned. "Did I tell you that I have wanted you very much?"

"I don't mind hearing it again."

He bent down, bracing his arms on either side of her, and kissed her breasts again, only to work further down her body. She enjoyed watching the muscles of his arms and back work as he moved, making her squirm under his featherlight kisses.

And then he touched her between her legs. Bared flesh that had ached for him. He dragged his finger down, parting her. Justine moved without thinking, bucking her hips, wanting more. His other hand dragged up and down on her thighs, squeezing as she flexed and squirmed. Then he found her wetness, delving into her to swirl the dampness onto his finger. He pulled it towards the hard nub that was the source of all her pleasure. His touch was light, and she wanted to beg for him to rub harder, but she was scared he would stop, so she stayed silent.

He lowered himself to his side, next to her, his hand continuing its soft ministrations. She bucked again, almost involuntarily. And then he bent down to find her nipple again. As he turned his attention to her aching breasts, his fingers moved faster and harder, and her head swam with it. It wasn't long before Justine's back arched and she bit her lip to keep from crying out.

When she was able to open her eyes again, he was back to stroking her softly. His eyes were full of pride and his lips were quirked with bemusement. "Oh, was that good for you?" she asked him, as if he were not petting her in the most private of places.

Karl smiled. "We could stop here and I would be satisfied."

Justine shook her head. "I don't want to stop. I want to see you fall apart."

He looked down. "If we stop now, it's not bad if we walk away from each other in a few weeks' time. If it's more—Justine—I couldn't let you go."

There was something in her that shifted, she heard his meaning. She knew that he didn't mean a possibility of a child, he didn't mean ownership. He meant that he was letting a piece of him go if they continued. Just as she would. "I don't want to stop," she repeated. Because she didn't want him to let her walk away.

They pulled off the rest of his clothing, and he took his time peeling off her stockings. Both of them were as vulnerable as they could be. He touched her face and she could smell herself on his fingers. That did feel like ownership. Like she had marked him.

"Is this your first time?" he asked.

She nodded.

"Then you should be in control. I want you in control." Karl shifted so that he was lying down. She pulled herself up and it was her turn to look and appreciate. She'd never seen a grown man naked before. She ran her fingers down him from chest, to stomach, to this new part. She looked at it, straining, and she took it into her hands.

He sucked in a breath at her touch.

Oh, that was interesting. "I don't know how you like to be touched."

Gasping again, he bucked his hips. "You seem to be doing fine."

She pumped again, just to see what would happen.

"Justine," he said, his teeth gritted.

Then, as he had teased her, she bent down and licked the very tip of his cock, where a bead of wetness had gathered.

He sat up, his eyes wide, his breath short. "There are two ways this happens."

She did not let go of the hot, hard cock in her hands. "I am listening."

"One is this way, the other is with you on top of me. But I cannot last much longer. So you must choose which way, because I cannot do both tonight."

It was disappointing in a way, that men couldn't keep going

the way women could. That the enjoyment would have to cease and rest for a time. But she did enjoy this control he'd given her. She pushed his shoulder. "Lie down."

Groaning in relief, he obeyed. She straddled him, thinking of why she learned to ride horses sidesaddle and understanding it finally. She rubbed her wetness onto his shaft, wondering if this is what she should do. But then his hands found hers, and together, they found her entrance.

"Slowly," he advised.

And so, little by little, Justine sank onto him, the feeling strange and new and odd. When she found herself all the way seated on him, she angled and moved, finding what felt good and what felt like too much.

"Does it feel good?" he asked, his brow furrowed.

"Yes," she gasped, and he threw his head back as she rocked forward. He held her hips and they found a rhythm together. It stopped feeling like he was inside of her, and more that they were one new, different thing altogether. He moved his thumb between her legs and found that hard nub once again, rubbing in circles harder and harder. That feeling of crashing was happening again, faster than it had before. She collapsed her hands down to his hard chest, bracing herself as she clenched in ecstasy.

He gasped some words—something that sounded very much like cursing—and clamped his hands on her hips, thrusting upwards roughly in a way that only added to the waves cresting over her. His back arched, and she held onto him as everything inside her felt different. He relaxed down again, and she let him pull her down to his chest, holding her there.

Her world changed. The smell of him, the smell of her mixed with him, felt permanent somehow. As if it hadn't been an act, but rather an alchemy. She was still herself, but now she was more with him beside her. She closed her eyes, feeling his heartbeat in her own blood, his skin on her skin, his breath matched with hers. There was nowhere in the world she would rather be.

KARL SLIPPED OUT of Justine's door, his waistcoat and jacket slung over his arm. Justine kissed him as he tried to exit, and he felt a surge of pride that she didn't want to see him go. Things between them felt different, they were different. If she didn't want marriage, then that was fine, and Karl would find a way. Whatever would keep her in his life.

"Ahem," came a voice in the passageway.

Karl pulled up straight as if he'd been struck. Turning, they both watched as Francis Brewer stood up, leaning against the wall of the passageway across from Justine's door. His rumpled clothes and mussed hair made it clear that he had slept there. It was not yet daybreak.

"Francis?" Justine pushed out of the doorway as Karl tried to block her path.

"I believe we can fetch the vicar now, can't we?"

"Wait," Justine said. Karl wanted to join in, but he was at a loss of what to say. In some ways, this was precisely what he wanted—but not if Justine didn't want it. Anything she was forced to do would diminish her, make her unlike herself.

"You cannot deny that you are ruined," Mr. Brewer said. "Accept your fate. Live with this one in the flea-infested hotels up and down this mountain range. You've made us a laughingstock, as you've been trying to do since you were born."

Karl did not like this way her brother spoke to her. No one deserved such contempt. As if what they had done was wrong. "There is no reason to fault your sister. I came to her room. I did this. If you wish to make insults, direct them at me."

Francis laughed, his shoulders slumped. "You have no idea what she's done, parading herself around, letting men run after her for years. Years!"

"And no one caught me," Justine said through gritted teeth. "Until now."

Karl looked back at her, realizing then and there that when she asked him here, to be with her, it was so that he would be the one who caught her. Whether she wanted to marry or not was immaterial. She wanted him, not any of the other English dandies. It was him. And he would be worthy of her.

"I will take my place at the altar with pride, if Justine wishes it." Karl faced her brother, but hoped she marked his words. His hand sought out hers. "But I will hear no more slander from you. I do not know how the English do it, but here, I would use my fists to silence you. Remember that and choose your words wisely."

At least Mr. Brewer had the decency to look shocked.

"Plan the wedding, Francis. But this isn't your doing. This is my choice. My desire," Justine said.

Karl could barely breathe. It was not the best proposal, he supposed, given that it was made by her brother, but Karl would make the best of what he was presented. "You will be my brother, and I will give you my respect. But not if you speak so poorly of my bride." Karl liked that word. Bride. It was so close to wife. Bound together through knots no one could untangle.

Mr. Brewer narrowed his eyes. "I suppose I should have said so earlier, but Mother and Father will arrive tomorrow."

"What?" Justine exploded out the door, knocking Karl's arm aside as if he were nothing.

"I wrote to them ages ago. They telegraphed to say they were on their way as soon as possible. So, congratulations. You'll have a family wedding."

Chapter Fourteen

JUSTINE DID NOT appreciate surprises that ended in her getting scolded. Unable to get more than a few hours of sleep, she escaped outside to think. Not that she was capable of contriving a big scheme, but she did have a great deal of emotions to feel, which might as well be the same as thinking.

The horizons beyond the mountains were lightening from dark purple to pink, then to orange and yellow. The cold of the rock seeped into her bum. The cold tips of her fingers felt good on her eyelids, which stung with an unexpected heat in wake of her lack of sleep. Her life would never be the same. Which was honestly something she'd been longing for even before the Matterhorn. Then why was she a little sad?

Because suddenly her future was entirely unknown, and a life with Karl could possibly keep her from returning to England forever. This was the moment, the point so obvious Ophelia could put a pushpin in a map for it, where Justine grew up.

After what she and Karl had just done, she could be a mother. But she would most definitely become a wife—likely within the week. Who knew what Francis and her parents would insist upon.

She heard the swish of grass above her. Normally, she would never be still enough to hear it, but this was an unusual morning. Turning, she saw Karl startle as he spotted her.

"Early morning hike?" she asked, her voice shockingly loud in the spacious dawn sky.

He cleared his throat. "You did not wake early enough to catch me this time."

"Would you have waited?"

"If I had known, yes." He strolled up to stand beside her rock. Sweat glistened at his temples, and the tip of his nose was red from cold. He sniffed and discreetly wiped his nose with the back of his wrist. Even his hands were ruddy from the cool, Alpine night temperature. "What has you up early?"

She gave him a reedy smile. "I'm getting married, haven't you heard?"

Karl huffed, which sounded something akin to an embarrassed laugh. "How could I not?"

They were quiet for a moment, and then Justine realized she was being rude by taking up all the space on the boulder. She scooted over to give him room. He gave her a questioning look, but when she patted the empty stone, he hopped up beside her.

"Justine, I—" Karl stopped, looking down at his hands. Justine watched as his fingers climbed over each other, trying to find a position of rest and failing. Finally, he looked in her eyes, and she saw the turmoil in his. "If you do not wish to marry me, then don't. I couldn't bear it if you thought I had trapped you in some way. A bird will not sing if she is caged against her will, and I want you to sing."

Perhaps because she was already feeling so many emotions at once, or because she was admitting to herself that her childish life had finished, his words penetrated deep. "It's because you don't want to cage me that I agreed to marry you, Karl."

"Agreeing from family pressure and jumping up and down saying yes are very different things. I would prefer the jumping kind for someone to marry me." Karl held her gaze, grimacing, almost as if he was bracing for her rejection.

She looked down at her own hands and held them up to tick off her reasons. "The reasons I would marry Karl Vogel. One, and I deeply regret saying this out loud, you are extraordinarily attractive. Straight nose, excellent teeth, jawline sharper than a carving knife, and shoulders broader than an ox. So aggravating." She glanced over to see how he was taking her complete inability to discuss her feelings directly.

"Number two, he lives in a place that I have fallen absolutely in love with. Number three, he, very annoyingly, can keep up with me physically. Very few can."

Karl laughed with what sounded like genuine delight. "Keep up with you? You keep up with me!"

"Number four," she said, louder to emphasize that she was still talking. "Karl Vogel has either already climbed all the best mountains and therefore knows the way, or knows how to climb all the best mountains and would absolutely do it with me."

"Number five, he doesn't mind if I drink brandy in the middle of the night."

At the reminder of the night they met, Karl's face melted into gentle peace. He leaned back and folded his arms, waiting for the rest of her enumerations.

"Number six, when he says he is not after my family's money, I believe him."

Karl nodded succinctly at that, but didn't interrupt.

"Number seven, he knows how strong I am and doesn't try to take that from me."

His expression turned grave. "Never."

"Number eight, if I say I don't want children, I think he would respect that, and if I said that I did, he would respect that, too."

Karl nodded, his eyebrows raised as if contemplating the new topic.

"Number nine, I'm fairly certain that Karl worships the ground I walk upon."

This caused a massive smile to break out across his face, and he reached for her, but she stopped him. It was this last reason that made her heart pound, and her stomach seize.

"And number ten, if I told him that I loved him, he wouldn't laugh at me."

This time she didn't stop him as he threaded his hands around her face and kissed her. She folded herself into his lap, allowing every emotion she had been feeling to open and lay bare to him, as if she were lining them up for his inspection. She did love him. She did. And marrying him would be no hardship, not really. It was a new adventure, and if there was one thing Justine Bad News Brewer loved, it was a new adventure.

Below them, the rustling of the goats' neck bells alerted them to the outside world. Karl looked at the sky, and then down below where movement could be heard in the hotel.

"I have to go," Karl said. "I help Tante Greta with the morning chores."

"Go," she said, shooing him. "But I'm going to stay a bit longer on my rock. I'm enjoying it here."

He gave her a boyish grin and trotted down the hill. She heard the bell for breakfast, but didn't feel like eating, so she stayed on her rock as the sun came up and perched over the mountains.

Worse, was that according to Francis, her parents would arrive that morning. She certainly did not want to explain to her mother what had happened. Nor did she want to be nearby when Francis told them, either.

Most likely, she considered, she would become the Frau Vogel to whatever mountaineering venture Karl next undertook. She didn't know any words of Bavarian German. Or Swiss German. Or really anything. Her French was terrible as well. But she would figure something out. She always did.

"Good morning," Ophelia called as she trudged up the hill to join her on her rock.

"Good morning. How did you find me?" Justine asked, scooting over to make room.

"Well, I went outside because that would be where you would go, and then I looked up."

"I'm not hiding," Justine said, just in case Ophelia thought she was.

"I know," Ophelia said, nodding.

"How is your father?"

"His eyes fluttered, and he's almost swallowing the broth now, not just letting it dribble out." Ophelia's tone was measured.

"But not really awake yet?"

Ophelia shook her head. "No. Not yet."

They were silent, looking out at the mountains. Justine picked at the lichen on the rock. "Turns out I'm getting married."

"I heard."

"Already?"

"Francis told everyone. Frau Brunner is very happy. She's singing in the kitchen. You can hear it all over the hotel."

Justine scrunched up her face. Even if Frau Brunner was happy, there would still be scoldings from Lady Rascomb. "And your mother?"

"She has a hard time not thinking about my father. But I believe her exact words were, 'It's the only way that girl was getting married, and I've said it since the day I met her.'"

Justine's cheeks heated. "That doesn't sound very complimentary."

"I don't think she meant you're loose, I think she meant you're stubborn." Ophelia's words were kind, but Justine could see the sadness coming off her as if it were water vapor.

"Oh." Justine looked at Zermatt, wondering if she and Karl would live there year-round. She wouldn't mind it. She'd figure out how to make cheese and bread, and all those things. Perhaps her father would still give her a dowry. That was something to think about. She'd insist on buying a very big stove.

"There's an Anglican bishop in town, it turns out," Ophelia said after a while.

"An Anglican one?" Justine frowned. There wasn't an Anglican church—only the funds being raised for one.

"Precisely. They laid the foundation stone last month for the new church. The bishop stayed on to enjoy the mountains."

"How do you know this?" Justine asked.

Ophelia looked at her in surprise. "Your mother, of course."

Justine's heart started pounding. "She's already here?"

"Apparently, they came in very early this morning. Francis met them. They've been very busy running around town already."

"But—" She must have been kissing Karl a bit longer than she thought she had. She couldn't see the front of the inn from here. Oh drat. If she didn't go down and show her face, this would be a disaster. Well, even more of a disaster. She slid off the rock.

"Before you go—" Ophelia grabbed Justine's hand. "Will being with Mr. Vogel make you happy? If not, I'll do what I can to stop this. I don't know what I could do, but something."

Justine smiled. Even if she had so many questions about what would happen in the future, not one of them was about whether or not Karl would make a good husband. "I think everything is going to work out, Fee. I really do."

Ophelia smiled back at her; sadness touched every feature of her lovely face. "Then I'm happy for you."

"I have to go greet my mother." Justine sighed. "I'm not looking forward to this."

"I know. She's already invited my mother for tea in her room this afternoon. I believe it won't be pleasant."

Justine winced. "I need to apologize to your mother. It's not her fault."

Ophelia slid down the rock and joined Justine on the ramble back down to the inn. Now that she'd said it out loud to Ophelia, Justine felt the feeling of assurance settle over her like a shawl. Everything would work out for the best. And maybe this was the only way she would have ever gotten married—being forced into it due to her indiscretion. The indiscretion that she couldn't wait to try again.

"If I try the Matterhorn again, will you do it, even though you'll be a married lady?" Ophelia asked, her voice sounding thin and pinched.

"Wild horses couldn't keep me away," Justine answered. "I wouldn't let you try this with anyone else. It's still us against the world."

They entered the inn, and Justine could hear her mother in the dining room. Her mother's voice was very distinct. And it carried. Justine looked at Ophelia, who gave her a pat on the shoulder as encouragement. Justine exhaled, hoping for the best, then swanned into the dining room with false confidence.

"Mama, so good to see you." Justine took her mother's hands and kissed her cheek.

"Congratulations are in order, daughter." Her mother pushed her hands back out so she could examine Justine. "You look as wild as ever. But at least happy this time."

"And is Papa here? Who came with you? I'm amazed you came to Switzerland at all."

Her mother's face fell into a thin line. "Francis wrote to say you were getting married after climbing the Matterhorn. We were ready to leave when his telegraph came that your expedition was hurt. We wouldn't abandon you out here, wedding or no!"

Something inside Justine's chest popped open, like a bubble that burst. They'd come. They'd come for *her*, not for the prospect of a wedding. Francis had thought of her safety. She'd put herself out of their reach, and yet they ran to her when she needed them. Her throat felt hot and thick.

"Francis also informed us of your wedding date, and I am glad we could make it here before you converted to Lutheranism or something else rash."

Justine swallowed hard. Wait. So her mother believed that this hurried wedding was not because of a night of indiscretion but rather a planned ceremony? "Er—"

Her mother gripped her hands tighter, smothering Justine's into a tight fist. "In fact, since you allowed Francis the pleasure of arranging the ceremony, I've just found you an Anglican bishop to preside over the wedding. Please tell me that you'll let him, and not whatever Lutheran pastor you've dug up. Please. For your mother."

"I will—" Justine looked around, still trying to figure out how to best handle this. "I will talk to Karl about it. I don't think he had his heart set on any particular pastor."

Her mother sighed in relief. "Thank goodness. This way your marriage will be recognized in England and I won't have to have any of those awkward conversations about if your children are technically bastards."

Justine frowned. "Wonderful."

"And where is Mr. Vogel? Is he nearby? I haven't met him yet. Your father is still up in the room. He's having troubles. Something about the dairy doesn't agree with him. But I would like to meet this young man. Oh," her mother blanched. "He is a young man, isn't he?"

Justine stifled a laugh. "Yes. Close to my age."

"That's for the best, anyhow. I can't believe how he managed to sweep you off—"

At that moment, Karl peeked into the dining room, his waistcoat hanging open, his hair a mess, holding the hatchet across his shoulder. He looked every inch a mountain woodsman, broad and capable and muscled. His blue eyes speared Justine. "Is all well? Do you have any needs I may address?"

As Justine caught her breath, she looked over to her mother, whose mouth gaped open.

"Karl, this is my mother," Justine said. "Would you like to be introduced?"

"I apologize, I did not know they arrived." He backed up a step. "Please excuse me, I must bathe before introductions. I'd like to be presentable." Karl nodded his head, almost as if he were bowing. "Ma'am."

Karl disappeared from the lobby, his footsteps heavy on the stairs.

"That's him," Justine said, clasping her hands to pinch herself.

"Oh my," her mother said, the admiration clear in her voice. Justine grinned. "Isn't he just?"

KARL SCRUBBED HIMSELF red. He shaved as close as he could muster, and he put on his second-best suit. He needed to be presentable for his future wife's parents. According to Tante Greta, they'd already found an Anglican bishop to perform the ceremony, and if it would be an Anglican wedding, then Tante Greta wanted every other tradition to be Swiss. Karl reminded her that he was Bavarian, but she said it did not count since he was here so much.

Karl wasn't sure which traditions she wanted, but he supposed Tante Greta would make sure it would happen. On the stairs, Karl met a portly Englishman. The cut of the suit was unmistakably British, and when he got closer, he noticed distinct dark brown eyes, filled with mischief. It had to be Mr. Brewer. He was a large man, much larger than Karl thought he would be, given how small Justine was.

"Good evening," Karl said.

"Evening, evening."

Karl slowed his steps to keep pace with the gentleman.

"Are you heading out to dine somewhere?" the large man asked.

Karl shook his head. "I am here to meet my bride's parents."

"Ah! How fortuitous!" Mr. Brewer stopped his slow advance. "You must be Mr. Vogel."

Karl gave him a shallow bow. "At your service."

"You must be quite something to have caught my girl's eye. She was never taken in by fools or dandies, thank the Lord."

"Thank you?" Karl could only take that as a compliment.

"Have you met my wife yet? She'll be impatient to take your measure. Come along." Mr. Brewer picked up his pace, and before long, Mr. Brewer presented him to the diminutive Mrs. Brewer.

Mr. Francis Brewer also arrived, and then Tante Greta bustled out and told him that Lady Rascomb had agreed to move Lord Rascomb from the dining room up to a guest room. That meant he had to forego discussion and help move the sick man and then clean the dining room so they might have a proper dinner with their new guests.

When Karl meant to protest, Tante Greta stopped him. "Show your future parents what a good boy you are," she said in German.

Karl made his excuses, and although he waited until the party had left the dining room to remove his coat, he did notice later that Mrs. Brewer was watching him as he and Tristan moved the heavy wooden bed frame upstairs.

Perhaps Justine's parents approved of him enough?

THERE WAS A gunshot.

Justine sat bolt upright in bed. Another one. Then firecrackers? Ophelia rubbed her eyes and turned over to look at Justine.

"What is going on?" Justine demanded. "Is it war?"

Ophelia laughed. "No, but it is your wedding day."

"Why are they shooting guns? It sounds like they're right outside the window!" Justine rushed over to peer out the curtain.

"They are right outside the window." Ophelia yawned. "Austrian custom. Bride awakes at dawn."

"What? That's ridiculous!"

"You better announce that you're up so I can get some more sleep," Ophelia said with another yawn.

Her blood pounded in her ears from the noise. There was no way she'd ever sleep again. "Nonsense. You hate sleep."

She pulled off Ophelia's blanket. Ophelia grumbled but gamely sat up.

Justine waved out the window at Herr and Frau Brunner outside, with Frau Erhart the healer, the young maid, and a few others she didn't recognize. They cheered her and laughed and, according to Ophelia, told her to meet them downstairs.

After they dressed and descended, Frau Brunner greeted them with fresh rolls and a pot of tea. Through Ophelia's halting translation, they told Justine what to expect for the day.

"Apparently they decided to forego the kidnapping," Ophelia said.

"Pardon? Kidnapping?" Justine swallowed a scalding sip of tea.

"It is a grandiose tradition here, from what I gather. I think it has something to do with how well your husband can protect you? By finding you? I'm not sure. My language skills are not perfect." Ophelia frowned as Frau Brunner again started talking at speed.

When it was time to dress for the ceremony later that day, her mother tsked over the fact that they hadn't time to get something new.

"Something from Paris," her mother said with a sigh. "My only daughter, and this is what she wears."

It was the most appropriate dress she had—her nicest pale frock, the one with the red buttons and satin sash. The very one Karl had peeled off of her. At least there had been time to get new buttons covered in a cream silk and change the ribbon sash to cream, so it could seem more like a wedding dress. Even as they were altering it, her mother noted a slight tear in the skirt.

"It's a good thing we are working on this today," she'd said. "You must be more careful with your things."

There was a knock at her door as her mother's lady's maid yanked and pulled and twisted her hair into place.

Frau Brunner entered, holding a length of lace over her forearm and a coin in her hand.

"Schuhe," the woman said, gesturing with the coin.

Justine looked at her mother, hoping she understood, but apparently Swiss matrimonial customs were outside of her scope of knowledge. Frau Brunner mimed putting the coin in her own shoe.

"You want me to put it in my shoe?" Justine asked. Frau Brunner nodded. She looked to her mother, who looked as baffled as she was.

Justine took the coin—a pfennig—and placed it under her arch inside the slipper. Frau Brunner said more, explaining the custom perhaps? But no one understood. Then Frau Brunner presented her with the lace. Again, Justine wasn't clear what to do with it. So she draped it around her shoulders, thinking it was meant to be like a shawl. Frau Brunner shook her head fiercely.

The innkeeper took the lace and draped it over her head, covering her face.

"Can you please fetch Ophelia?" Justine said to her mother's lady's maid. "I believe we need a translator. I can't see a thing."

Once Ophelia arrived, she listened intently to Frau Brunner's lecture. She gave thoughtful nods, and Justine wanted to shake her.

It was Justine's *wedding* day, and she couldn't see, and apparently would have to hobble everywhere she went due to a coin in her shoe. Top it all, she was tired from being woken up at the crack of dawn by gunfire, and she hadn't even seen Karl, whom she supposedly was going to be marrying later.

But it didn't bother her that she was technically being forced into marriage, since she had decided to marry Karl anyway, that night they'd spent sweating, curled up in her narrow bed. She could be angry about not knowing where she'd live next year, or even where she would tomorrow. Would she sleep on a pallet in front of the fire here at the inn as well? She had no idea.

But it made the whole thing exciting. Who knew what was coming next? The one thing she could bet on was more mountains. More hikes in the woods. That which made her happier than anything else. And she was going to be walking with Karl, who was her second-favorite person. Because really, who could be better than Ophelia?

It was a backwards way to get to happiness, but Justine was fairly certain she was stepping into it in her own way.

"I think I understand now," Ophelia said, her eyes still on Frau Brunner as she turned to Justine. "The coin in your shoe is to give you good fortune in your married life."

Justine's mother harrumphed, no doubt disturbed that no one who spoke English knew about Karl's family except Karl, and he was pleasantly evasive about his financial prospects.

"And the veil is so that no evil spirits recognize you and carry you away before the wedding." Ophelia said it slowly, glancing back to Frau Brunner, asking something in German, and received a confirmation.

"They seem awfully concerned about brides being stolen away here," Justine said. "I'm not sure what that says about Switzerland."

"The lace is very becoming," Justine's mother said, holding the lace up. "Very fine craftsmanship."

"Mine," Frau Brunner said, tapping her chest with her hand.

The pride of this woman, how she honored Justine with her loan. Tears pricked Justine's eyes. "This belonged to you?"

"Ich—" Frau Brunner stopped and turned to Ophelia, speaking in German again.

"She made it," Ophelia said. "It was for her wedding to Herr Brunner. She said she put all her love into it, and hopes that it will bring as much happiness for you and her nephew."

Justine was not sentimental, at least, not in her own opinion. But this was more generosity than she could take. She stood and pulled Frau Brunner into a tight hug, whispering her thank-yous in English and in German. When she pulled away, she could see the redness in Frau Brunner's blue eyes as well.

When it came time, they rode donkeys over to the site of where the Anglican church would one day stand. For now, the one foundation stone marked the territory. Wooden benches had been brought out for guests, and while it was meant to be a church wedding, Justine was glad it was outside. Glad that the mountains could attend, watch over them, bless them in whatever way mountains could.

She'd decided to forgive the Matterhorn. She'd done what the Matterhorn always did. The Ladies' Alpine Society had turned back due to the injury of one of its members, an honorable and admirable thing to do. The Matterhorn tested them, and they emerged with honor. The next climb would come in due time.

Karl was already at the church site, looking handsome in his best suit, the gold braid covering the military-style jacket. She stumbled dismounting the donkey, lace obstructing her sight. She hobbled a bit from the coin in her shoe. She could hear her mother sniffling already. But this felt right and good. And she had the rest of the Ladies' Alpine Society there, cheering her on. Prudence pressed a bouquet of wildflowers into her hands, and Eleanor kissed her cheek through the lace veil.

"You are going to love being married," Eleanor promised, mischief in her voice.

The ceremony went so fast, Justine almost didn't believe it had happened. At least, until Karl raised the veil, kissed her soundly—in front of her parents!—and they adjourned to a donkey cart with a bag waiting for them on the board.

"Boiled sweets," Karl said, when she looked at it with eyebrows raised.

She peeked into the bag to find at least a pound of brightly colored paper twists. "This is an awful lot of sweets for two people."

Karl laughed, climbing into the donkey cart and putting out his hand to pull her up. At least she didn't have to keep her face covered anymore. She could see. Frau Brunner pinned the veil back, so she still had lace cascading down to her shoulders, and her mother admitted it was very becoming.

"We throw the sweets to the children as we go back to the inn. To celebrate our joy, and to give back to our community as they welcome us."

Justine liked the idea. It was better than people throwing things at them. As soon as they hit the streets of Zermatt, children appeared, as if they heard the siren song of sugar. Justine threw handfuls out and they skittered across the cobblestones. This was the most fun she'd had in *ages*. Well, public fun, anyway. She grabbed two handfuls and threw them both in the air. "I want to do this every day!"

Karl laughed. "I will see what I can do to put sweets in our budget."

At the inn, Frau Brunner pulled her into the kitchen and handed her a small box. Guests were arriving, and Herr Brunner was serving beer and wine and schnapps. Justine hadn't ever been in the kitchen before, and just like the veil scenario earlier that day, she hadn't a clue of what was going on. It had to be another gift, but Frau Brunner kept pushing her to the cooking stove, where a steaming pot of soup cooked.

"Ophelia?" she called, hoping her voice carried through the heavy wooden walls.

Frau Brunner shook her head. She mimed taking something from the box, tossing it in the soup, then pointed at Justine.

Justine frowned and opened the box. It was salt. "You want me to salt the soup?"

"Salze, ja." Frau Brunner nodded at her, trying to make her get on with it.

"I don't know how much to use." Justine was out of her depth. Oh no, would she be expected to cook for Karl? It had not occurred to her that they would be so poor as to have to cook for them both. She had no idea how to do anything in a kitchen.

Frau Brunner kept gesturing to the pot, so Justine took a pinch and tossed it in. The pot was rather large, and more cauldron-shaped, so perhaps more? Frau Brunner urged her again, so Justine dug out a handful and threw it in. Frau Brunner looked worried.

"Oh no, was that too much?"

"Gut, gut," Frau Brunner said, shaking her head and pushing Justine out the door and into the dining room.

The rest of the afternoon was fun, and not at all like the weddings she'd attended in England. This was loud, full of music and dancing and drinking. They spilled outside and danced and she listened to men yodel and clapped as women danced. The older men wore the traditional lederhosen, and she was still not sure she was ready to see men's bare knees, but see them she did.

As the sun set, Karl pulled her away from the crowd. "It is time for us to go."

"But the party—"

"It is time." Karl's voice was smooth and rough, and she realized that she hadn't paid much attention to him today. She'd been so focused on these strange traditions, and old men's knees, and tasting the soup that was clearly over-salted. Whoops.

He handed her up into the donkey cart, and she scooted over to make room for him. Crested carriage with matching horses, this was not. The sweet smell of hay still permeated the wood. "Where are we going?"

"To a cottage nearby. We will stay there for a few nights. Then I wanted to ask you to go to Augsburg with me. I would like for you to meet my parents."

He sounded nervous to her, so she leaned over and put her arm around his. "That sounds fine. What about my parents?"

"I invited them, but your father insists on returning to England. They will leave in two days."

"What about—"

Karl smiled at her, and it struck her suddenly that this was her husband. She'd *married* him. This competent, giving, strong, kind man. "Herr and Frau Moon will be returning to England at the same time as your parents and your brother. Lord Rascomb's health will determine when they return. Moving him to Zurich is too difficult at the moment."

Justine nodded. They might stay for weeks, but Justine knew the second they could safely get Lord Rascomb down the mountain, they would return to England as well. Ophelia needed her parents more than she needed Justine right then anyway. She might as well go to Augsburg.

Karl pulled the cart to a stop in front of a gorgeous chalet. It was meant to be a herder's hut, but this was if the herder were a prince in disguise. It was larger and had massive windows—a terrible idea for keeping warm in the winter, but it was summer and beautiful. Pretty red and white flowers had been planted, making the building as welcoming as any she'd ever seen.

Karl got down and held out his hand as if to hand her down, but instead, he blocked her path, pulling her into his arms. "You are my wife."

Justine leaned down to put her arms around his neck, reveling in being taller for once. "And you are my husband."

He threaded his hand up to her cheek, pulling her down for a kiss. What started out as tender and full of the excitement of the day quickly turned passionate as they both realized what this night was meant to be for them.

When Karl pulled away, Justine was gasping, feeling a now-familiar ache in her belly and between her legs. Karl handed her down, as if he were a gentleman. "I have to deal with the cart," he said, his eyes roving over her in a way that was most definitely ungentlemanly. "You go inside. Start unbuttoning."

Justine blushed, and he chuckled.

"I like making you blush," he said, pride showing in his expression. "Challenging, but worth it."

"I hate you," she said, even though they both knew she meant the opposite.

"I love you too," he said. Was he staking a donkey? Yes. But he was staring into her eyes, connecting in a way she'd never connected with anyone else.

She swallowed hard, stopped short by his clear declaration. "I love you," she whispered, testing out the words on her tongue. When they flowed out of her mouth, she realized that she meant it. She loved him in a way she'd never expected to be able to do.

It almost felt like a parlor-trick—the way it had snuck up on her. The way he'd so easily slipped through her defenses, earned her esteem, and then quietly made her love him.

He beamed in response to her whispered declaration, and it didn't matter that the sun was behind the mountains, because Karl was her light.

Epilogue

Augsburg, Bavaria

"THIS IS YOUR parents' house." They descended from the hired hack in front of a tall, flat-front, ornate baroque building.

"Yes." Karl smiled at her as if there was nothing surprising about the filigreed front of the five-story building.

Each window was topped with inlaid stone ornamentation, and painted filigrees to draw the eye to them. The top of the house was nothing like what she might find in London, even in the most expensive Belgravia. These top floors looked carved, like a mantel clock, making it difficult to see the rooflines. It was ostentatious. It was curls upon ornamentation and—was that gold filigree?

It was downright shocking. She loved it.

"I thought your parents were traders. Merchants." Justine hadn't bothered pressing Karl about his family. Why would she? When they were waved down by the hack driver to go straight to his parents' house from the train, instead of stopping at the apartment Karl had leased for them, she was expecting a cottage on the edge of town. Not . . . this.

But then, when she'd thought of Augsburg, she'd pictured a farm town the size of Zermatt. Not a beautiful, bustling city full of ancient watchtowers and churches and guild halls. London prided itself as being the center of the world, but it could learn from the beauty of Augsburg.

"They are traders. That's how my Onkel Peter met my Tante Greta. He was bringing goods to Switzerland."

"I have noticed that when I ask something about you or your direct family, you end up trying to distract me with things I already know."

Karl grabbed her hand, and kissed the back of it.

"Does this mean we can afford a cook?" she asked.

"Yes," Karl said, not elaborating.

"I won't have the chapped hands of a washerwoman?"

Karl frowned at the dove-gray gloves she wore. "Only if you wish it."

Suddenly, she was struck with a fear she'd never even thought of before. These were upper-class people, and Justine was a terror in society. What would they think of her? Would they like her? Flashes of evenings spent at tense, scowling, formal dinners came to her.

Then the door opened, and a woman in a ruffled blue gown trimmed with ebony ribbon stood there. "Karl!" she called, and then said something more in German that Justine couldn't understand.

His grip tightened on her hand, and he pulled them forward. "My mother," he whispered to her. As soon as they were at the threshold, she pulled him into an embrace. Karl pulled away enough to introduce Justine, and then his mother pulled her into the embrace as well.

So much for awkward introductions. The woman turned, still gripping both of them, and propelled Karl inside, smacking him lightly on the bottom as he went. Then this formidable woman turned her blue eyes on Justine. She was so much taller. So much bigger. But she had Karl's same eyes, and that made Justine want to trust her kindness.

"Meine Tochter," she said, and then, with a smile, said in perfect English, "My daughter. Welcome."

Frau Vogel moved inside and Karl reached for her hand. "Are you all right?"

Justine squeezed his hand. "This is going to be quite the adventure, isn't it?"

"You'll need to learn to speak German," he said. "Or at least Swiss."

With his mother out of the room, Justine reached up to her tiptoes. "Didn't you know? I can do anything. Besides, you'll teach me."

Karl snorted. "I am not a good teacher."

"I don't know, you've already taught me loads." Justine smirked at him, gratified to see his cheeks flare with heat.

"That does not count," he whispered, glancing at the doorway where his mother had just disappeared through.

"Of course it does. New skills, all that."

Karl's eyes were round as saucers, and Justine smiled with satisfaction in making her new husband blush. What was the translation of Bad News in German? Because she was determined to earn the moniker here, too.

The End.

About the Author

Edie Cay writes steamy feminist historical romance. Her debut, A LADY'S REVENGE won the Golden Leaf Best First Book (2020), as well as the Indie Next Generation Book Award (2020). The second in her series, THE BOXER AND THE BLACKSMITH won the Hearts Through History Legends Award, A Man for All Reason in 2019 as an unpublished manuscript, and then went on to win the Best Indie Book Award (2021). The third book, A LADY'S FINDER was a finalist for a Lambda Award, the most prestigious LGBTQ+ literary award in the world. A VISCOUNT'S VENGEANCE garnered the Best Indie Book Award for Regency Romance as well in 2023.

Previously, she published short stories, poems, and non-fiction in small presses. She co-wrote and starred in several short films and documentaries from MadLaw Media, including "Big 5 Dive" about scuba diving in the Great Lakes, and "How to Be Sexy," a fictional short about confidence and self-worth.

She obtained dual BAs in Creative Writing and in Music from Cal State East Bay, and her MFA in Creative Writing from University of Alaska Anchorage. She has been a professional musician, bookstore employee, and a healthcare worker.

She has participated in several anthologies, including Unlocked, The Grand Mistletoe Assembly, and the upcoming Beneath the Midwinter Moon.

Her next series will be about Victorian women alpinists, out in August 2024 from Dragonblade Publishing.

She is a founding member of the historical fiction collective The Paper Lantern Writers, and helps edit and publish their anthologies. She gives presentations at conferences around the world on the history of women's boxing and other aspects of

Regency culture and writing.

In addition to fiction, Edie writes and reviews for the Historical Novel Society. You can keep up with her on her website, www.ediecay.com, or follow her on Instagram or Facebook @authorEdieCay.